When the Stars Fall

Book Two

The Sisters, Texas Mystery Series

Becki Willis

Clear Creek Publishers

ISBN: 1947686046
ISBN 13: 9781947686045

TABLE OF CONTENTS

1	1
2	13
3	24
4	33
5	44
6	58
7	72
8	82
9	85
10	94
11	102
12	113
13	121
14	131
15	138
16	150
17	160
18	166
19	184

20 194
21 206
22 223
23 229
24 236
25 253
26 261
27 270
28 278
29 294
30 301

Note from the Author 313
More Books by Becki 314

1

"Excuse me, ma'am. Did you just say you were going to kill someone?" Madison Reynolds repeated the words to make certain she heard correctly.

"I certainly did," the woman on the phone said emphatically. "And I meant it, too. I'll kill that man dead if he thinks he can cheat on me after almost forty years of marriage!"

Madison closed her hazel eyes and issued a brief plea for patience. "Mrs.... Burton, did you say it was?"

"Yes. Yes, that's right, George Gail Burton."

"Mrs. Burton, I think you may have reached us in error. This is *In a Pinch Temporary Services*."

"There's no error. I'm in a pinch, and I want to hire you to find out the details of my husband's torrid affair. He's seeing some hussy from Naomi. That's where all the trollops live, after all!"

"I take it you live in Juliet," Madison murmured, trying not to take offense. Her best friend Genesis Baker lived in Naomi. The two towns, known commonly as The Sisters, were divided by a railroad track and a long history of rivalry.

"One of the first families to settle our fair city. And I'll not have our family name sullied now, with the likes of that woman!" George Gail Burton spat.

"I'm tempted to ask who 'that woman' is, but I really am afraid you have the wrong impression about our company, Mrs. Burton. We're a temp agency. We fill in when employers are left in a pinch."

"I'm telling you, I'm in a pinch and it's only going to be temporary, because if I find out that scalawag really is cheating on me, someone is going to wake up dead!" Her voice grew more shrill as she threw out the threat.

Madison tried once more to instill reason into the conversation. "I think you might be confusing our services with those of a private detective agency."

"The only confusion here is whether or not you want to take my money. Lucy Ngyen said you charge one thousand dollars. Is that correct?"

"I'm afraid Mrs. Ngyen may have given you the wrong impression. That may have been what she paid, but—"

Before she could explain her pricing structure, the other woman broke in, "All right then, two thousand."

Madison's mouth fell open and her eyes went perfectly round. She sat up straighter, suddenly interested in what the woman had to say. "What—What is it you want me to do, Mrs. Burton?"

"I want proof. Proof that my Curtis is cheating on me. I want you to follow him, take notes of when and where they meet, snap off enough pictures so there's no doubt to what they're doing. I want hard evidence when I confront him and that two-bit hussy!"

Madison's conscience warred with her avidity. She needed the money. Her gig at the car dealership was winding down and she had only a few odd jobs lined up. As long as Mrs. Burton understood she was not an official investigator and was merely performing amateur surveillance, surely there was no harm in taking the job.

Forcing herself not to be greedy, Madison pushed out a sigh and said, "Two thousand is too much, Mrs. Burton. Depending on the level of surveillance you desire, I'm sure one thousand dollars is more realistic. We'll need to meet to sign a contract and discuss what you expect from me."

"I expect you to clear the air, once and for all! After thirty-nine years, I know something is up with that man, and I plan to find out exactly what it is. Tell me when and where, and I'll bring you your money. Is cash money acceptable?"

"Cash is good."

"Where is your office?"

It was the first time Madison encountered the question and it left her momentarily confused on how to best answer. "Why don't we meet somewhere neutral?" she finally countered.

"Good idea. Don't want to tip our hand that I've hired you. We'll meet out in public, and I'll say I just wanted to shake the hand of the woman who single-handedly got Don Ngyen out of prison."

"Chief deCordova might have some argument about that," Madison protested. Not to mention that the accused Vietnamese man went no further than the River County jail.

"Katie Ngyen does my nails, and she says you're the reason her brother-in-law was set free," George Gail insisted. "The chief of police was satisfied to let him take the blame for killing Ronny Gleason, but you saw differently. You're worth every penny you charge, Katie and Lucy say."

"Oh. Uh, well, thank you." Madison frowned at the odd compliment. In truth, she charged a very modest hourly rate, but Lucy Ngyen insisted on paying her one thousand dollars, and now it seemed George Gail Burton was prepared to do the same. Who was she to argue? Even though her new client couldn't see her, Madison shrugged. "Why don't we meet at *New Beginnings Café*? I'm free today after noon."

"Two o'clock, then?"

"Yes, that sounds fine."

"Get a table and I'll find you. And Mrs. Reynolds?"

"Yes?"

"I really wouldn't kill anyone, you know."

Madison slid into a booth at *New Beginnings* a few minutes before two. There were only a handful of other customers scattered throughout the old building, but she chose a booth in the far corner to ensure privacy. Shrugging out of her sweater, she tossed it on the seat beside her and waved to her best friend who stood behind the bakery display.

All the food served at the café was delicious, but the bakery items were undoubtedly the best. After years of living away, Genesis came back to Naomi last summer and opened the restaurant with money she inherited from a previous employer. She revamped the old building so that it was a pleasant mix of old and new, created a menu every bit as eclectic, and dedicated one special corner to her love of baking.

Madison and Genesis first met and became best friends the summer of their eighth-grade year, when Madison moved to Juliet to live with her grandmother. For the next four years, the girls were inseparable. They were even roommates at Sam Houston State University in Huntsville. Their lives followed different paths after that, but they remained close. Genesis took a break in traditional study and went to France to learn to be a pastry chef, while Madison stayed and earned her degree. As Genesis began a career that took her to exciting places and exclusive events, Madison met Grayson Reynolds and began a family. They both lived out their own personal version of a fairy tale life, until Madison's marriage began to fall apart two years ago. Last November, the rest of her world crumbled when Gray was killed in an automobile accident and she discovered they were flat broke. She had little choice but to pack up her fifteen-year-old twins and move back home to Juliet. They were living with Granny Bert again, but she was trying to get back on her feet with her new business venture.

Genesis came forward with a small plate of cookies and placed it in front of Madison. "Compliments of the house. Maybe it will sweeten your deal." When she grinned, charming dimples appeared in both cheeks.

"Thanks, Genny." Madison gazed out the window beside her, which overlooked the parking spaces. "I don't even know what George Gail Burton looks like."

"Oh, about my size or a little larger. Shorter than you, maybe as tall as me. Short reddish-blond hair she wears in tight curls. Like her personality, her makeup is usually pretty dramatic."

Madison watched as a very plump woman got out of a late-model SUV and paused to fluff her cap of sandy-red curls.

When she turned toward the café, Madison got a glimpse of vivid blue eye shadow. "I think that's her," she muttered. "That, or it's the woman from that old Drew Carey sitcom."

Genesis followed her friend's gaze and confirmed George Gail's identity. "Yep, that's her."

"Genesis Dawn Baker, you always accuse *me* of having the carnival mirror. If you think you're anywhere near the same size as that woman, you're the one looking through distorted glass!"

Genny merely wrinkled her nose and moved away as the bell jingled above the café door.

At least George Gail Burton dressed more modestly than the sitcom character did, Madison noted. In contrast to her dramatic makeup, the woman making her way toward the back of the building was dressed in a smart, demure pantsuit in dark navy.

"You must be the famous Madison Cessna Reynolds!" She beamed the words while she was still several feet away.

"Uhm, yes, I suppose so." Madison peeped around self-consciously to see if anyone had overheard the 'famous' part. One nearby couple glanced her way and she saw Cutter Montgomery grin from where he perched at the bakery counter, but for the most part, no one paid attention.

"I've heard all about you! May I join you?" George Gail continued to put on a show, just in case anyone watched.

"Of course."

It was a tight squeeze, but the woman wiggled into the booth seat across from Madison. "Think they bought it?" she whispered loudly, leaning her ample bosom over the table-top. "Maybe I should ask for your autograph to make it more believable."

Madison bit back a smile. Not a soul looked their way. "I think we're good. You did a good job pretending."

"Why, thank you." George Gail seemed genuinely pleased with Madison's comment. "Actually, I did a little acting back in high school, but that was years before you came here. And I have a part in the church Christmas play every year."

"So, you graduated from The Sisters?"

"Class of '75," she chirped with a big smile.

"And your husband?"

"The same. We were high school sweethearts. Actually, I knew back in the sixth grade that I was going to marry Curtis, even before Trudy Huffman and I went to see that fortuneteller at the State Fair in Dallas. It just took him a few years to figure it out and propose to me. Men can be dense like that, you know."

"So, you've been married for almost forty years and dated for several years before that. Why do you suspect that your husband is suddenly cheating on you, after all these years?"

George Gail's double chin quivered. Tears welled in her eyes. Madison wondered if a river of blue eye shadow would pour down her face if she actually cried. "Because I found this." She reached into her oversized purse and pulled out a cell phone. She slid it across the table toward Madison. "Go on. Open it."

With a bit of a frown, Madison hesitantly did as she was told. She worried for a moment about invading someone's privacy, but George Gail sensed her reluctance and said, "Don't worry; it's in my name, so technically the phone is mine. I'm giving you permission to read the text messages."

Madison swiped her finger across the bottom of the screen to unlock it. As she did so, a series of text messages popped up on the screen.

"Go on, read them. Just read what he and that hussy have been saying to one another!"

Does she know?

Not a clue.

When can we meet?

2:00 Wed.

Our usual place?

Yes. Can't wait to see your boobs.

Madison looked back up at George Gail. She had to admit, the messages did appear incriminating.

"Can you believe it? After I've given three children, my entire adult life and most of my childhood to that man, he goes off and has a torrid affair with that trollop!"

"What is it you would like me to do, Mrs. Burton?" Madison asked gently. It seemed fairly cut and dry to her.

"I just admitted my deepest, darkest secret to you. Please, call me George Gail. And I told you on the phone what I wanted. I want you to follow the weasel, get photographs and details. I want to flaunt it all in his face, just like he's flaunting *her* in mine!"

"Who, exactly, is 'her?'"

For the first time, George Gail seemed unsure of herself. She made a face as she admitted, "Well, I don't really know. The number is blocked; text messages only."

"Then how is he flaunting her in your face?" Madison wondered the thought aloud, just enough for the other woman to hear.

"It was a figure of speech. But I'm sure he'll do just that, once their affair goes public! He'll bring her to his family reunion and to all the ranch rodeo events, get her to ride on the

Fourth of July Parade float with him, have their picture made together for Christmas pictures, do all the things he and I once did together."

Before the woman could dissolve into a flood of tears and smeared makeup, Madison broke in. "I think you may be getting ahead of yourself, George Gail. You don't even know for sure he's having an affair, much less that he will go public with his mistress and ask you for a divorce."

"Divorce! Who said anything about a divorce?"

"Well, uh, I, uh..." Madison stammered incoherently, realizing she had put her foot into her mouth with the thoughtless statement.

With a glum sigh, her companion propped her elbows onto the table and cradled her full cheeks. "I guess that's to be expected, isn't it? That's the way it usually goes."

"Honestly, George Gail, there could be a perfectly good explanation for all this."

George Gail raised perfectly groomed eyebrows, stretching the blue shadow to new heights. "Really? Why else would they be meeting behind my back to look at her boobs?"

"Well, uh... your husband's not a gynecologist by chance, is he?" Madison asked hopefully. "Or a plastic surgeon?"

"He's part owner in the cattle auction in Naomi."

"Yes, I heard they opened a new one off the highway," Madison murmured with a nod.

"He's partners with Jimmy Adams and your uncle, Joe Bert Cessna."

A light of familiarity came to Madison's eyes. "Okay, that's where I've heard his name before. And you and Aunt Trudy are good friends."

"We have been since first grade," George Gail confirmed. "I've been too embarrassed to tell her about any of this."

"Have there been any other clues? Has he been keeping odd hours, staying out late, that sort of thing?"

"If you know anything about the auction business, you know the hours are completely erratic. The sale starts at noon every Friday. If people bring in three hundred head, the sale is over by two that afternoon. If they bring in three thousand, the sale isn't over until two the next morning. They often have special sales in the middle of the week or hold cattle over in the pens, so he spends a lot of time at the sale barn. Your uncle has his own ranch to run and Jimmy is the Ag teacher at school, so it's Curtis' responsibility to be at the barn most of the time."

"Has he been... less attentive to you lately?" Madison phrased her question carefully.

"What? Oh, you mean... no, no!" A blush stained the other woman's cheeks, causing a similar shade to invade Madison's face. "My Curtis is a very amorous man. No change there."

"So, you're basing your assumption of an affair solely on these few text messages?"

With a huff, George Gail reached into her purse again. "You obviously won't take me seriously, not until I've paid you. So here." She slid a bank envelope across the table. "You count it. One thousand dollars, in cold, crisp cash."

Madison opened the flap and glanced inside, noting several hundred-dollar bills.

"Didn't you see the other messages on there?" George Gail demanded. She scrolled back through the phone, flashing the screen toward Madison with every offending message.

Like the pink behinds best.
Work the ride.
Hope we pull this off.

"There's definitely some hanky-panky going on!" she declared. "You'll take my case, right?"

"Again, I must caution you that I'm not a private investigator."

"Can you operate a camera?" George Gail asked in an exasperated tone.

"Yes, of course."

"Can you take note of times and dates?"

"Well, yes."

"Can you drive a car?"

"Of course." She didn't technically own one, not since her late-night rendezvous with an old pickup truck and a train, but she was driving a loaner from the dealership. As soon as her Uncle Glenn returned from his vacation, she planned to buy it. His return, of course, would mean the end of her job at Cessna Motors, but perhaps he would take the money in this envelope as the down payment.

"Then I don't care what you call yourself. I just want you to follow my husband, see where he goes, who he meets at what time, and take photographic proof that he's cheating on me. Can you or can you not do that?"

Madison could already think of a dozen things that could go wrong.

She could also think of a thousand things that could go right.

Slipping the envelope into her purse, Madison accepted the challenge in the other woman's blue-shadowed eyes. "I can do that, George Gail," she said with confidence. "First, I'll need a little more information, and you'll need to sign this contract."

Simple as that. *In a Pinch Temporary Services* had a new client.

2

When Madison arrived at the three-bedroom house she shared with her grandmother, she saw both the old Buick and the brand-new motor home parked in the driveway. She considered herself lucky to catch the elderly woman home; just because Granny Bert was eighty didn't mean she was a homebody. Her grandmother's recent resignation as mayor of Juliet simply meant she now had more time to run the roads.

"Granny?"

Madison made two sweeps through the house before she became concerned and started calling for her grandmother in earnest. "Granny Bert, where are you?"

She eventually heard the muffled voice from somewhere above her head. "Up here!"

"In the attic?" She more or less muttered the words in confusion as she made her way to the hallway and the attic's pull-down staircase. Tugging on the string to open the portal, she called again, "Granny? Are you in the attic?"

"Come on up," her grandmother's voice called from the overhead space. "But be careful. The dad-blamed stairs closed up on me."

Madison hadn't been up to the attic in years. She used caution as she climbed the simple staircase and stepped into the lofty space that had fascinated her as a child. Tugged into odd angles and stretched across the varied corners of the old craftsmen-styled home, the attic was large and rambling, and more crowded than she remembered. She spotted her grandmother beneath the low beam of a dormer, sifting through boxes by light from the window.

"How long have you been up here? Are you all right?" Madison asked in concern.

"I'm fine. Been here for quite a while, but I knew you'd be home sooner or later and come looking for me." Bertha Cessna brushed away her granddaughter's worry with a casual shrug.

"What are you doing up here, anyway?"

"Looking for some papers."

"Do you need help?" Madison offered, ducking under a rafter to come closer.

"Oh, I found what I needed an hour or two ago. I've just been visiting old memories. Seeing some of this stuff again is like discovering an old friend all over again."

Madison understood what her grandmother meant when she glanced around, and her eyes fell on a familiar object. "You used to let me play with the hats in that old trunk," she remembered with a smile. "I would pose in front of that antique mirror and pretend I was somebody important."

"You've always been somebody important, girl."

Little words of encouragement such as those had helped Madison through many hard times. Granny Bert might be crusty—and certainly unconventional—but Madison knew she had her undying love and support. Even when she couldn't depend on her flighty parents, she could always depend on her grandmother.

"So, what's that box you're digging in?" she asked conversationally. "Would you like me to carry it down so you can look through it in better light?"

"Are you implying I'm too old and feeble to carry it down myself?"

Madison laughed at the fiery comeback. "No, I figured you would have your hands full with whatever you came looking for to begin with."

Granny Bert's only reply was to nod toward the box she pilfered through. "These are pictures of the Big House, back in the day."

That was what locals called Juliet Randolph Blakely's old estate. It dominated an entire city block and sat in a prominent location off Second and Main, a grand three-story structure that always reminded Madison of a wedding cake.

"I'm sure it was really something back then," she murmured. After one hundred years, it was in sad need of new paint and some major updating.

"Oh, it was. And it will make a fine home for you and the twins."

"Granny, I told you I can't afford to buy the Big House, even if I wanted to."

"So, you're saying you don't want to live there?"

"I didn't say that. Not exactly. But you must admit, it needs a lot of repair. That kitchen layout is a nightmare."

"It was designed for the times, back before microwaves and dishwashers and pot-fillers. It still has a wood stove and an icebox, mind you. Back then, room to roll out biscuits was more important than saving steps between the stove and refrigerator. But all that can be remodeled, you know. You have to look at the potential. There's plenty of room in that house for you and your young'uns."

"Plenty of bedrooms and common rooms, yes, but very few bathrooms," Madison grumbled.

"It's a grand house, Maddy, if you just give it a chance. I've always loved that old house, and it would make me pleased as punch to see you living there."

"Why me?" Madison asked, not for the first time.

"I told you, everyone else is all settled. Except for your father with his chronic sense of wanderlust, all my boys have homes of their own. Same thing for my other grandchildren. But you need a house and the Big House needs an owner. More importantly, it needs a family to live in it. Seems like a perfect fit to me, even if some of the pieces have a few odd shapes."

Still unconvinced, Madison chewed her bottom lip. "I don't know..."

Granny Bert ignored the negativity and continued, "Mama used to take me to work with her and let me play in the kitchen, or on that long, covered porch out back. While she whipped up dishes for Miss Juliet's dinner parties and afternoon teas, I would slip off and traipse all over that mansion. It has more than one hidden passage, you know." Her old eyes twinkled with the memory. "Your Great-Uncle Jubal and I would get into a mess of trouble hiding in some of those places, trying to spy on the grownups. A time or two, we heard things not intended for young ears, and one time I plumb near got stuck in a narrow spot beside the library fireplace!"

Enchanted by her grandmother's story, Madison forgot her misgivings about the house. "Did Miss Juliet ever catch you?"

"No, but it's a wonder she didn't hear us giggling from behind the walls. We thought we were awfully smart, slipping through all those secret places."

"So why did she have secret passages? I know they did that sort of thing back in Civil War days, but she built the Big House fifty years later. What—or who—did she have to hide?"

"There's no telling what she was thinking. Her daddy had the house built for her, an exact replica of the one he was building for Naomi across the railroad tracks. But rumor has it that both girls made a few modifications, no doubt trying to make her own house more special than the other. Miss Juliet was all about show, always concerned about appearances. She probably put in secret hallways, so the servants wouldn't be seen carrying her dirty underwear!"

Madison laughed along with her grandmother, imagining uniformed maids carrying bundles of bloomers and old-fashioned corsets. Rose Hamilton, Granny Bert's mother, was the main cook at the mansion. Did she ever have to carry dirty dishes through those hidden halls?

Shaking the visuals from her mind, Madison cocked her head. "So, I've always wondered, Granny. Why did Miss Juliet leave the Big House and almost everything else she owned to you?"

"She left some money and property to my three brothers," Granny Bert was quick to point out.

"Very little, compared to what she left you. She practically gave you her town."

A look of sympathy flooded her grandmother's wrinkled face. "For all her airs and fancy ways, Miss Juliet was a lonely old woman. She wanted children so badly, but her husband died just a few weeks after they were married. I was just a baby when Mama first brought me along to work, and I think Miss Juliet liked to imagine I was her little girl. She would invite me to have tea with her and she would show me her books. She loved to read, you know. I think it was her escape from a sad, miserable life. Even after I married your grandfather and started a family of my own, I would visit her at least once a week. Sometimes, I think she may have lived her life through me."

"Maybe that explains why she left everything to you, even though you're so different from her. Maybe you were brave enough to live the life she couldn't bring herself to live." Blake, Madison's teenage son, made a similar observation when she told him Granny Bert was heiress to the town. "And maybe she knew if her town were to survive, it needed a new direction, one with strong leadership."

"If you're trying to say I'm pushy and uncouth, you may have a point." She grinned as if the attributes were favorable.

"You married the love of your life, raised four sons, have seven grandchildren and a slew of great-grandchildren. You've been mayor of Juliet, a River County elected official, you love to travel and do new things, you have friends from all walks of life, and Willie Nelson wrote a song about you. You have to admit, you're about as different from Miss Juliet as you can be."

"Don't forget the motorcycle and bungee jump."

Madison laughed. "Yes, you drove a motorcycle for years before you wrecked it racing my father, and for your seventy-fifth birthday party, you took everyone bungee jumping. I'm sure the most daring thing Miss Juliet ever did was serve red wine with fish. You know she had to admire your enthusiasm for life."

"She didn't have it easy, you know." Granny Bert couldn't help but defend her friend and benefactor. "Her mother died when she and Naomi were babies, and their father spoiled them so. There was just the two of them, but they never could get along. Their daddy had to give them each their own house and their very own town, because the older they got, the bigger the rivalry."

Familiar with the old story, Madison nodded in empathy. With no son to inherit his cotton plantation, cotton king Bertram Randolph divided his dynasty into three distinct entities. Each daughter received plats to a town she could develop and manage to her own liking. Upon his death, the rich farmland went to his oldest and most trusted employee, Andrew deCordova. It was a blessing Bertram Randolph never knew the final fate of his beloved daughters.

"And then their father got sick, and they both fell in love with his new doctor," Madison recalled the sad legend.

"They say Darwin Blakely was a real looker. Had some fancy doctoring degree from Philadelphia. Trouble is, the man couldn't make a decision without seeing which way his pecker blew."

"Granny!"

"Oh, don't act so scandalized," her grandmother chided. "You sound like Miss Juliet. She pretended she'd never heard a dirty word in her life, but I traveled those secret halls enough to know better. She was known to cuss up a blue streak once in a while, when she thought no one was around to hear. Most of the time, the words were directed at her own sister and poor little niece."

Madison could certainly empathize with her. "Can you imagine how humiliated she was, a new widow who discovers another woman is carrying her late husband's child? Her very own sister, no less?"

"The man finally decided and chose Juliet, but it was little consolation once he died and Love was born."

"Do you think Miss Naomi named her baby that on purpose, to further humiliate her sister?"

"With those two, you never know. But you forget… in that day and age, the humiliation was on Naomi, having a child out of wedlock."

"You knew Love, didn't you?"

Granny Bert nodded. "My mama never was one to put on airs or snub another soul. She didn't cotton to the notion of not being able to talk to neighbors, just because they lived in the town of Naomi when she lived in Juliet. She was good as gold to everyone she met, and she encouraged me to make friends on both sides of the track. But the one person I wasn't allowed to talk to was Love Randolph. She felt she owed Miss Juliet that much."

"What about later, when you were an adult?" Madison wondered.

"By then, it didn't matter. Love married Hugh Redmond and died giving birth to their second child."

Madison remembered going to school with some Redmond kids. Even though they had the money to buy nice clothes and nice cars and make-believe friends, they were never quite part of the "in" crowd at school. Back then, old prejudices still ran deep.

"I'd like to think the towns have finally evolved, have finally learned to be more tolerant of one another. What does it matter that a hundred years ago, someone's great-grandmother was born out of wedlock? What does it matter which side of the track you live on, what town your mail is addressed to? We share the same schools and public utilities. But I met with a new client today, and she is convinced that if her husband is having an affair, it's with a trollop from Naomi. That's where all the trollops live, according to her."

Granny Bert gave an unflattering grunt. "She must not know Sheree Blackburn, Angie Jones, or Lana Kopetsky," she mumbled, only half under her breath. Louder, she asked, "Who's your new client?"

Madison hesitated. Granny Bert could be an invaluable source of information, but she could also be an undeniable gossip. "I—I'm not sure I'm at liberty to say."

Her grandmother merely snickered. "I understand. Customer confidentiality and all that. And you're probably undercover again, right?"

Madison squirmed uncomfortably, answering the question without saying a word.

"Okay, so I won't go around blabbing that you have a new client. I can be discreet. Who do you want to know about this time?"

Again, Madison hesitated. She needed to follow Curtis Burton without being seen. Her only hope of catching him with his mistress was to catch him unaware, and that would be impossible if he heard about her surveillance through the grapevine. She warred with her options for a moment longer, before taking advantage of Granny Bert's uncanny knowledge of everything that went on in The Sisters.

"What do you know about Curtis Burton?" she finally asked.

"A fine, God-fearing, church-going man. Good father and husband. Your Uncle Joe Bert's best friend and business partner at The Sisters Livestock Auction. Practically raised that boy myself, he was in and out of the house so much. He was friends with your own daddy; all my boys, in fact." Granny Bert peered at her over the top of the opened box. "You can't seriously be mentioning the name 'Curtis Burton' and 'trollop' in the same sentence. That man is as faithful as the sunrise. He dotes on George Gail, crazy makeup and all."

"Granny Bert, you have to promise me that what I am about to say to you doesn't go beyond these walls." Madison stressed the words with a piercing gaze.

"Scout's honor."

"You weren't a scout. And don't bother with crossing yourself, either," she warned, seeing her grandmother's hand movements. "We aren't Catholic."

"Just tell me what you know, girl," Granny Bert said impatiently.

"Not until you promise."

"I promise." She made the oath, but her nose wrinkled in distaste.

"George Gail found text messages between Curtis and some unknown woman. I have to admit, they look pretty incriminating."

"Who was the other woman?"

"She doesn't know. And the phone number was blocked. She's hired me to follow her husband and find out where he goes and who he's seeing. But remember, Granny, you mustn't say one word about this to anyone, especially not to Aunt Trudy! George Gail is too ashamed for even her best friend to know about this."

"There has to be another explanation. I refuse to believe that Curtis Burton would cheat on his wife. He's been in love with that girl since they were in junior high, but he was too afraid to tell her until they were in high school. I was the one to coach him on how to finally ask her out! You can't tell me he would cheat on her, not after all these years."

"Yeah, well, even the best ones are capable of cheating," Madison said, allowing bitterness to seep into her words.

"Not Curtis Burton," her grandmother insisted.

"We'll find out soon enough. George Gail has a dentist appointment tomorrow at two, and I'm supposed to follow Curtis when he meets this mysterious woman."

"Won't do you any good, because that man is not cheating on his wife. But I suppose you need to at least make a show of earning the money she's paying you. If he spots you following him, just create a diversion," her grandmother advised as she shoved the box she had been digging through into Madison's arms and motioned for the stairs.

"How on earth do you—"

"Never mind how I know how to spy on someone. Here, take these on down to the kitchen table. I'll come down and make us both a power shake. How does kale and cabbage sound, with just a pinch of grapefruit juice and honey?"

As Madison stomped noisily down the attic steps, she muttered against the cardboard box, "It sounds like I should have never given you that juicer for Christmas!"

3

Madison felt guilty about leaving her job at Cessna Motors to take on her newest assignment.

In truth, there was nothing at the dealership needing her attention; she had already done payroll, all the filing was complete, and the phone lines were particularly quiet that day. Still, she asked Granny Bert to cover for her while she slipped out to spy on Curtis Burton.

George Gail made certain her husband came home for a late lunch. Madison nibbled on her own sandwich as she watched the house from two blocks away. Five minutes after George Gail left for her dentist appointment, Curtis Burton crawled into his blue pickup truck and pulled out in the opposite direction. Madison allowed him a good head start before trailing slowly behind.

This was her first surveillance mission and she didn't want to blow it. When he made an unexpected stop just one block after turning onto Main Street, she feared he had spotted her. But he pulled up in front of *Posey's Petals & Plants* and went inside without even glancing her way.

The string of quaint wooden houses along Main Street's east side had long ago been converted to businesses. *Posey's* sat on the corner, across from the Big House. Per Miss Juliet's strict requirements, any side buildings or unattractive necessities for the nursery were relegated to the back of the property, well hidden from the street view; and of course, only lush plants and gardens could face the prized mansion.

Madison dawdled at the stop sign down the street, thankful no cars were behind her. A few minutes later, she watched as Curtis came out of the florist carrying a small bouquet of fresh flowers. As he folded his long, thin body back inside his pickup, Madison pulled slowly away from the stop sign and followed him as he crossed the railroad tracks and headed into the town of Naomi.

Madison hated to admit it, but so far, George Gail's assumptions of an affair seemed to be correct, especially when the blue pickup pulled into the parking lot of the *Bumble Bee Hotel.*

Madison parked across the street, where she had a clear shot of Curtis Burton as he carried the flowers up the front steps of the old mansion turned hotel and disappeared inside. She snapped off a few pictures, zooming in on the small bouquet he held in his hands and the look of anticipation upon his face. She was a bit surprised to discover Curtis was still a very handsome man.

Madison soon grew bored as she waited for Curtis to come out. How long could an afternoon liaison take, anyway? She finished her lunch, listened to the entire Bryan Adams *Tracks of My Years* CD two times through, filed her nails, and sent a dozen or more text messages as she sat in the car.

Staring at the hotel once again, Madison willed the door to open. She could only stare at a yellow and black house for so long, she decided, before her eyes began to cross and her stomach felt nauseous. Her skin even began to itch and there was a humming in her head, as surely as if bees buzzed about.

Except for the bright color scheme, Naomi Randolph's old home looked identical to the Big House. But like their original owners, the houses were as different as the sisters themselves. Juliet's pristine white mansion had always been haughty and elegant, cool and inaccessible except for formal invitations to visit. The Big House now stood vacant and empty, echoing the life of the lonely woman who once lived inside.

Across the railroad track, Naomi's old home was still vibrant and alive. Long before her death, she had painted the house a robust yellow trimmed in black and opened it to the public. Now her granddaughter ran *The Bumble Bee Hotel,* a three-story structure that featured community rooms on the bottom floor, lodging on the second, and two extravagant suites on the third floor. The grounds served as an outdoor venue for weddings, parties, and family reunions.

There was little activity, however, on this Wednesday afternoon in early February. Madison was getting a crick in her neck from staring in one direction for so long. She considered giving up when the front door finally opened, and Curtis Burton stepped outside.

She snapped off a few more photos, documenting the time of his departure. Instead of a bouquet, he carried a piece of paper in his hands and wore a satisfied smile on his rugged but handsome face. He reminded Madison of a movie star from an old western. Tall and thin with a long handlebar mustache and the air of timeless strength and virility. Judging from the hour and twenty minutes he had been inside, she decided he was definitely virile.

Madison ducked as he pulled out of the parking lot and drove past her. A good five minutes passed before a woman came out of the hotel, carrying a bulky leather bag and a familiar bouquet of flowers.

"Now we're getting somewhere," Madison mumbled aloud. She took several pictures of the small woman in the fur-lined leather jacket. Even though the weather was sunny and mild, she wore the coat cinched at her tiny waist with matching fur-lined boots beneath black leggings. A fur bubble hat sat smartly upon her coiffed head.

Madison felt a stab of sympathy for her client. This woman was everything George Gail wasn't: small, dainty, and fashionable.

Who am I kidding? I'm none of those things, either, Madison thought wryly.

At five feet seven inches, Madison's arms and legs were too long and thin to ever be considered 'dainty.' She might be slim, but she was hardly small. She had broad shoulders and 'a good understanding in life,' which was Granny Bert's way of saying she had big feet. And fashionable? Madison refused to glance down at her own sad wardrobe, not after taking in the other woman's appearance.

As she zoomed in on the woman's face, she saw that the smartly dressed home wrecker wasn't a day under sixty.

The woman gracefully tucked her petite form behind the wheel of a late-model Lincoln. She took a moment to slide on designer eyeglasses and adjust her seatbelt before putting the car into gear. Jotting down the license plate number and car details, Madison noted the window sticker on the back glass.

There were no trendy women's gyms here in The Sisters, but the franchised brand might be found in Bryan-College Station or Waco; even Houston was within easy driving distance.

Judging from the woman's attire and overall aura of sophistication, Madison guessed she wasn't a local. She must be meeting Curtis here from out of town.

"Well, this poses a problem." Madison spoke aloud to herself as she trailed behind the white Lincoln through the streets of Naomi, heading toward the highway. She had enough gas to follow the car all the way to Houston, but did she have the time? The kids would be home from school soon. She promised to take Bethani to a friend's house to practice for cheerleader tryouts, and Blake would undoubtedly be starved after baseball practice.

On the other hand, if she let the car out of her sight, she might never find to whom it belonged. She couldn't very well ask Chief of Police Brash deCordova to run the license plate number, not after he made it clear she shouldn't be "playing junior detective."

Deciding to follow at least long enough to know which direction it turned, Madison kept back at a safe distance.

The highway bypass was another new addition to The Sisters since Madison moved away. The handy overpass sailed right over the railroad and the towns spreading out on either side; newly constructed double lanes raced off in either direction, eager to offer an escape route. For most towns, a new highway meant new growth, new businesses popping up alongside the roadways, even when that growth often meant the death of the old downtowns. But here in The Sisters, the land bordering the highway was still controlled by the deCordovas and the estates of Juliet Blakely and Naomi Randolph.

By rare mutual agreement, only two businesses were allowed access to the highway trade: one on the southbound side of Juliet, the other on the northbound side of Naomi.

To Madison's surprise, the car crossed the highway and immediately took the Juliet exit on the other side of the highway, pulling into the convenience store's parking lot. *Was I that obvious?* she worried. *Does she know I'm following her?*

Madison parked several spaces down from the Lincoln and gave the woman time to go inside before she opened her car door. Maybe she could get in line behind the woman at the register and get a peek at her driver's license when she opened her wallet or overhear someone calling her by name. If she was meeting Curtis Burton at their 'usual place,' she may have been in here before. It was worth a try, especially if it kept Madison from following her all the way to another town.

The fashionable woman was nowhere to be seen along the aisles of the small convenience store, nor at the back counter where questionable-quality pizza was offered. That left only the restroom.

Madison stepped inside the ladies' room, just in time to see the middle stall door closing. She caught the tail end of the woman's conversation.

"No, the wife doesn't suspect a thing!" She laughed merrily.

She's bragging about her affair? For the sake of George Gail, herself, and unsuspecting wives the world over, Madison felt a rush of fury at the woman's cavalier attitude. *Unbelievable!*

"Okay, I had to make a pit stop. You know my bladder's not what it used to be," the woman chirped into her cell phone. "I'll meet you there in about forty minutes. Tootles."

Madison flinched as the woman carelessly tossed her fur-lined coat over the top of the stall's door. She resisted the urge to barricade the hussy—as George Gail called her—inside the stall. The woman may have looked dignified, but obviously she was no better than the trollop George Gail accused her to be.

A soft thump suggested the trollop hung her purse from the hook on the other side of the door.

Unbidden, an old story Granny Bert told Madison years ago came to mind. According to her grandmother, a woman's purse was stolen from a similar hook, keys and wallet still inside. A good samaritan called the next day to report finding the purse and arranged a meeting to return it. As the story went, while the grateful woman was gone, the thief used her own house key to go inside the house and steal her blind. To this day, Madison always took the time to wrap her purse strap around the hook or to stash her bag elsewhere.

A wicked idea slipped inside Madison's mind. George Gail had paid her a thousand dollars to learn the woman's identity, but even if she followed the Lincoln all the way to another town, there was no guarantee of success. But there was another way.

And Granny Bert *had* suggested a diversion.

Ignoring her conscience, Madison dug into her pocket and found a roll of breath mints. She swiped a piece of toilet tissue from the adjacent stall and wrapped it around the mints several times, leaving a long twisted 'tail' sticking up. She waited until she heard another rustle of clothes and was certain the home-wrecking woman was otherwise occupied, then rolled the mints along the floor beneath the middle stall.

In what she hoped sounded like a frightened voice, Madison squealed, "Oh my gosh! What is that? Is that a rat?"

The home wrecker immediately shrieked. Madison's hand slipped over the door, snagging the purse as she heard the commotion on the other side. She could just imagine the woman jumping to her feet, black tights tangled around her knees, frantically dancing around the tiny space and scanning the back wall for a glimpse of the rodent.

"Oh, it *is* a rat!" Madison cried again, even as her hand made quick work of jerking the wallet from the designer purse. A silver compact came out alongside the expensive wallet and clattered to the floor, adding to the noise and confusion. As it rolled into the stall, Madison added urgently, "Watch out, there it goes again!"

Obviously terrified, the woman inside blubbered incoherently. Her heels tapped out a frantic tempo on the tile floor as she hopped from one foot to the other. By now, she was in actual sobs.

Tamping down feelings of remorse, Madison flicked the wallet open and quickly scanned the driver's license inside.

Claudette Ellingsworth
562 North River Oaks
Naomi, Texas

She's a local? From right here in Naomi? Madison absorbed the surprise as she quickly slipped the wallet back inside the purse, yelled another warning that the rat was along the wall, and quickly dropped the purse over the stall door. Not bothering to find out if the strap snagged on the holder, she headed for the exit.

"I'll call for the manager!" she assured the frightened woman as she hurried out.

By the time she reached the front of the store, guilt washed over Madison. That had been a cruel trick to pull. What if the woman were so frightened, she had a heart attack, or got tangled in her state of undress, fell, and broke a leg?

She's breaking up a home and George Gail's heart, a stubborn little voice reminded her.

Still, Madison stopped at the cash register and reported there was a woman in the restroom in obvious distress. Madison quickly left the store, her conscience feeling somewhat better.

And then, as Granny Bert would say, she left Claudette Ellingsworth to her rat killing.

4

"Madison?"

The voice on the other end of the line was scratchy and low. Madison scowled, pulling her phone away to check the name on the caller ID through sleep-blurred eyes. "George Gail? Is that you?"

"Yes, it's me."

"Why do you sound so odd? Are you all right?" For a moment, Madison considered the possibility Curtis Burton discovered his wife's suspicions and had done something to harm her. A crazy thought, she knew, but what did you expect at one o'clock in the morning? She peered at the clock to confirm the time.

Beside her, Bethani rolled over in bed and grumbled a sleepy, "Is that another alarm?"

"No, honey, go back to sleep," Madison purred. One of the many downsides to her previous job at the commercial chicken houses had been the automated alarms at all hours of the night. If feed lines emptied out or temperatures changed too drastically, the computer called with an alarm and she was required to go out to the farm to manually reset it.

Madison twisted away best she could and hissed into the phone, "Do you know what time it is?"

She could all but hear George Gail nodding her head, fleshy cheeks jangling. "1:18."

"Why do you sound so muffled?"

"So Curtis won't hear me. I'm in the hall closet, standing between his hunting jackets. I couldn't sleep, not without knowing what you found out today."

You won't sleep once you find out, either, Madison thought sympathetically. She lumbered out of the bed and moved into her own closet, so she wouldn't disturb Bethani or the other two occupants of the house. "George Gail, I just started my surveillance today," she reminded her client.

"Yes, I know, and you followed him. Did you see who he met?"

"Look, it's one in the morning. Can't this conversation wait, at least until daylight?"

"You know, don't you? You know who my husband is seeing, and you don't want to tell me!" the other woman correctly guessed. "Is it Lou Ann Shellburger? She's always flirting with him in church!"

"What? No." Madison had trouble imagining the timid second-grade teacher flirting with any man, much less a married one, and right under his wife's nose.

"Denise Adams? She called here the other day, claiming to have a question about selling her mother's cows. It's her, isn't it?"

"No."

George Gail guessed at least four more women before she made a desperate accusation. "I bet it's Genesis Baker! I know she's your friend and all, but Curtis is always at her café. He carries on about how delicious everything is, and how she's added a red velvet cupcake to her line, his very favorite kind! It's her, I know it is!"

"Oh, for heaven's sake, it is not Genesis!"

"Then who is it?" George Gail demanded.

"It's Claudette Ellingsworth!" The words no sooner left her mouth, than she tried to recall them, but of course, it was too late. Madison clamped her hand over her loose lips, horrified to have allowed sleep deprivation and exasperation to make her blurt out the truth in such a fashion. Where was her compassion? Her professionalism?

"Caress?" George Gail breathed in dismay. "Beautiful, dainty little Caress, the *movie star*?"

"I thought her driver's license said Claudette." She had read the name upside down, so perhaps she had it wrong; the description sounded right, though.

"The DMV may know her as Claudette, but the world knows her as Caress." George Gail's voice was borderline reverent. With the next breath, it turned bitter. "And now she has her claws in my husband, that back-stabbing hussy! I'd like to give her a taste of her own medicine!"

"I—I don't know for certain if anything is going on between her and your husband, George Gail. I just know that they met."

"Where? Where did they meet?"

"In—In Naomi."

"Where in Naomi?" the other woman insisted.

She would have to tell her sooner or later. "At the *Bumble Bee*," Madison admitted grudgingly.

George Gail gasped. "I—I…" She stuttered an incoherent thought before quickly mumbling, "I'm sorry to have wakened you. Good night."

"George Ga—" The phone clicked off before Madison could finish.

Pushing fingers through her hair, Madison lamented breaking the news to the shattered wife in such a heartless fashion and in the middle of the night, but the damage had been done.

Now they would both have a restless night.

Madison didn't look good in dark circles, but there they were, smudged beneath her eyes.

After hanging up with George Gail, sleep was evasive. Around three a.m., she gave up all pretenses and got up to start her day. Luckily for her, the internet was open twenty-four hours and welcomed her on-line presence as she searched for a cheaper cell phone plan.

Even on a full night's sleep, her day would have been hectic. Her tight schedule didn't allow for dealing with an irate customer at Cessna Motors or spending an hour on the phone with her insurance company, who seemed to blame *her* for last month's accident. She hadn't exactly encouraged being rammed into a train from behind, but the company failed to take that into consideration while bickering with her over every dime of the claim. By the time she locked up the office at three o'clock, she was late to Blake's baseball game. She only caught two innings before she had to leave to meet with a new client for *In a Pinch*. As with George Gail, she met him at the café.

As soon as the client was out the door, Genesis slid into his recently vacated seat. "Penny for your thoughts."

Madison pretended offense. "As badly as I need money, and you only offer a penny?"

"What if I throw in a cup of coffee and Gennydoodle cookies?" she asked, motioning to the very items in her hand.

"Sold!" Madison laughed. "What would you like to know?"

"Why the long face? You looked pretty forlorn when I walked up, despite the fact you just signed a new client." At her friend's inquisitive expression, Genesis explained, "I saw you whip out the contract. So, who was he and what did he want?"

"His name is Murray Archer and he's a private investigator from the Houston area. He's working for an insurance company and needs 'eyes and ears' on a local level. Basically, he wants me to do all the legwork for a paltry little sum, while he rakes in the big bucks and claims all the glory."

"So of course you took the job," Genesis guessed.

"Of course. Even a paltry sum is better than no sum at all."

"Not that I'm complaining, but you really need an office. Especially now that you're on a roll; two clients in one week."

"How much do you charge for booth rental? That's about all I can afford."

"Is that the reason for the long face?"

"No, I was thinking about George Gail. What can you tell me about some Caress person? Attractive older woman, very petite, snappy dresser, drives a white Lincoln."

"You mean Caress Ellingsworth, another of Naomi's claims to fame, right alongside Tug Montgomery and Glitter Thompson. She's a former soap opera queen from one of those old daytime shows that got canceled. *Bleeding Heart* or something like that."

"*So Beats the Heart*," Madison nodded in recognition. "My mother-in-law was addicted to that show. She was devastated when it was canceled, especially since it was in the middle of her favorite character's big life-saving operation. She never knew if she lived or died!"

"Hey, that was Caress' character! I've heard her mention the storyline several times. She still gets fan mail from people wanting to know if she made it through the ordeal. They seem to get the character and her real life all mixed up!" Genesis laughed.

"What can you tell me about her? Is she married?"

"No, but she has an on-again/off-again relationship with none other than John-Paul Noble. She moved here permanently, but he still goes back and forth to LA."

"*The* John-Paul Noble?" Madison squeaked. "The John-Paul Noble you and I once drooled over in *Hatchet for Hire*?"

"Yep, the one and only 'Sam Hatchet,' star of our favorite television series and some of my most vivid fantasies." Genny's dimples appeared again as she flashed a smile.

"You're telling me John-Paul Noble has actually stepped foot in Naomi, Texas? Why have I never heard this before?"

"He hasn't been here since I moved back, but I understand he calls this his second home. That is, when he and Caress are 'on' again."

Madison stared at her friend in amazement. John-Paul Noble was a legendary actor, best known for his outlandish playboy lifestyle and his long-running private detective series. New episodes of the drama may have ended years ago, but it lived on forever in re-runs. A dozen or so movie roles kept his name in the headlines, and rumor had it he was favored to star opposite Jennifer Lopez in an upcoming thriller. His name was often mentioned with references to New York and LA, even Paris and Rio; not once had the media reported his connection to tiny little Naomi, Texas.

"Wait a minute," Madison said with a sudden frown. "Isn't he a lot younger than Caress?"

Another dimpled grin. "You know his reputation; John-Paul is a non-discriminating man-ho. He loves women of all ages, shapes, colors, and form. He and Caress first got together when he had a recurring role on the soap."

Madison rattled her head to clear it. "So, what on earth is Caress doing here in Naomi in the first place?"

"Her grandparents were from here. I think she's somehow related to Molly Shubert, whose husband runs the pharmacy."

"I thought his wife died a few years ago," she murmured in confusion, remembering the news from Granny Bert. "Something about a prescription drug overdose?"

"So I heard. Rather convenient, wouldn't you say, for a pharmacist's wife? He remarried a couple years ago and has a new family, but that's a whole other story." Genny waved the train of thought away, not wanting to get sidetracked. "Why the questions about the former soap queen?"

Madison glanced around to make certain no one was close enough to overhear her words. "I followed Curtis today. He met this Caress person at the *Bumble Bee Hotel*."

"Curtis Burton? I told you, that man is as faithful as they come!"

"Then why did they meet at a hotel, of all places?"

"I have no idea, but there has to be a plausible explanation. Curtis would never cheat on George Gail. Not only does he adore her, he's simply not the type."

"Well, George Gail wants to know the truth. I was just sitting here wondering if my own life would be different right now, if I had been as brave. Even if I couldn't save my marriage, maybe I could have saved my pride. Maybe I could have saved the business."

"Madison, you aren't to blame for what Gray did." Genny's tone was adamant. "Gray destroyed your marriage. He was the one to run your business into the ground and leave you destitute. He is to blame, not you."

"You're right. I know you're right. I just like to wallow around in self-pity every now and then," Madison admitted. She took in a deep breath, held it in her lungs for a moment, then released it slowly. Her technique was obvious but effective. When she opened her eyes, they held renewed energy. "So," she said, changing gears with the new topic, "how are plans coming for your Valentine's Day Mixer?"

Genny's blue eyes sparkled. "I think this is actually going to be a success! Everyone seems to be really excited about it."

"Most everything you do is successful, Gen. You just have that golden touch."

Her friend's short burst of laughter was followed by a crinkled nose. "Except for in my personal life. It has more of a rusty grunge than a golden glow."

"And whose fault is that? Who never takes time for herself, always busy putting others first?"

"You?"

"And you, my friend. You should be celebrating Valentine's Day one on one with someone special, not hosting a party for an entire town."

She waved a dismissive hand through the air. "Maybe next year. This year I wanted to do something special for the community. They've welcomed me with open arms and made these first months in business phenomenal. I want to give something back by throwing this party."

"What can I do to help?"

"So far, everything is going according to schedule. I have the band booked, the decorations all lined up, the food planned and ordered, extra workers scheduled, the advertisements underway." She ticked the items off her fingers as she ran a mental checklist.

"Sounds perfect," Madison smiled. She was truly proud of her friend for her creativity and success.

"Oh, and I have our dresses ordered."

"Dresses?"

"Since you and I are acting as hostesses that night, I have a little something special for us to wear."

Madison groaned. She and her friend had decidedly different tastes in clothes. "Please tell me there are no ruffles. I hate ruffles."

Genesis gave her a mysterious grin. "All I will say is that you are going to be a knock-out. Brash deCordova had better step up his game, or he'll find he's missed his chance with you. Again."

Stifling a yawn, Madison attempted a low-level threat. "If I had the energy, I would insist on seeing the dress before agreeing to help with the party."

"You've already agreed," Genny reminded her.

As Genesis touched up their coffee, Madison turned bleary, unseeing eyes toward the window. She idly watched as a white van pulled up outside, but she paid no heed to the fancy graphic painted on its side panel.

Madison's sleep-deprived mind was elsewhere as her eyes lazily tracked the woman getting out of the van on the passenger side. She was dressed in a tailored red wool business suit and could easily grace the cover of a magazine, prompting

Madison to make an abrupt declaration. "Valentine's Day dress aside, I need a new wardrobe."

"Agreed, but what brought on this sudden realization?"

"Next to Caress Ellingsworth, that woman out on the sidewalk, and even George Gail herself, I feel like a dowdy little ragamuffin."

Genesis followed the tilt of her friend's head to the fashionably dressed woman getting out of the van. She immediately muttered beneath her breath, something about being two days early.

"Have you ever seen that woman before?" Madison asked. "She looks a little overdressed for Naomi. Maybe she's Caress' daughter. They have the same flair for style."

"Uh, Maddy, there's something I've been meaning to tell you."

"Oh, wait," Madison continued to speculate. "Maybe she's that man's daughter. You know, your customer that's always bragging about his daughter who works in television. Mr. Pierce or somebody."

"Mr. Pruett. Tom Pruett. No, I don't think that's his daughter."

Madison missed the nervous tone in her friend's voice as she yawned, yet again.

"Are you listening to me? There's something I need to tell you." Genesis' tone became more insistent. She took Madison's arm and shook it to capture her friend's attention.

Blinking in surprise, Madison looked down at Genny's firm grip, then into her worried blue gaze. "What's going on, Genny?"

"I, uh, I have a surprise for you. You know that Granny Bert offered to sell you the Big House, now that you've decided to stay in The Sisters."

"Yes, but we all know I can't afford it, no matter how great of a deal she offers me. And I certainly can't afford to remodel it." There was a bit of a wistful sigh hidden in her words. Ever since her talk with Granny Bert in the attic, the house had been on her mind. It did, indeed, have potential, but all that potential added up to more money. Money she didn't have.

"What if I told you I might know of a way to remodel?"

Madison frowned. "What are you talking about, Genesis?"

"Have you ever heard of the television show *Home Again,* where they restore old houses for people to live in?"

"I've never personally seen it, but I've heard people talk about it."

"Well, I took the liberty of contacting the show and sending in a few shots of the Big House. The producers were interested enough to say they would send out a team to look at it, day after tomorrow." Genesis slid her gaze toward the van. A man now joined the woman on the sidewalk. "Apparently they're early. And apparently, they're interested enough that the show's star has come to see it for himself. That's the main carpenter and anchor of the show, Nick Vilardi."

Madison stared at her friend in total surprise, even as the bell jingled above the door and the occupants of the van stepped inside.

Television-land had come to The Sisters.

5

The next five minutes were a blur for Madison.

She sat dumbly in her seat as Genesis popped out of the booth and hurried toward the door. As Genesis greeted the newcomers with animated features, Madison's sleepy brain tried to make sense of it all. Something about a television show and a way to buy the Big House. Something about the sexy hunk shaking Genny's hand. The words floated around in her head without making a connection.

Genny's bubbling laughter drifted back to the booth where Madison sat. One by one, the trio at the door turned around to look at her. Almost as an afterthought, Madison nervously wiggled her fingers in greeting.

An exaggerated head movement from Genny finally propelled her into motion. She was aware of the eyes upon her as she stood awkwardly from the booth and straightened her simple cotton blouse. She was particularly aware of the light of appreciation within the man's gaze.

At least she wore one of her better outfits today, a starched cornflower-blue oxford shirt with black slacks and her favorite boots. Like most of her wardrobe, the classic outfit was tasteful and timeless. She ignored the little voice in her head that reminded her it was also ageless; it could have as easily come from her grandmother's closet as her own.

Thank goodness she had cut her hair recently, she thought as she raked her fingers through the shortened ends. After years of wearing it long and straight, a sudden bout of wounded pride prompted her to give the stylist free rein on the style. The result was a very flattering bob that highlighted her cheekbones and made her nose look smaller and her eyes larger. The new layers added softness to her angular face and ended at a jaunty little angle just below her chin.

"Maddy, I want to introduce you to these people. This is Nick Vilardi, star of the hit remodeling show *Home Again* and his producer, Amanda Hooper. And *this* is Madison Reynolds." Genesis made the introductions as if Madison were the celebrity.

The blond woman in the red suit smiled warmly as she thrust out a hand in greeting. "Mrs. Reynolds, what a pleasure to meet you."

Madison's smile was hesitant and more than a bit confused. "Hello."

"And I'm Nick."

The deep voice, kissed with the faintest of Italian accents, immediately resonated with something deep within Madison. She lifted her startled gaze into a pair of dark-blue eyes the color of a stormy sky.

She thought she was prepared for the sizzle she instinctively knew was coming. Madison braced herself, but she literally jerked the moment his hand enveloped hers. A shot of electricity ricocheted through her arm, setting off sparks throughout her body. Embarrassment flooded her cheeks with a rosy-red hue, but for the life of her, Madison couldn't pull her hand from his.

The man wasn't handsome, not in the traditional way. Good looking, yes, but there was an odd symmetry to his face. His nose was slightly crooked, his thick, dark brows not quite even. The distinct grooves in his cheeks were charming now, but she wondered how much the creases would deepen and change through the years. Still, there was something arresting about his face. Something powerful. Other than Brash deCordova, it had been years since any man, even Gray, caused her such a physical reaction.

Surprise flashed in the depths of his stormy-blue eyes. Did he feel it, too? Or was he merely taken aback by her flinch? His voice seemed to have a new layer of warmth as he said, "It is definitely a pleasure to meet you."

He still held her hand. Warmth crept up from his fingers and swirled low in her belly, in places Madison forgot even existed. She knew she should pull away, but she was held captive by the magnetism of his touch.

Maybe I'm dreaming, she reasoned. I'm having one of those dreams where you try to move, try to speak, but your body won't cooperate. Or maybe I'm sleepwalking. I'm so tired…

There was something intimate about his gaze. Their handshake lingered past the two-to-five second rule, stretching well into the ten-second range. As he finally released her hand, his fingertips brushed softly over her palm, setting off a new wave of erratic heartbeats.

She had never seen his show, but Madison was suddenly his biggest fan.

Amanda Hooper spoke up, filling the awkward silence. "Miss Baker tells us you have an intriguing house you'd like for us to see. Is this a convenient time for you?" Her smile was expectant.

"Well, I, uh, I—" Madison knew she was stuttering, but her mind refused to work properly. "I—I suppose so," she managed to say.

"Wonderful! We can take the van." The television producer gave a bright smile that said everything was decided.

"Would you give us just a minute?" Genny was already taking Madison's arm and tugging her friend toward the back booth. The moment they were out of earshot, she whispered, "What is wrong with you? You act like you're in a trance!"

"I think I am. What did you *do*?"

"I told you, I sent in pictures of the Big House to have them consider it for the show. And don't worry, I have the key."

"How did you...?"

Seeing the dazed expression on Madison's face, Genny gave her arm a comforting pat. "Don't worry. Granny Bert and I took care of everything. Go get your purse while I tell the staff I'm leaving."

She stepped away before Madison could ask questions. Genesis asked Shilo Dawne Nedbalek to watch the café in her absence.

"Who is *that*?" the young woman asked in a dreamy voice. The waitress' eyes were glued to the man at the door. "He looks kind of like the guy on that TV show *Home Again*."

"Don't tell anyone, but that's exactly who it is."

"It is? You're kidding! What's he doing here?" Shilo Dawne all but squealed.

"I'll tell you later." Genesis turned to the young man sitting at the counter. It was a known fact that Shilo Dawne—along with almost every other female in town, young or old—had a crush on the handsome young firefighter. "Cutter, keep an eye on her for me, while she keeps an eye on the café."

"I don't see what all the fuss is about." There was a slight sulking tone in the young man's voice. Was he jealous of the way Shilo Dawne all but drooled over the television star? "You're staring at him like the heavens opened up and dropped him down to earth."

When Genesis glanced up at him, his accusing gaze centered on her, not the waitress. She merely laughed. "Hey, that's the same way most women in town look at you!" she quipped. Her eyes wandered back to the man of topic. "But you have to admit, he does have something magnetic about him."

"And he's definitely pulling me in," Shilo Dawne muttered in agreement. For once, she was completely immune to Cutter Montgomery's presence.

Genny grabbed her cell phone and keys from behind the counter, laughing as she gave Cutter's arm a sympathetic pat. His face scrunched with a deep scowl as he watched her walk away.

"Are we all ready?" Amanda Hooper smiled. She opened the door for Genesis to follow her out.

At the back booth, Madison called home to say she was running late. As she hurried to join the others, Nick Vilardi politely waited for her. He put a hand to her back as he held the door for her. Madison braced herself for his touch, prepared this time for the jolt of awareness that pricked her spine and radiated inward. His hand remained lightly on her as he fell into step beside her on the sidewalk.

Madison stole a glance at him. He was taller than Gray, yet not quite as tall as Brash. *Tall enough I can still wear my boots,* she mused. Gray never allowed her to wear heels, insisting she was already tall enough. Unlike her late husband, the television star had a powerfully built body, more sinew than flesh. *Macho* was the word that sprang to mind and echoed within her soul. Long after he dropped his hand, she felt the reverberation of his touch.

Amanda Hooper kept up a steady chatter as they followed her to the white van. As Nick hurried around the women to slide open the side door, she asked Madison, "So what made you call the show? Are you a big fan?"

"Honestly?" She slid an apologetic glance Nick's way. "I've never seen the show."

Genny spoke up and saved her friend from further embarrassment. "Actually, I'm the one who called. And yes, I am a fan. And I know the Big House will be exactly what you're looking for."

"The Big House?" Amanda echoed.

"What the local people call Juliet Blakely's old mansion."

"Well, let's go see the Big House," Nick said, offering Genesis a hand in climbing into the van.

Genesis guided them over the railroad track and into the town of Juliet. Two blocks, and they were there.

Like its twin on the other side of the tracks, the estate encompassed an entire city block and featured a three-storied house with tiers and curves and plenty of lattice edging. Large old trees, mostly oak and massive pecan, dotted the yard. A few pines mixed in here and there for year-round color. Tucked behind the house was an assortment of necessary outbuildings: a carriage house turned garage, the gardener's shed, a sagging gazebo, and a battered caretaker's cottage.

Gazing at the Big House through the windshield, Nick let out an appreciative whistle. The women were already out of the van while he still ogled the mansion.

"We can use the walk," Madison said, scurrying ahead to the foot gate. An elaborate white wrought-iron fence surrounded the property and featured an electronically operated gate for automobiles, but the smaller footpath served their purpose well. She opened the gate and led the way up the cobbled path edged with flowerbeds and small shrubs.

Nick Vilardi craned his neck, trying to see everything at once. Pure wonder stole over his features. His mouth hung open as his lips curled upward in a smile. The look of enchantment somehow made him even more attractive, something Madison hardly needed. She was trying her best to ignore him so that she could get her reeling senses back under control.

"Amanda, I haven't even seen the inside yet," Nick murmured, still looking around, "but I want this house."

"It is magnificent, isn't it?" his producer agreed. Turning to Madison, she was clearly impressed. "And this house actually belongs to you?" It was more of a rhetorical question, meant as a compliment.

"Well, not exactly," Madison admitted.

"What?" The barked word came from Nick Vilardi, as he snapped his attention back to the woman unlocking the front door. The smile immediately died on his face and suspicion crept into his eyes. "Is this some sort of prank? If you dragged us all the way out here..."

"Nick, before we jump to conclusions, let's hear what they have to say," Amanda said calmly, but the friendly light had gone from her eyes.

Madison huffed out a sigh as Genesis quickly explained, "As I mentioned, I was the one to call the show."

"Oh, so *you* own the house." Amanda looked relieved.

"No, Granny Bert owns it. Madison's grandmother. But she's offered to sell the house to Madison."

Amanda Hooper was clearly confused. Nick Vilardi looked angry.

"I'm afraid I don't understand." Irritation made the producer's words sharp. "Why did you call our show, if neither of you own the house? We came all this way to see a home we could remodel for the actual owner, not a prospective buyer."

"Please, let me explain," Genesis said. "This is a very historic home, built in 1915 by the founder of this town, but obviously it needs some major work. Madison's grandmother wants to see that the mansion remains in the family and is restored to its former glory, but that will take a great deal of money. Please don't be angry with Madison. Granny Bert and I took it upon ourselves to call your show and invite you here. Madison knew nothing about it."

Amanda was not appeased. She fairly snapped. "Exactly what were you hoping to accomplish by inviting us here?"

Genesis pointed toward Nick and offered a simple reply. "His exact reaction."

Seeing their scrunched foreheads, she hurried on to explain. "I think if you'll just step inside, you'll understand why I called you. This house would be perfect for your television show. I can see an entire season being dedicated to its transformation, but of course, that's not my call. Madison doesn't have the money or the means to restore this house on her own. It will require a very talented and capable carpenter, someone who really knows their business. Please, just come inside and see if you agree."

Genny's heartfelt speech was so compelling, the couple followed her inside without another word.

One step into the foyer, and Nick Vilardi was practically drooling. He dropped to one knee and ran his hand over the old wood floor, his touch almost reverent. The finish was worn in places, its shine dull to none, but the beauty of the wood grain was undeniable. He rapped on the floor with his knuckles. "This is quarter-sawn hickory," he said in awe. "This is all original! And considering the age and the high traffic pattern, it is in remarkable shape."

Excitement glowed in his eyes as he peered around the room, his hand still touching the floor as if to stake his claim. "Look at that lattice work in the corners. The carving on that chair rail." He stood so he could wander around the entryway. He seemed to be talking to himself, as much as to them. "The plaster is in poor shape, but that can be easily fixed. And that staircase! That banister is absolutely amazing."

He gazed around the room again, his mouth hanging agape as his dark-blue eyes danced with imagination. When his attention zeroed in on Madison, she felt the jolt of his passionate enthusiasm. "This is incredible."

Genny grinned, displaying her dimples. "Just wait until you see the rest!"

Madison swept along with the others, trying desperately to hide the fracas brewing within her. The passion on Nick Vilardi's face did strange and wicked things to her. It was all she could do to ignore the man and concentrate on the tour.

Madison had been inside the old house countless times. She had always thought it special, always thought it pretty in an outdated sort of way. But as they walked through the rooms today, seeing it through the eyes of a master carpenter, it was as if she were seeing it for the first time.

What she once saw as simple wood wainscoting in the library, Nick Vilardi pointed out as exquisite burled walnut panels. He explained the process in harvesting the natural phenomenon and pointed out the movement in the wood's grain, comparing it to granite. He gave her a brief history of the front parlor's inlaid Italian marble fireplace, explaining why that particular cream and mocha color pattern was so rare, particularly for its day and age.

As a teenager, Madison had been amused with the panoramic scene painted around the dining room walls, but there was sheer delight in Amanda Hooper's face when she saw the creation. She immediately identified the work of renowned twentieth-century artist Seymour Addison. The visual story of a Southern cotton plantation told upon the old walls was of museum quality, she said. When she named an estimated worth of the artwork, Madison's mouth fell open and Genny's eyes bulged.

The foursome walked through the remainder of the first floor, confirming what the women already knew; the stained-glass windows were exquisite, pocket doors connecting small rooms together to function as one large room were ingenious, and the kitchen was atrocious.

The stairs, Nick claimed, were a masterpiece all in themselves. Madison loved the way they turned and twisted all the way up to the third floor. She loved all the neat angles, the spacious landings at each quarter turn. She saw them as simple wood risers, stiles painted white with dark stained steps, conveniently created wide enough to transport furniture. Nick saw them as not only art, but as a piece of history. He pointed out the different woods used in construction. He explained that the mix of hickory, oak, and mahogany was a clue to its authenticity and made the structure all the more valuable, both historically and financially.

The second floor was dedicated to bedrooms and a small library. As an avid reader, Juliet Randolph Blakely made certain she had plenty of books and ample space to read them. All six bedrooms on the second floor had their own sitting room, and two featured a corner turret. In contrast to the generous accommodations, there was only one bathroom to share among them.

"I can't get over these staircases," Amanda said as she ascended the flight to the third floor. "The workmanship is amazing."

Only three rooms comprised the uppermost level. Pocket doors sectioned off the turrets, which were originally intended as sitting rooms. The space between them was one long, narrow room.

"A ballroom?" Amanda asked in glee, clasping her hands together. "How absolutely fabulous!"

"Look at those floors," Nick murmured. Once again, he went down on bended knee to examine the hardwood flooring that still held a faint glimmer of its original polish and shine. "Incredible. Absolutely incredible."

"Now do you see why I brought you here?" Genesis beamed.

A light shone in the stormy-blue depths of Nick Vilardi's eyes. It could be described as excitement, perhaps zeal, but

Madison decided the best description was hunger. There was no doubt he craved this house and the opportunity to restore it to its former glory.

"So, what it is that you propose, Miss Baker?" he asked, slanting a crooked eyebrow her way. His voice was a mixture of caution and eagerness, flavored with a touch of skepticism.

"That you restore this house so that Madison and her children can live here."

"You're married?" The surprise was evident in his voice as his eyes flew to Madison. She thought she saw disappointment flash in his eyes, but there was no denying the censure there.

"Widowed," she corrected quietly. She waited for the look of pity that usually followed her announcement, waited for the sense of guilt that normally snuck upon her. Propriety dictated she feel grief over the title, particularly so soon after Gray's death; her apathy most often created more guilt than any sense of actual mourning.

"I'm sorry to hear that," Nick replied with sincerity.

"Widowed and homeless, with teenage twins," Genesis announced, bobbing her blond head for emphasis. She refused to meet her friend's eyes, knowing they would be ablaze with embarrassment and indignation. In her opinion, now wasn't the time for pride, not when she was trying to make a deal. "She's in the process of buying the house from her grandmother, but there's no money in her budget for renovations, not the way they should be done. A house like this deserves special attention, don't you agree? And that is why I called you. Would you or would you not be interested in featuring this house on *Home Again*?"

"Of course we're *interested...*" Amanda's voiced trailed off with a silent 'but.' She shot a glance at Nick, whose stormy-blue eyes reflected his thoughts on the matter.

"Could we have a few moments alone?" he suggested.

"Of course! Take all the time you need."

"Do you mind if we take a few photos?" Amanda asked.

"Take all you like," Madison offered. "We'll go on downstairs. You can join us when you're done."

"Yes, take your time," Genesis agreed. "We'll wait for you in the dining room. Now that you've educated me on that mural, I want to take a closer look at it."

At the reminder of the mural, Amanda's eyes glowed, exactly as Genesis intended.

Madison waited until they cleared the second floor and were descending the final staircase to hiss, "I couldn't believe you back there! Why did you tell them I was homeless?"

"Because you are."

"I am not homeless!" she denied in an adamant whisper.

"You live with your eighty-year-old grandmother because the bank forced you to either sell your home at a loss or have it go into foreclosure." Her gentle tone softened the harsh truth of the words.

Madison looked glum. "I've lost just about everything I have, Genny. Do you have to take my pride, as well?"

"Aw, honey, I'm not trying to hurt you, I'm trying to get your house remodeled for free!"

"Free? Are you crazy? There's no way they will remodel this place for free. It's going to cost a fortune."

"Yep," Genesis agreed glibly as they reached the bottom step. "Which is why you can't afford it and they can."

"But for free? There's no way."

"Didn't you see that look in Nick Vilardi's eyes? He's already in love with this house. That look on his face tells me he's not about to let this jewel get away. And Amanda will go along with it, if for no other reason than the dining room mural."

"Where did you learn your negotiating skills, by the way? Having her meet us in the dining room was almost cruel."

"Not cruel, strategic. If for some reason they decide to pass, one more look at those walls will definitely change her mind!" Genny grinned with unabashed confidence.

"You should be the one working at the used car lot, not me," Madison mumbled.

Clearly unconcerned with her friend's implied insult, Genesis looked down as her phone binged. Fishing the instrument out of her pocket, she frowned as she read the text message across the screen. "It's the restaurant. I swear, I can't leave that place for ten minutes without things falling apart!"

"And you love every minute of it!"

"Yeah, I do," she admitted with a guilty grin. "Excuse me while I call Shilo Dawne and see exactly what she means by 'the shit just hit the fan.'"

6

As Genesis went into the dining room to make her call, Madison wandered into the front parlor. She tried to imagine a time when homes necessitated so many rooms. The elegant home she and Gray occupied in Dallas featured both a formal living room and a comfortable den, but for years, Granny Bert had managed comfortably with one single room to serve both functions. Juliet Blakely, however, needed a formal parlor, a ladies parlor, a library, a formal dining room, and a breakfast room. Combined with the kitchen, a butler's pantry, one bathroom, a laundry room and several functional porches, the first floor of the Big House had a sprawling footprint.

Oh, and she couldn't forget the hidden hallways. Where were they, by the way?

"Hello?" a familiar voice called from the foyer.

Madison recognized the pleasant baritone. "In here!" she called back. "Front parlor, to the left."

Brash deCordova re-snapped the leather strap over his holstered gun as he stepped into the room. Adjusting the firearm securely at his side, the police officer eyed her with concern.

"Everything all right?" he asked. He sounded cautious, perhaps anticipating trouble.

"Yes, yes, everything's fine."

He came closer, bringing with him the hint of spicy cologne, security, and old high school dreams. As always, it was a heady combination, all wrapped up in a handsome, sexy package.

Madison liked to think she outgrew her teenage crush years ago, but the butterflies in her stomach danced a different tune.

"Are you sure?" he worried. "Excuse me for saying so, but you don't look fine. Something's wrong."

His words brought to mind a similar compliment from a few weeks ago, when first their paths re-crossed. She had just found a dead body, and she looked and smelled worse than death itself. That day, the actual words had been silent, the message clear: she looked horrible.

His words also brought to mind a true compliment a few days later, this one as warm and flattering as his brown eyes when he saw her cleaned up and properly dressed. That was the beginning of several subtle attempts to flirt with her.

It brought to mind the eager way she craved his attention, even when she believed him a married man. Madison's hand instinctively went to her shortened hair, remembering how Brash had unknowingly inspired her new hairstyle. Much to her chagrin, she admittedly wanted to impress him, in spite of her firm belief in marriage vows. She almost allowed him to kiss her, still believing he had a wife. Never mind that she had resisted at the last minute. She chastised him for cheating on the mother of his child, but his reaction was one of hurt, not shame; he had been divorced for over ten years. He was disappointed that her opinion of him was so low. Since that time, encounters between them were awkward and few.

His words brought to mind the situation she was in now, with no money, no home, no clear path for the future. They brought to mind the dilemma of the day; walking through the Big House—seeing it through the eyes of Nick Vilardi and Amanda Hooper—made her yearn deep in her soul for something that could not be. She would love to own the house, to be the one to restore it and fill its vacant halls with love and laughter, to finally make the empty old house a home. The irony of today's tour was that it showed her how much she wanted to live here, and how impossible that dream really was.

Brash's words brought to mind Nick Vilardi, and the fool she had made of herself. How embarrassing, jerking like that from a simple touch. When had she become so pathetic? It seemed to be a special talent she had, behaving like an idiot in front of men she was attracted to.

"Maddy?" Brash repeated, coming close enough to touch her cheek. "Tell me what's wrong."

Ridiculously close to tears, Madison closed her eyes and leaned her cheek into his large palm. "That would take too long," she whispered.

"I have time, if you do." His words were warm and reassuring, the first real promise she hadn't done permanent damage to their budding… what? Relationship? Romance? It was still too new and fragile to even have a name.

Madison opened her eyes to look into Brash's face, hopeful she might find the answer there.

Her attention, however, was snagged by the smiling man entering the room behind Brash. Nick Vilardi stepped into the parlor with his producer close behind.

Nick's stormy-blue gaze went immediately to the uniformed man touching her face. When his eyes flickered back to hers, they held a quick flash of accusation. The look was gone in an instant, right along with the smile from his face.

Brash felt Madison stiffen, even as he sensed the presence of others. He tried to bite back the irritation of being interrupted. Maddy had been on his mind for days now, weeks, if he were being honest with himself. Ever since he saw her again for the first time in twenty-odd years.

He had spent several restless nights since then, thinking about his botched attempt at a kiss, wondering what would have happened if he had been successful, dreaming about what she would taste like, what she would feel like in his arms. He had always known she had a crush on him back in high school, but he had foolishly taken her feelings for granted. He had thought about dating her back then, but somehow never got around to it. Soon life took them down opposite paths and he all but forgot about the tall, slim brunette, until suddenly she was back in town, and in trouble. She not only discovered a dead body, but someone tried to kill her. Twice. He almost lost her, before he hardly even found her again.

A frown creased Brash's handsome face as he dropped his hand and turned to see the object of her attention.

A couple stood in the doorway behind them. Something about the lean muscled man —maybe the groomed but shaggy eyebrows, the deliberately casual cut of his hair, the designer label on his blue jean jacket—suggested an air of wealth; something above a day laborer, at any rate.

His eyes traveled behind the man, to the woman standing at his back. She was an attractive blonde with modest curves beneath her bold red outfit. Judging from their distance apart, the couple was more likely business acquaintances than lovers. The assumption was confirmed by the fleeting expression in the man's eyes when he looked at Madison.

Brash didn't know who the man was, but he had no right to look at Maddy like that, not his Maddy. He ignored the little voice that reminded him she wasn't *his* to begin with.

Before Brash could mark his territory, the other man spoke. His words were as stiff as his movements. "I didn't realize you were expecting company, Mrs. Reynolds."

"I—I wasn't. He's not," Madison stammered. "Company, that is." She added the last lamely, as she realized she was making a fool of herself in front of both men now, at the same time. *It's so much more efficient this way,* a sadistic voice said in her head.

Why was Maddy acting so guilty? Brash wondered. You would think they'd been caught making out. Which, he acknowledged, wasn't at all an unpleasant thought.

Brash stepped forward to instinctively shield her body with his as he extended his hand. He introduced himself in his 'official' voice, the one reserved for exerting his authority. "Brash deCordova, chief of police here in The Sisters."

"Nicolaus Vilardi."

Brash appreciated the way the man used a firm, confident grip to shake his hand. He looked the lawman straight in the eye, something many men were too intimidated to do. Nicolaus Vilardi came up a few notches in Brash's esteem.

Moving aside to make room for the woman behind him, the dark-haired man swept an arm in her direction. "And this is my producer, Amanda Hooper."

"Ma'am." Brash nodded in polite greeting as he took her hand, noting the unusual violet color of her eyes.

She darted a nervous glance at Madison as her hand lingered in his. "We do have permission to be here, don't we?" She looked back at Brash, her eyes dropping to the police insignia embroidered on his jacket.

"What? Oh, yes, of course!" Madison laughed in understanding. "Brash is… a friend."

"Brash. Brash deCordova." Nick tried out the name on his tongue as recognition dawned in his eyes. He nodded as he wagged a finger at the officer. "You played for Texas Tech, then went on to the NFL before coaching college ball. I knew I recognized that name!"

Brash gave a self-conscious laugh. "Careful, you're telling my age now."

"I remember that game you had against Alabama. Your team was down by thirty points at the half, but you came out throwing in the third quarter and went on to lead the upset of the season. Man, that was a great game!"

"It was, at that," Brash agreed with a whole-hearted smile. "So, what brings you to The Sisters? And did you say Miss Hooper is your producer?" There was no ring on her finger, so he assumed 'Miss' was the correct title.

"We're here with our syndicated cable show, *Home Again.* And yes, Amanda is my producer and the main reason our show is such a success." The smile he gave the woman was generous and sincere, and caused new ripples to work through Madison's stomach. Nick's forehead scrunched in a scowl as he belatedly added, "But why does everyone keep referring to this as The Sisters? I thought we were in the thriving metropolis of Juliet, Texas."

"Sister cities," Brash explained, giving him the short version. "This side of the tracks is Juliet, the other side is Naomi. Collectively they are known as The Sisters. But what's this about your TV show?"

"Miss Baker called us to look at this magnificent house." Nick glimpsed around and frowned. "Where is she, by the way?"

Amanda remembered exactly where she was. "The dining room," she reminded her colleague. "Shall we go find her and tell her our decision?"

Nick glanced at the man in uniform before sending Madison a quizzical look. There were multiple questions in his gaze.

Was it all right to discuss their deal in front of the officer?

How close of a 'friend' was he?

And why, his gaze demanded, had she reacted to his touch so passionately, if she was involved with another man?

The curious light in his eyes darkened into mild accusation. His look challenged her to define her relationship with the lawman, right then and there.

Brash felt Madison stiffen once again.

Before she even spoke, he knew she was dismissing him.

Madison looked up at Brash, begging him to understand with silent eyes. "Brash, I appreciate you stopping by, but everything is fine here."

"You're sure?" His voice was low and intimate. He studied her long enough to make her squirm.

Could this be any more awkward? Madison inwardly cringed. Both men were watching her, waiting for her answer.

The air between the men stirred with challenge. Nick Vilardi's earlier admiration of the football player fell flatly to the floor. She could all but see Brash's hackles rise.

"We just have a bit of business to discuss," she told him. She refused to look Nick Vilardi's way. Even across the room, she could sense his air of victory. Not stopping to think her actions through, she put a hand on Brash's arm and blurted out an awkward invitation. "Why—Why don't you come by the house later? For dinner. Lucy Ngyen brought fried rice."

For some reason, the Vietnamese woman thought she had to feed Madison's family now. Every few days, she brought something by the house, some offering of thanks for Madison's part in freeing her son. Today, she delivered a huge portion of rice to the dealership, adding another unexpected detail to Madison's day when she had to drop it off at home before going to the game.

Brash declined the invitation with a note of regret in his voice. "I can't tonight."

Oddly enough, Madison felt a rush of relief. She wasn't ready to start a relationship with anyone right now, and certainly not one spurred by foolishness. What did it matter what Nick Vilardi thought? She owed him no explanation.

Her relief was short-lived when Brash asked lowly, "Rain check?"

She jerked out a nod, dropping her hand from his arm. "I'll talk to you soon," she promised, but her eyes didn't quite meet his.

Even as Brash said polite goodbyes to Nick Vilardi and his pretty producer, Madison turned abruptly and hurried from the room.

&

"I'm counting on you, Shilo Dawne."

Madison caught the last of her friend's conversation as she entered the dining room. She watched as Genesis hit the 'end' button with a frown.

"Trouble at the café?"

"The entire town. Make that plural, as in *towns*." With an exaggerated sigh, Genesis elaborated. "Louise Crowder saw the *Home Again* van pull up at *New Beginnings*. So did Molly Schubert and Delores Morse. They were also watching as you came out of the café, and, I quote—'clinging to that handsome carpenter like a vine to a brick building.' They are convinced the show came to do a feature in Naomi, but you somehow hijacked them and convinced them to explore the fairer city of Juliet. The three of them plus three customers from the pharmacy came marching across the street, demanding to know how you managed to snag the TV show away from Naomi and why someone at the restaurant, presumably myself or Shilo Dawne, didn't stop you. In the meantime, Tanisha Dewberry and Latricia Jefferson passed the van as we turned onto Second Street, and they immediately called Jimmie Kate Hadley, who just happened to be in the café drooling over Cutter Montgomery. When he heard all the commotion and the buzz about the famous TV star, Cutter got disgusted and walked out without paying his bill. Of course, I'm hardly worried about that. There does, however, seem to be a mild riot taking place at the café as we speak, and I'm afraid to look out the front door. I hear the van is already surrounded by gawkers and curious residents from both sides of the track."

Madison stared at her friend, mouth agape with fascinated horror. She had forgotten how quickly news traveled in a small town. She managed a small chirp. "*I* hijacked them?"

"Don't look so wounded." Genesis hooked her arm through her friend's. "You can't take this personally. It's just a bunch of busy bodies stirring up trouble between the towns again."

"But I had nothing to do with all this!" Madison's voice was borderline shrill. First the mean trick she pulled on Caress Ellingsworth yesterday, then the fiasco with Brash and Nick, now the ire of half the town of Naomi. Hardly her finest week.

"Of course not," Genny murmured soothingly. She threw a glance overhead. "Have they come down yet?"

The answer came through the door before the words could die away. Amanda chuckled at Genny's eager anticipation. "From the third floor? Yes. Off the cloud? No. Nick is still floating around on number nine."

Nick offered a dimpled and charming smile. "Guilty as charged."

"So, what is the verdict?" When Genesis squeezed her friend's arm with a nervous pinch, Madison knew she wasn't as cool and collected as she sounded.

"This is an amazing home," Amanda stated the obvious. Her hand moved lovingly over the mural once more, her eyes taking on an enamored glow. She visibly forced her attention away from the story on the wall as she turned to the women with a bright smile. "And we think it would be a wonderful addition to the *Home Again* line-up!"

Genny squealed in delight and clapped her hands together, skewing Madison's arm into an awkward angle as she did so. As Madison disentangled herself from her friend, she wore a pragmatic wrinkle on her brow.

"Mrs. Reynolds?" Amanda asked in concern. "You don't seem as pleased as I thought you would."

Nick Vilardi merely watched her, his own forehead crinkling.

"Please, call me Madison. And of course I'm pleased. I'm just… cautious. How much money will I be out of pocket?" These days, it seemed everything came down to money.

"That's a very fair question, and one that is more in Nick's line of expertise than mine. Nick?"

The carpenter took a step forward at her invitation. "At this point, I only have very rough estimates, of course. The first order of business will be to see how sound the foundation is that in itself could be a deal-breaker. Then we would need to draw up a design of the finished product and get estimates for supplies. I can have a very crude estimate by tomorrow, but it will take at least a week to get a better idea of actual costs and to check out the foundation."

"But you have a ball-park figure." It was a statement, not a question. "You must have some idea of how much it will cost to renovate this house."

He appreciated her direct approach. He knew the figure would make her intriguing hazel eyes cloud with worry, but he wouldn't sugarcoat the truth. "A full restoration could climb into the hundreds of thousands," he told her honestly. "If this were to be a museum, or to maintain the home's full historical value, the costs could be staggering. But I understand this is to be your family's home, and it needs to be functional for a modern family. Assuming the roof and the foundation are in sound shape, if we gut and remodel the kitchen, keep re-modeling on the second and third floors to a minimum except for adding bathrooms, paint inside and out and replace rotting boards, and bring the plumbing and wiring up to code, I think we could safely put the estimate at just over one hundred thousand."

Madison regretted having loosened herself from Genny's grip. She grabbed for her friend now, needing the support as the astronomical numbers swirled around in her head. She gave a short, humorless laugh. "Surely you're kidding."

"I know it sounds rather low, but I think we can pull it off," Nick said with enthusiasm.

"Low? Low! You think one hundred thousand dollars is *low*?" Even to her own ears, Madison's brittle voice sounded shrill. She did an abrupt about-face. "I'm sorry." She threw up her palms and waved them in denial. "It seems we have wasted your time. I apologize for the inconvenience, but this entire idea is simply ludicrous. There is absolutely no way—*no way*!—I can possibly afford to have this house re-modeled."

She started to walk away, but Nick Vilardi's hand, warm and tingle-inspiring, even now, shot out to stop her. "Please, don't go," he said in beseech. "You didn't let me finish."

She waited without saying a word.

Still holding her arm, Nick gave her a pleased smile.

"The show is prepared to cover half the costs of renovations, meaning your part would be just over fifty thousand. In fact," he darted a brave glimpse at his producer, daring her to contradict him, "I'm certain I can promise you a firm fifty thousand and not one penny over."

"Barring that the roof and foundation are in good shape," Amanda quickly pointed out.

Madison shook her head adamantly. She felt the despair welling inside her, the feeling all too familiar. She had heard similar words, similar numbers, right before the bank threatened to foreclose on her home in Dallas. If she could produce a lump sum to appease the board of directors, they would renegotiate the terms of her loan. She could stay in the home she and Gray shared with their children. The problem was, coming up with that kind of cash was no more realistic today than it had been three months ago.

"I'm sorry," she said, shaking her arm free of his hold. "That may be a very generous offer, but it is still out of the question. I simply don't have that kind of money."

"How much do you have, Mrs. Reynolds?" Amanda asked in a clear, direct voice. It echoed in her candid eye contact. "I want you to know we are *very* interested in this house."

Madison's brows drew together. "You don't understand. This isn't some ploy on my part to get a better deal. I don't have the money."

"Again, I ask. How much do you have? How much can you invest in the restoration of this home?"

It was hard to squeeze the words past the tears that thickened her throat; harder, still, to squeeze out the truth. "Nothing," Madison whispered in a raw voice. Shame gathered in her eyes in liquid form. "I have no money at all."

She ran from the room, needing to put distance between herself and the brief but beautiful dream of restoring the Big

House. What had she been thinking? What had Genesis been thinking? She had no money, absolutely no money at all! Not even enough to buy the house at a bargain, much less restore it. It had been a foolish, hopeless dream.

Madison threw open the front door and ran down the cobbled walk, her eyes downcast as she maneuvered the uneven stones. She shielded her eyes as she ran, trying to keep the tears at bay. When she reached the gate, she struggled with the latch. Her hands were too unsteady to open it. As she haplessly rattled the latch back and forth, she became aware of the buzz of voices around her.

With startled eyes, Madison looked up at the small crowd assembled around the *Home Again* van. A dozen curious faces stared back at her as a hush fell over the crowd.

The gate swung suddenly outward and she stumbled forward. It was the only catalyst needed to take the crowd off mute. A dozen voices buzzed again, all full of questions, some with accusations. Madison stood on the sidewalk in utter shock, even as the more aggressive onlookers surged forward and their excited tones took on a menacing note.

Brash swooped in to rescue her. With a strong arm flung around her waist, he literally dragged her forward and away from the crowd. In a move normally reserved for fleeing reporters and paparazzi, Brash opened the front door of the police cruiser and quickly tucked her inside. He demanded the crowd stand back. He jogged around to the driver's side, slid inside, and whisked Madison away, just as Genesis and the *Home Again* duo stepped out of the mansion.

7

"Oh. My. Lord."

Stunned, Madison sat back against the seat of the police car. If she had the energy, she would slap her face with both palms. She made a half-hearted attempt anyway. Her hands fell limply to her lap, pulling her mouth into an odd sag as they traveled downward.

Hysterical laughter welled up inside her. It came bubbling out, mixed with the tears from earlier. "I—I can't believe this town! What was I thinking, planning to live here permanently? This—This place is unbelievable! They were like vultures back there!"

Brash frowned, throwing a glance into the rearview mirror. The crowd swarmed forward, already forgetting about Madison the moment they caught a glimpse of the television star. Putting thoughts of the simple-minded mob aside, he zeroed in on what she said.

He tried to keep his voice even. Casual. "You're staying?" he asked in what he hoped was a conversational voice.

"Maybe." She hedged the question before admitting on a sigh, "Yes. Yes, I decided to stay. But what was I thinking? I don't have any money!"

Her wailed words didn't make sense to him. "I guess I'm confused," he admitted. "Wouldn't it cost more to live in Dallas than it would here in Juliet?"

"Yes, but Granny Bert offered to sell me the Big House. And for one crazy moment, I thought it might work. But even pulling strings, Nick Vilardi says it will cost over fifty thousand dollars to remodel." She angled toward Brash with wide, shell-stocked eyes. "Where on earth would I get fifty thousand dollars?" she demanded.

He didn't answer immediately. He seemed intent on crossing the railroad track, taking the ramp across the highway, and driving west out of town. They passed the convenience store and the entrance to The Sisters ISD. Brash didn't speak until he turned onto the farm-to-market road. Even then, his voice held a cautious note. "Didn't your husband have life insurance?"

Madison couldn't restrain the whimper that leaked from within her weary heart. "Yes. But he borrowed against it." She refused to acknowledge why and how he spent the money. Her voice was low as she made the painful admission. "It took every penny that was left to get out from under my mortgage in Dallas. I sold at a loss."

Just for a moment, she allowed herself to mourn the beautiful house on Willow Circle: two stories, triple garage, in-ground pool, upgraded everything. And, for the past two years, an empty bed. She mustn't forget the empty bed. That bed made it so much easier to leave the house behind.

"I'm sorry, Maddy." When Brash offered his hand along with the heartfelt sentiment, Madison latched on to both.

She was hardly surprised when he curved left, onto the white-rock road that led beneath a sprawling metal sign. Familiar icons—cattle, cotton, horses, and oil derricks—danced across the plate metal arch supporting the words 'de-Cordova Ranch, est. 1918.'

The same true-to-life images repeated in the fields themselves. A lone oil well stood in the distance, silhouetted against the late afternoon sun. On one side of the road, cattle and horses grazed in pastures thick with winter oats; on the other side, row after row of dormant fields held the promise of cotton yet to come. Madison stared at the empty fields as they zipped past, until the horizontal lines made her dizzy.

"Where are you taking me, Brash?" she belatedly thought to ask.

He flashed her a smile, the one that made her heart melt in high school. Truth be known, her heart was feeling rather soft and pudgy right about now, as well. "A little late to ask, don't you think?" he teased.

"That's the problem. I can't think right now. My mind is a mess."

"Give me a few minutes. I think I have the cure."

He gently withdrew his hand from hers so that he could use both hands on the steering wheel. He took a fork in the road to the right. The path was rough and bumpy, but Brash dodged the holes best he could and knew when to accelerate, when to slow down. A few more twists and turns through empty cotton fields, a curvy path along a wooded tree line, and soon they topped a knoll, coming to an abrupt stop.

Madison stifled a gasp as she saw nothing but river and sky beyond the windshield. They perched high upon a red bank of the Brazos River, angled as if teetering on its brink.

"Whenever I need to think, this is where I come," Brash confided. "It makes me feel like I'm flying."

"I feel like I'm falling!" She laughed, but the sound came out in a nervous warble.

"Just take a couple deep breaths and look around you. We're perfectly safe. And further from the edge than you think." He grinned as he placed his hand over hers in reassurance. He transferred his gaze to the scene around them, his tone sobering. "This has always been my special place. Sitting here, looking out over the sky and the river, it helps me feel grounded. It clears my mind and helps me put things in perspective."

Trying to be brave, Madison drew in an unsteady breath. She did as he suggested, surveying the magnificent scenery before her and praying they did not fall. Just in case, she clung to the security of his strong hand.

After several minutes without tipping forward into the river, Madison began to relax and loosened her death grip on his hand. Instead of moving away, Brash turned his palm over and wove his fingers through hers. Very casually, as if it were the most natural thing in the world, he pulled their joined hands over to rest on his knee.

"Okay, so maybe it's not so bad," she admitted. She pretended to be talking about the steep red-dirt banks edging the muddy waters below. She also pretended not to notice how her pulse raced at his touch.

"Told you so," he said with a satisfied smirk.

A comfortable silence settled between them. Madison rested her head against the back of the seat and studied a ripple in the water as it worked its way downstream. If only her troubles could float away as easily.

"Uh-oh. What happened? Why the sudden frown?" Brash asked. His thumb made slow, lazy circles over her fingers.

"I was trying your technique of clearing my head. It didn't work."

"Maybe you didn't do it right. See that big limb right there, beginning to pull away from the bank and bob up and down in the water?"

She followed the line of his pointed finger. "I see it."

"Okay, so imagine one of your problems on it. What's something that's worrying you right now?"

"One thing, or twenty-seven?"

"Start with one."

"I'm trying to be both mother and father to my fifteen-year-old twins. I'm afraid I'll mess up." She admitted the last on a raw whisper.

"Okay, put your insecurities right up there on that log." He leaned in toward her, his eyes trained on the log. He visually boosted the imaginary load onto the wood, flinching when the limb bobbed for a moment, almost as if it bore the actual weight of her troubles. Madison darted her gaze between his animated facial expressions and the scene down on the river, fascinated at how he played out his part. He smiled when the log balanced itself in the current and began drifting downstream.

"See? Now watch. There your insecurities go, floating south."

They watched the log as it slowly inched down the river.

"Uh-oh," Madison said at one point. "It's beginning to stall. And it's turning sideways, right there in the middle of the stream."

"Let it go, Maddy." He said the words as if she had some control over the course of the drifting log. "Just like the log, parenthood hits a few snags now and then. You have to go with the flow. And you're doing great." His voice was steady and reassuring. Calming. "You're a good mom, Maddy, a good parent. A good provider. Have faith in yourself. And, look. The log is moving again, floating on down the river."

He released her hand to point, but they still connected on a completely different level. Maddy offered a nervous, hopeful smile in answer to his more confident one. Maybe he was right, maybe she worried too much about her parenting skills.

Brash's voice was still soft and steady. "Next problem."

"I live with my grandmother. My teenage daughter and I share a bed. How are you going to fit *that* on a little bitty ole log?" she challenged.

"Okay, okay." He studied the water for a moment before opening the car door. "This requires a closer look," he explained. The engine had cooled enough for him to hoist himself onto the hood of the patrol car. Peering back through the windshield, he beckoned her to join him.

Madison reluctantly crawled from the car and allowed him to help her onto the hood beside him. This was only one of the crazy things she had done this week.

She was barely settled when he bumped his shoulder against hers. He pointed upward this time, to the sky. "There. See that cloud? That big, puffy white one? Imagine it's your bed. A big, fat, fluffy mattress."

"Hmm. It's drifting." The cloud floated effortlessly across the expanse of blue until, incredibly, it began to separate. "It's splitting into two." There was a touch of awe in her voice. She turned to him with an astonished smile. "How'd you do that?"

"Faith, my dear." His exaggerated tone held the perfect pitch of sage wisdom. He immediately switched to nonchalance. "So soon you'll have separate beds. Next problem."

Madison grinned, getting into the spirit of the game. She would hit him with something hard this time. "Today I realized just how much I would love to remodel the Big House. But it's going to cost a minimum of fifty thousand dollars. That kind of obstacle isn't just going to float away on a breeze, you know."

"Look down there at the river, Maddy. Can you see the rocky bottom from here?"

"No. The water's too muddy. And too deep."

"But the bottom's down there, you just can't see it as plainly as you would like. In this exact spot, the water is deep and cloudy, but move along a little way. It gets clearer, more shallow. Sometimes you have to travel upriver, sometimes down, but eventually you can see the bottom. It's the same way with your money troubles. You might not have everything all at once but give it time. Eventually, you'll be standing on solid ground again."

A silly grin spread across Maddy's face. She was clearly impressed. "You're pretty good at this, you know?"

"I've had plenty of practice. I come here often enough with my own troubles."

"So, let me return the favor. What problem can I carry away for you, kind sir? I see a nice steady current coming down the river. Let me toss your latest problem right into the water and let it travel off downstream, never to worry you again." She giggled as she emulated tossing something into the river.

"My current problem, eh?" He seemed to contemplate the matter, his blue eyes twinkling as he looked over at her.

Maddy's gaze collided with his, triggering an instant spark. The look in his eyes changed, just like the rhythm of her heartbeat. She tried to hear his lowly spoken words over the clamor.

"Well," he drawled thoughtfully, his attention dropping to her mouth. "It seems there's a pretty lady who's back in town, but she has a rather low opinion of me. Any ideas on how to solve that little problem?"

"Maybe her opinion's not as low as you think," Maddy murmured, her own eyes slipping down to watch the slight smile skip along his generous lips. An hour ago, it was Nick Vilardi who made her pulse race. Thirty minutes ago, she decided she wasn't ready for a relationship with any man. But right now, she craved the feel of Brash's lips upon hers. It was a familiar ache, born twenty-something years ago, but it had never been this strong, this viable. She drew in an unsteady breath and whispered, "Maybe you should let that worry float away on a cloud."

For one crazy, heart-stalling moment, she thought he would kiss her. She wouldn't be foolish enough to stop him this time. She even leaned forward, encouraging him with her silent invitation.

As he began to move, the police radio squawked. The beauty of the moment was shattered. As Maddy blinked in confusion, Brash muttered a complaint and slid off the car to answer the call.

After a brief conversation with the dispatcher, he poked his head out of the car. "I'm sorry, Maddy, but I have to get back. There's a problem in town."

Madison hopped down from the hood and returned to the front seat, where Brash had pushed the door open from the inside.

"Sorry 'bout that," he apologized as she tucked her long legs inside the car. His eyes registered true regret.

"I completely understand," she insisted. "You told me you had plans for the evening, yet you took time out of your schedule to bring me out here and make me feel better." She smiled. "Thank you for that."

"Did it work?"

"Magically."

"Told you," he said again, his smile smug. He put the car in reverse and retraced their tracks across the pasture. Despite their latest botched kiss attempt, the silence between them was comfortable. Brash broke it by saying, "So you never did tell me the whole story about the television people. Why are they in town?"

Madison relayed the story as they traveled back into Juliet. After Brash's insightful assessment of her financial situation, fifty thousand dollars no longer sounded quite as scary; it was still impossible, but somehow less frightening.

"Where do you want me to drop you off?" he asked.

Madison almost had to think about it. "My car is at *New Beginnings*," she remembered. "Hopefully all the hoopla will have died down by now."

"Oh, things should be rather peaceful at the café," he predicted. He pursed his lips ruefully. "That's because, according to dispatch, most of the town is at *The Bumble Bee Hotel*, once again swarming around the television van and its occupants. They can't even get out, for fear of being attacked by eager fans."

In response, Madison bit her lip and stifled a helpless laugh.

It was past dusk when he pulled up at the café. Brash shoved the gear into park and jumped out to open Madison's door. He walked her the few steps to her own car door, where he held it open as she slid in behind the wheel.

"Thank you for coming to my rescue earlier. And thank you for the very insightful exercise in getting my head on straight."

"Your head's always been on straight, Maddy. That's one of things I've always admired about you." He smiled down at her with the compliment.

"Sometimes it doesn't feel that way," she admitted, tugging on her neck as if to make sure it was secure.

Brash placed his large hand over hers, letting his thumb trail over her cheek. "Things have a way of working out for the best, you know."

"I know," she acknowledged softly.

"And Maddy?"

"Yeah?"

He leaned in closer, his voice dropping with an intimate promise. "One of these days, I *am* going to kiss you."

She was woefully out of practice, but she offered him what she hoped was a flirty smile. "I think I might just hold you to that, Chief."

8

Nick Vilardi shut the door behind him with a firm 'click,' allowing the stiff smile to die upon his lips. Sometimes it was hard to remember that these aggressive fans paid his salary. No matter the inconvenience, he had to smile and pretend to enjoy the way they clung to his arm or yanked on his clothes.

Not that he didn't appreciate their enthusiasm. After all, it was what allowed him to make a living doing what he loved most: working with wood and restoring old homes to their former glory. Without the fans, there would be no sponsors, no syndicated show. No career.

It was just that he was a private person. He would be perfectly content to hole up in one of his old houses and not see another soul until the job was completed. Sometimes it was difficult to remember to share his time and attention with others. It was an effort to welcome the cameras and the crowds, to allow them to see his love affair with wood. It was even harder to let them claw at him, constantly pulling and tugging and asking for more; one more smile, one more hug, one more autograph as the camera flashed in his eyes.

Nick shrugged out of his jacket and slung it across the foot of the four-poster bed. It had been a long day, first traveling, then touring the magnificent old mansion only to find a resistant owner—and not even the actual owner, at that!—topped off by the throng of eager fans who stood between him and his bed. His stomach growled in hunger, but he wasn't sure he was up to fighting the crowds again. Maybe he would take Genesis Baker up on her offer to have dinner delivered to his room.

He took his phone from his pocket and flipped back through the photos he had taken at the Big House, as locals called it. He didn't need the digital images to remind him of the stately old mansion; the impressions were burned into his mind, filling his head with grandiose visions of its restored state.

He had to have that house.

No matter what it took, he would find a way to persuade Madison Reynolds to jump on his bandwagon. And if for some reason she didn't, couldn't… well, he would find a way to make it work. Even if he had to fund the project himself, he would be the one to restore this house. The thought of someone else doing the work—or worse yet, doing *inferior* work, like that done here at the *Bumble Bee*—was unacceptable. Almost physically painful.

The house, he knew, was going to be an obsession with him. One look at its magnificent staircase, at its hand-hewn floors, and he was a goner, instantly in love with the stately old house.

Yet oddly enough, when Nick settled his weary body into the easy chair and closed his eyes, it wasn't the elaborate curve of a banister that he saw, but the graceful curve of a long, slender neck, and the wide hazel eyes of the widow Madison Reynolds.

9

Madison tried going to bed early that night. Granny and the kids had already eaten by the time she got home, so she reheated a plate of Lucy Ngyen's fried rice, gobbled it down, and announced she was going to bed. She had only been asleep for a short time when her cell phone rang.

Madison was in no mood for pleasantries. "George Gail, you have to stop calling me in the middle of the night!" she hissed by way of greeting.

"It's 11:52. You were in bed?"

"Yes, I was in bed! Asleep!"

"Oh."

She heard the air deflating from George Gail's lungs. She imagined her blue-powdered eyes drooping in disappointment. With an exasperated sigh, Madison attempted to disguise the irritation in her weary voice. "What did you need, George Gail?"

"He left. He got a call and said he had to go out, something about an emergency at the sale barn."

"I assume you mean Curtis." With great reluctance, Madison eased out of bed and made her way to the closet. These late-night calls were getting ridiculous.

"Of course Curtis! He just up and left, the minute she called!"

"Do you know it was her?"

"Well, no, not exactly. He took his phone with him. But I'm sure it must have been her! Who else would it have been?"

"Maybe someone at the sale barn?" Madison suggested. "Doesn't someone stay there all night, before and after sale day?"

"Yes, but—"

"I'm sure it is exactly what he said, a problem at the barn."

"I heard a woman's voice! I know it had to be her!"

"Even so, what do you want me to do about it?"

"I want you to follow him."

"I'm already asleep!"

"Not anymore, you're not."

Madison forced herself to count to ten. "George Gail," she began, carefully schooling her voice into a semblance of calm, "when you hired me, we didn't discuss middle-of-the-night phone calls. This has to stop. I—"

"I'll give you another five hundred dollars!" the distraught woman blurted out.

"What?"

"Consider it overtime. I'll pay you five hundred dollars if you'll follow him and see where he went."

"Wouldn't it be easier if you just went to the sale barn and saw for yourself whether or not he was there?"

Madison could hear the disdainful sniff over the phone. "I guess business must be awfully good, if you can turn down five hundred dollars cash."

It was a low blow, delivered right where it hurt the most: her pocketbook. Standing just inside her closet with the door slightly ajar, Madison had a glimpse of her bed. It looked so warm and inviting. Her bank account, however, looked cold and empty. She heard herself asking, "What—What exactly did you want me to do?"

"Find out where he really went. Take photos. That's all you have to do. You should be back home in an hour, tops."

She gave the bed one more longing perusal. "You're sure you don't want to go yourself?"

"I can't. I've already had a glass of wine. Maybe two."

Madison shoved her feet into a pair of tennis shoes, muttering aloud about a wild goose chase. "Do not call me tomorrow night. I can only go so long without sleep."

George Gail all but squealed her appreciation. "Thank you, Madison. I knew I could count on you!"

Madison stuffed the phone into the pocket of her flannel sleep pants as she tugged a Texas A&M sweatshirt from its hanger. Never mind that the maroon clashed with her orange Halloween-themed pants and their dancing ghosts and goblins; no one would see her anyway. She grabbed her purse and camera before slipping out the front door, into a night turned cold and foggy. Good thing the loaner car had a dependable heater, unlike her grandmother's Buick.

The heated seat feature was nice, too, she decided fifteen minutes later, as she wiggled against the warmed leather. So far, there was no sign of Curtis Burton at the sale barn. She circled the perimeter twice, looking for signs of his pickup and for the so-called emergency. From what she could see, there was no activity at all at the sale barn. Even the cows slumbered.

She texted George Gail to see if he had returned home, but the answer was a shouted NO, in capital letters.

Five minutes later, George Gail called her. "Never mind," she said, her voice a bit slurred. "You can go home now."

"He's back?"

"No, but he called. Something about a trailer breaking down full of cattle."

"Are you all right? You sound strange."

"I finished off the wine. It always makes me sleepy."

"I'm glad you had sense enough not to drive," Madison told her. Putting the car into gear, she didn't bother to hide her growled retort, "Just wish I had the same sense!"

"I'm sorry, Madison. Go home and go to bed."

"What was that noise? Are you outside?"

"Um, the television is on. Go on home and go back to bed."

"Believe me, I will!"

Despite her emphatic reply, Madison's foot faltered on the gas pedal. Something bothered her about George Gail's sudden change of heart. Thirty minutes ago, the woman begged her to follow her husband, not believing his excuse. Suddenly, she believed him and wanted Madison to go home—insisted upon it, in fact. It didn't make sense.

Since she was already out, it wouldn't hurt to drive a few streets over and see if Curtis Burton's truck was parked in front of Caress' house. *Although surely the man would have sense enough to park down the street*, she reasoned. He was having an affair, after all.

Madison looked for the blue pickup as she turned onto North River Oaks. There was only one vehicle parked alongside the entire street; the rest were tucked into garages and snuggled beneath carports.

She slowed as she passed the house bearing the address 562. Hardly movie-star status, but clearly the nicest house on the block. The lights were still on and the blinds were wide open. Madison could never understand why people left their blinds open at night. Didn't they realize how easily people could see inside? Like right now, she could see Caress standing in what was obviously the dining room, talking with someone. Madison only got a glimpse of the other person as she drove past, but she knew the short, stocky blur wasn't Curtis Burton.

"I guess he was telling the truth," she muttered aloud. "So that means my work here is done and I can go home to my nice, warm bed."

Madison rolled to a stop at the bottom of the hill, dutifully obeying traffic rules even though she was the lone traveler on this foggy night. Fog settled in low, swirling around her headlights. A hazy tuft of murk bobbed in front of her, reminding Madison of the shadowed visitor at Caress' home. Something about the person pricked at Madison's subconscious...

The shape, she realized. The rounded shape definitely didn't belong to Curtis, but could it possibly belong to George Gail?

She made a U-turn in the road and proceeded back up the hill, rolling to a stop across the street from Caress.' From there, she had a clear view inside the house.

Caress appeared to be shouting now, her features fully animated. It was difficult to see much about her visitor. The person was slightly taller than Caress, but much heavier. It was impossible to tell anything about their age or even gender; the khaki-colored trench coat was universal. Either sex could wear the sporty little fedora. With no hair visible beneath the hat and no facial features showing, Madison couldn't rule out the possibility of it being George Gail. The size and shape were about right.

Madison thought about the background noise from George Gail's call. She claimed it was the television, but it sounded more like a car engine. Was George Gail just drunk enough to confront Caress herself? Was that why she insisted Madison forget the stakeout and go home to bed?

Madison watched for a few more minutes as the argument appeared to escalate. At one point, Caress shoved the other person, pushing them completely out of view. The one Madison dubbed 'Trench Coat' stormed into the frame again angrily, broad back to the window, advancing toward Caress. Even Madison could sense the menacing atmosphere. She watched as Caress shrank back in fear.

Madison gasped aloud when she saw Trench Coat's hand suddenly dart out, striking Caress across the cheek. The actress' reaction was so melodramatic that Madison wondered if the two of them were rehearsing for a scene.

The two people inside the house engaged in a brief push and shove contest. Caress slowly edged out of view of the window, except for the occasional slender wrist shooting forward with a slap or shove. Just because she was the smaller of the two didn't mean she was the weaker; the sixty-something woman gave as good as she got.

"Okay, this has to be pretend." Madison spoke aloud in her car, trying to convince herself she witnessed a make-believe fight. Otherwise, shouldn't she call the police?

And say what, exactly? That she was sitting outside, spying on the occupants of a house as they had a domestic argument? Never mind that the blinds were open and she could plainly see inside, even at this distance. Propriety dictated she refrain from looking.

What about domestic abuse? Shouldn't she at least report it? The problem was, she saw Caress push first. And there was something about the way Trench Coat held his or her body, something about the hands… They were almost feminine. And if that was the case, it wasn't domestic abuse. Caress and her guest were fighting.

Is there a law against that? An ordinance, maybe?

What if she called the fight in and the person turned out to be George Gail, after all? Getting her own client arrested would probably mean forfeiting the bonus money for tonight. Madison still couldn't get a clear view of the face or see the telltale blue eye shadow, but that didn't rule out George Gail, come to stake her claim on her husband. She wouldn't be the first woman to confront—or to accost—her husband's mistress.

Just for a moment, Madison imaged the satisfaction that must come with such a brave act. She imagined lifting her palm, swinging it back with self-righteous fury, and slinging it forward. She imagined the feel of a resounding 'smack!' against a smooth, creamy cheek, that little sting of pleasure and pain that came with delivering a heartfelt slap.

"Don't go there." She spoke sharply, pulling herself back on task. No time for daydreaming, not when she had a decision to make. Should she call the police or not? Brash would want to know why she was there in the first place and then she would have to explain her latest gig, not that it was any of his business. What she was doing was perfectly legal.

She hoped.

In the end, she decided to call George Gail. She would probably wake the other woman—which she definitely deserved—but at least Madison would know her whereabouts. And if she didn't answer… well, there would be no clear determination, but it was still worth the chance.

There was no answer on the other end of the line.

Madison watched the scene playing out through the plate-glass window. If a phone rang from within Trench Coat's pocket, neither person gave any indication of the intrusion. They continued to argue without pause. In truth, in the few moments while she dialed the phone, the scuffle had turned into an all-out brawl. Caress flew forward, flinging her small body onto Trench Coat. Then she staggered backwards, pushed by the force of a lowered beefy shoulder.

No matter who the other person was, the fight was real. Madison's breath hung in her chest. There was another body-smack from Caress. Was that something in Trench Coat's raised hand? Madison strained to get a better view, but a flurry of sudden movement changed everything. Trench Coat surged forward, knocking Caress to the ground and out of Madison's line of vision.

"What's happening?" Even to her own ears, Madison's voice was shaky. She had a sinister feeling about what was transpiring inside the house. If only to soothe her own taut nerves, she talked aloud inside the car. "Where is she? Where's Caress... where's Trench Coat? Oh, wait, I see movement… Trench Coat! Now where's Caress?"

As she watched, Trench Coat lumbered slowly up, teetering for a moment to regain equilibrium. Madison saw a flash of something red before Trench Coat turned away, quickly moving out of Madison's line of vision.

Madison was intent on watching for signs of Caress. When a car came flying out of Caress' driveway, headlights glaring directly at her, she never thought to duck. She was like the proverbial deer, caught in the blinding headlights. The car careened past her in a blur and flew down the hill. Even if her mind had been in working order, the dark fog made it impossible to see any details about the vehicle.

Madison sat in her own car for another long moment, willing Caress to appear at the window. A cold sense of dread welled within her. By now, Caress should be up and moving. She should be at the door, demanding her guest to return and apologize. She should be on the phone, sobbing for a friend or an official to come to her aid. She should be showing some of that fighting spirit Madison witnessed earlier.

The memory of something red haunted her mind.

With shaking hands, Madison punched in the number on her cell phone.

"911. What's your emergency?"

Her voice was weak, but her words strong. "I—I think I just witnessed a crime."

10

Brash killed the siren as he pulled up to the house on North River Oaks. He left the strobe going, casting red and blue lights into air thick with fog and gloom.

He informed dispatch of his arrival on scene before crawling out into the chill of the night. He was the first to arrive, but he would hardly be the last, not if a crime truly had taken place here. Details were sketchy, but the caller mentioned a possible homicide.

Thankfully, murder wasn't a common crime here in The Sisters. Theft, yes. Illegal drugs, unfortunately. Even illegal gambling. But murder? Other than Ronny Gleason's death last month, the last murder had taken place over two years ago. Even that had eventually been ruled as involuntary manslaughter.

Snapping on a pair of latex gloves, Brash studied the house from where he stood. Single-story brick home, nice yard, drive-through carport with one car parked beneath the double space. A white late-model Lincoln, just like the one Caress Ellingsworth drove. No name had come in with the address, but he thought the former actress lived somewhere on this side of town.

Across the street, a car door opened and he saw a familiar long leg slide out to touch the pavement.

Maddy.

Tamping down the surge of pleasure that came with seeing her twice in one day, he took one glimpse at her pale face and knew her presence was no coincidence.

"What are you doing here?" The words came out sharper than he intended, but at least they brought a flash of color into her ashen cheeks. Anger had a way of doing that.

She lifted her chin with defiance as she crossed the street in her long, smooth stride. "I'm the one who called 911."

"You?" He threw a glance to the house behind him, trying to establish the connection. None came to mind. "Why were you here?"

She didn't answer directly. She tipped her head backwards, indicating the car behind her. "I was parked over there. I—I saw a fight take place in the house. Then someone ran out of the house and drove off in that direction, but I never saw Miss Ellingsworth again after that. I, uh, I think something bad happened to her."

A dozen questions ran through his mind. Why was she sitting out here in a parked car after midnight? How did she know Caress to begin with? Why was she always in the thick of trouble? Why was she dressed in a baggy sweatshirt and those ridiculous pajama pants, instead of the threadbare t-shirt he had seen her in before, the one that turned almost translucent when wet? Why did he still wonder what it would be like to kiss her, even now, when he had other things that he should be focusing on? And where was his backup? Shouldn't the emergency crews be here by now?

Brash shook his auburn head, hoping that by doing so, some of the answers might fall into place. He settled on asking the question upper-most on his mind. "Again, what are you doing here, Maddy? It's after midnight, and you don't even live in Naomi."

She answered with a question of her own. "Shouldn't we go in and check on her?"

"*I* should check on her," he corrected her. "*You* should stay here." He turned away abruptly, then wheeled back around to say sternly, "And don't think I haven't noticed how you keep avoiding my question."

Madison squirmed uncomfortably beneath Brash's long, pointed finger and his laser-blue gaze. So much for their new flirtatious banter. She knew he would demand a straight answer sooner or later, but she hoped it would be later. Maybe by then, she could invent a plausible excuse for her presence here tonight without ratting out George Gail.

She breathed a sigh of relief when Brash dropped his inquisitive stare and started up the driveway. Madison scampered behind him. No way would she stand out here on the sidewalk in the dark.

The driveway led to the side entry, where the door stood slightly ajar and a porch light shone like a beacon into the fog-shrouded night. Brash didn't acknowledge her presence, but he had to know she was right behind him.

He knocked as a perfunctory gesture. After a brief moment, he carefully pushed the door open wider. "Miss Ellingsworth?" he called into the empty room. "Caress? Are you home? May I come in?"

There was no answer in the quiet house. Stepping across the threshold, Brash twisted back toward Madison, his look nothing less than a glare. "Do not touch a thing!" he warned darkly.

Too nervous to speak, Madison started to nod in agreement, then changed to a negative shake. Realizing that still wasn't quite right, she nodded again. Brash rolled his eyes and turned away, leading the way through the room.

As he called for Caress again, Madison glanced around the utility room. It appeared even former daytime television stars were burdened by menial tasks such as laundry. If she expected wispy pieces of satin and silk complete with boa feathers, she was sadly disappointed; the laundry basket contained typical undergarments, no different than most Naomi residents, or so she supposed. For a moment, Madison imagined a dozen backyard clotheslines, all draped with sexy underwear and plenty of red satin. A nervous giggle escaped her lips, earning her another angry glare from Brash.

The laundry room opened into the kitchen. All new stainless-steel appliances winked beneath pendant lighting. Top-of-the-line amenities decked out the small but efficient space.

"Miss Ellingsworth, we've come to check on you." Brash's voice echoed across the empty tiled floors.

Madison clutched his arm and stopped him mid-stride. "In—In there," she whispered, nodding toward the dining room that opened off the kitchen.

He glanced down at the death grip she had on his arm. His tone softened as he gently suggested, "Why don't you stay here, Maddy, and let me take care of this?"

"I—I'm going with you," she said bravely. The truth was, she was too frightened to stay behind. Logically, she knew that whoever had harmed Caress was long gone; she had seen them leave with her own eyes. But right now, logic didn't play into the emotions shooting through her.

Brash curled his body into a protective shield so that he led the way through the doorway, while still allowing her to cling to his arm. Madison hovered close behind him, colliding against his broad back when he stopped abruptly a few feet past the dining room table that seated eight.

"You might want to go back into the kitchen, Madison." This time, his somber tone came out flat.

Scrunching her face up in preparation for what she knew would be an unpleasant sight, Madison peeked around the solid form of the police chief. At some point, her hands had come up to cling to either side of his waist.

The first thing she noticed was the odd angle of Caress' legs. Instead of the feathered slippers she expected to see, a pair of thick socks cloaked the older woman's feet, even though they lay too far apart to be in a natural pose. She was already dressed for bed, an odd mix of satin gown and flannel robe.

Hidden half behind Brash, Madison did not immediately see the knife, but she saw the damage it had done. Caress' clothes were ripped in long, angry slashes. At first, all Madison could see was the side of the other woman's body, spilling out of the thrashed night clothes. A very inopportune thought flashed through her mind: *that* was the boob Curtis Burton couldn't wait to see? She expected something full and perky, not something wrinkled and sagging.

Madison was immediately ashamed of herself, even before she saw the blood. A tiny shift to the right, and her vision was suddenly awash in red. The dark liquid still gurgled out of the half-dozen knife wounds on Caress' chest and throat, the cruor collecting beneath her body on the once-white carpet.

Who puts down white carpet? And in a dining room? Again, inappropriate thoughts swirled around inside Madison's head, but it was better than letting the hysteria overcome her. It bubbled just below the surface, much like the blood in Caress' abdomen.

Madison hid her face in Brash's back, unable to take any more of the grizzly scene. She breathed in the scent of him, spicy cologne mingled with the starch of his uniform and a slight hint of sweat. It was a comforting combination, one she could grow dependent upon.

"Madison." His voice was gentle but firm. "You need to go back into the kitchen. I have to attend the body."

Madison slipped away without protest. She swallowed hard, refusing to look back over her shoulder, even to get a glimpse of Brash's compassionate eyes. She stumbled back into the kitchen, just as the paramedics and the firefighters came storming into the room. She slid up against the counter, making room for four extra bodies in the small confines of the galley-style kitchen.

"Miss Maddy? Are you all right, ma'am?"

Leave it to Cutter Montgomery to take a moment to check on her. She already had a soft spot for the handsome young firefighter, and this gesture endeared him to her all the more. He had been the first to respond when she found Ronny

Gleason's mutilated body in the chicken house; she would always remember Cutter's calm, reassuring presence that awful day, and how he called to check on her later in the afternoon, even when no one else thought to do so.

"Yes." She managed a nod and a weak smile. "She's in there."

Cutter put a comforting hand on her shoulder and gave it a squeeze. "Hang in there, ma'am," he murmured before he passed through the space and joined the others round the body. Another law officer trailed him into the room.

Bits and pieces of their initial probe floated out to her.

"A dozen or so lacerations, all presumably inflicted by knife, five of them deep and potentially life-threatening."

"…level of violence suggests a crime of passion. The attacker must have known the victim."

"Wounds are deep and severe. Whoever did this was strong."

"And very angry."

"…next of kin?"

"Might call Darla Mullins. They're good friends."

"What time did this happen?"

"Eyewitness puts time of death around 12:45."

"Witness? Who's the witness?"

"Madison Reynolds."

"…that found Ronny Gleason? What are the odds of finding…"

Madison stifled a cry. What, indeed, were the odds of finding two dead bodies within a few weeks of one another? And here in The Sisters, no less? Leave it to her to be a longshot.

She heard Brash again, barking out orders about preserving the scene and taking photographs. As more emergency personnel arrived on the scene and neighbors came out of their homes to see what the commotion was all about, Brash directed the flow of traffic in—and mostly out—of the house. He posted Cutter at the door to keep unessential people from entering.

Madison wondered how she had managed to make the very short list of 'essential' people. So far no one had taken her statement, other than to confirm a timeline and to question positive identification of the assailant. Since she had no idea what the person looked like, her eyewitness account would have to wait, at least until they had secured the scene.

That left her very little time to come up with her story.

11

Madison knew enough not to touch a thing. She had watched enough television to know that, theoretically, the police could fingerprint every room of the house, analyze DNA from obscure objects, or find trace evidence on mundane surfaces that might eventually track down the killer. She also knew enough about the small community of The Sisters to know that, realistically, none of that would be done. At best, the three-man team of police officers would do a visual survey of the room; seeing nothing amiss—only one place setting and one water glass in the sink, all washed and turned upside down to dry—they wouldn't waste precious resources by processing the room.

Still, she was careful not to contaminate any potential evidence. She tried not to lean against the granite counter top, but her legs soon grew weary and her back ached from holding herself upright.

When she could take it no longer, she called out to the volunteer fireman who manned the door between kitchen and dining room. "Cutter, I need to sit down. Can I go out to my car?"

He shot a glance into the dining room, where Brash was busy taking photographs. "It's probably best if you don't, ma'am."

"I don't think I can stand here any longer," she confessed. She was tired and cranky and wanted to rest.

He hesitated a moment longer. "I tell you what; I'll take you out to the firetruck. You can wait for the chief there."

She nodded, willing to take what she could get. He spoke to someone in the other room, then came around to take Madison's arm and escort her out. As they stepped out the door she and Brash arrived through over an hour ago, she was momentarily stunned by the amount of people and vehicles that had accumulated in such a short time. All three patrol cars, two firetrucks, an ambulance, and a half dozen personal vehicles crowded into the driveway and spilled out into the street, where a steadily growing crowd strained to get a glimpse of what was happening. Two men wearing jackets from the fire department stood between the crowd and the house, holding busy bodies at bay.

Madison's mind flashed back to the day she found Ronny Gleason's body and something the chief of police told her. He reminded her things were done differently in the rural communities than in the city where she had been living. Here, the volunteer fire department was a valuable asset to the law agency, filling in gaps where needed. With only three officers to serve both towns, the skeletal crew often depended on the VFD to be first responders and to provide traffic control, medical attention, a chain of command, and whatever else was needed. Even now, Cutter Montgomery took on the responsibilities of a law officer, rather than the welder by trade and volunteer chief and fireman that he was.

"Madison!"

Someone called her name from the crowd as she walked toward the firetruck parked beneath the awning. She saw Genesis trying to rush forward, waving her arm to get her attention from among the crowd, but her friend was stopped short.

"Stand back," one of the firemen on crowd control cautioned in a stern voice.

Immediately leaving Madison's side, Cutter approached the invisible barricade. "It's okay, Perkins. Let her through."

Feet apart, hands on hips, the other man shook his head in refusal. "deCordova said no one gets in."

Cutter's voice took on a steel edge. Even though the man on the line was a dozen years his senior, Cutter's tone hardened with authority. "I said let her through." He motioned for Genesis to come forward, then threw his arm around her shoulders to guide her past his glaring fellow fireman.

Until then, Genesis forgot what she was wearing. The minute she had gotten Madison's text, she jumped from bed, threw on a pair of jeans and loafers, and flew out the door. She belatedly realized her top was a cute little cross between sleep shirt and baby doll, a thin pink jersey knit with ruffles and the glittery words *'Just because I sleep alone doesn't mean I sleep ugly.'*

She saw the way the other man leered at her. Without even a jacket to hide behind, Genesis curled her shoulders inward to hide the fact she wore no bra. Cutter followed the man's gaze, noticing her provocative top for the first time. Genny's cheeks flooded with color when she saw the surprise in his hazel eyes.

Once again, Cutter immediately came to the rescue. Throwing a menacing glare at the gawking Perkins, Cutter shrugged out of his own jacket. "Cold, Miss Genny?"

She was grateful for the way he shielded her body with his own as he draped the warm material around her shoulders. It smelled of leather and spice, and a pleasant hint of woodsy smoke. Cutter squeezed her shoulders before releasing them, offering her encouragement and a warm smile.

"Better?"

Snuggling into the warmth of the jacket, wondering about the sudden goosebumps that appeared on her arms, Genesis smiled back. "Much. Thank you, Cutter."

"My pleasure."

"Montgomery!" someone bellowed from the house. "Quit flirting with the ladies and get back in here!"

"Duty calls." He was still grinning down at Genesis, despite the fact a dead body lay inside, growing colder by the minute. He stood aside so the two friends could see one another. "Genny's here, Miss Maddy. Everything will be fine now."

His voice was so calm and reassuring, both women couldn't help but believe him.

By the time Brash worked his way to Madison, the clock struck two.

"Sorry this took so long," he apologized the minute he slid into the front seat of the firetruck. Even though he was obviously harried, concern showed in his blue eyes. "How are you holding up?"

"About as expected."

He turned a speculative gaze at Genesis. "What are you doing here?"

"She texted me."

"Ah, yes, the Bobbsey twins."

Genesis made a face. "I guess you'd like to be alone with Madison."

Yes, but right now, I just need to question her.

Did he say the words aloud or in his head? When neither woman's face registered surprise, he supposed the impulsive thought remained his secret. His only answer was to lumber back out of the truck and open the door for Genesis. "When we're done here, she can go."

She peered around his broad chest to her friend. "I'll wait for you at your car."

Before getting back inside the truck, Brash asked Madison, "Do you want to do this here or somewhere else? We can go back inside, if you like."

"No!" She had already spent over an hour inside the house with a dead body, thank you very much.

He settled his large frame into the driver's seat, pulled his trusty notepad from his front pocket, and twisted to level his blue gaze upon the woman in the contrasting maroon and orange outfit.

"So. Madison."

The heavy tone of those two words was enough to weigh on her nerves. She raised her chin a notch and looked at him as coolly as she could manage through sleep-deprived eyes. "Yes?"

"Explain to me why you were in front of Caress' house to begin with."

"That's where my car was parked."

He completely threw her with his next question. "Do you let your kids get away with that stunt?"

"Wh—What stunt?"

"When you ask your teenage kids a question, do you honestly let them get away with a smart little answer like that?" He didn't wait for her reply, charging right in with an angry, "I *know* your car was parked there, Maddy. What I want to know is *why* your car was parked there."

She had practiced her answer. Determined not to reveal her client's involvement just yet, particularly not until she could talk to George Gail and be assured that she was passed out at home at the time of the murder, Madison found a plausible excuse for her own presence. She pasted on what she hoped was a sheepish smile and looked at Brash through her lashes.

"I—I was star gazing," she admitted timidly.

"It's too foggy outside to see a dad-burned star unless it fell onto your nose!"

"Not that kind of star." She crooked a finger toward the house and tapped the air. "That kind of star."

He was clearly dumbfounded. "Caress?"

"She's a famous soap star, you know." Madison tried to look suitably impressed. "Until a couple of years ago, she was the Heather Lothario of the soap screen."

"Who?"

"Heather Lothario. You know, *Music to the Soul*?"

He stared at her blankly.

"*Two for Vegas*?"

She might have had a third eye, the way he stared at her.

"Oh, come on, surely you've heard of *Made You Say It*? You have a teenage daughter. How could you *not* know who Heather Lothario is? She's a huge star!"

"These are television shows?" he guessed.

"These are movies, Brash. Huge box office hits. Huge."

"I don't have time for movies. And I know what you're doing. You're stalling. And I'm still waiting to hear why you were parked in front of Caress Ellingsworth's house tonight."

"I told you. I was watching for a glimpse of the famous actress."

"So, you're telling me you've become a Peeping Tom."

"Peeping Tom suggests slinking around among rosebushes, peering through the gap in the curtains. I was sitting out in my car, on a public street, looking through a window that had the blinds fully opened."

"So, you've become a stalker."

"Stalker is a harsh word, don't you think? I was merely looking through a window. Anyone could do the same." She pointed over her shoulder to the crowd out on the street. "See, all of them are doing it now."

Brash muttered a curse beneath his breath. "Have they been watching the entire time?" he stormed angrily, rooting around for the handheld radio clipped to his side.

"Don't worry, they can't actually see her. I couldn't see them, either, when they fell to the floor. But when only Trench Coat came back up, I knew something was wrong."

"Trench Coat?" he asked, then held up a finger as in 'hold that thought.' He barked into the radio, demanding someone close the blinds in the living room. Only when he saw the disappointment on the faces of the crowd did he turn his attention back to Madison. "Trench Coat?" he repeated.

"The person who attacked Caress. He was wearing a trench coat, so I nicknamed him that."

"You nickname people while you watch them commit murder?"

"If I had known he was *murdering* her, I would have called the police immediately!"

"Why didn't you anyway, Madison?" The quietness of the question was more unnerving than his yelled words.

"I—I thought she was just having an argument. In the privacy of her own home. I didn't think it was illegal."

"Obviously this was much more than a simple argument."

"I didn't know that at the time. It started as a shoving match, a slap here and there. In fact, Caress' reaction was so melodramatic, I thought it was some sort of rehearsal at first. By the time I realized it was real, it—it was too late."

He recognized the distress in her eyes, the guilt etched upon her face. He put his hand on hers. "It wasn't your fault, Maddy. You had no way of knowing Caress' life was in danger, not if it happened the way you described."

"It just seemed to escalate so quickly," she murmured, recalling the scene that went from face slapping to murder in the time it took to make a quick phone call.

Brash withdrew his hand from hers and got back to business. "Tell me more about Trench Coat."

"Only slightly taller than Caress, but definitely bigger. Broader." She hulked up her shoulders to indicate the extra width. "He was wearing a long khaki trench coat and a hat, and had his back to me the whole time. I never saw a face. Not even a hair color."

"So how are you certain it was a man?"

Madison studied him covertly. Was this a trick question? Did he suspect George Gail? Maybe he already knew about the affair between Caress and Curtis.

"Well, I—I guess I just assumed…" she murmured.

"You know what they say about assume."

She nodded and muttered one of Granny Bert's favorite axioms, "It makes an 'ass' of 'u' and 'me.'"

"So, her attacker could have been a woman?"

"Again, I only saw the person's back, and they had on a coat."

"So that's a yes?" he persisted.

"I guess it's possible. Whoever it was, he or she was bigger and stronger than Caress, but she didn't seem to be afraid of them. She gave as good as she got." Madison's voice faltered. "At least, until there at the end…"

"Start at the beginning and tell me exactly what you saw."

Madison relayed the details the best she could. Brash had her clarify several points, taking notes on his pad. They exhausted the subject, and after thirty minutes, she thought he was finally through questioning her.

"One last thing, Maddy," he said.

"Yes?"

He nailed her with one look. "Tell me why you were really outside Caress Ellingsworth's house tonight."

The man doesn't miss a thing! she fretted silently. "I—I told you."

"I know what you told me. Now tell me the truth."

"I swear. I was watching for Caress." She returned his honest gaze, for she spoke the truth. Just not all of it.

Brash nodded solemnly. "And I believe you."

She almost grinned. Before a smile could work its way across her weary features, he squelched her sense of relief. "What I want to know is *why* you were watching Caress. And before you give me some song and dance, please remember it's almost three in the morning, and Genesis is sitting out there waiting on you."

"I don't know why you don't believe me. I wanted to see what Caress really looked like."

"At midnight."

"I felt like it would give me the opportunity to see the real woman, not just the actress."

Brash mumbled something that sounded like, "You're a pretty good actress, yourself." Pushing out a tired breath, he spoke loud enough for her to hear. "I never took you for the type to follow those daytime soaps."

"There's a type?"

Brash had finally reached his limit. "Cut it out, Madison!" he demanded, his face set in hard, haggard lines. "If you aren't going to tell me the truth, get out of the truck!"

His angry tone stung. Madison relented, but only slightly. She still felt the need to protect her client.

"Okay, you're right," she grudgingly admitted. "I didn't watch her soap opera. But my mother-in-law did. She was a huge fan of the show and was devastated when it was canceled. I couldn't sleep tonight, and I ended up here in front of Caress' house, innocently looking through the picture window. And that, I swear, is the truth."

His anger dissolved, right along with his energy. Brash dropped his dark-auburn head back against the seat and allowed his shoulders to sag, if only for a moment. "Go on home, Maddy," he said quietly.

"Are you—are you still mad at me?"

"I'm not mad. I'm frustrated." He made the admission with his eyes closed. A full beat went by, in which Madison wondered if he had actually fallen asleep.

No such luck. After a brief respite, he opened his eyes and looked at her. "You may be telling me the truth, but it's not the whole truth. Which leads me to believe you're playing junior detective again, after I distinctly told you not to."

"I—I..." she sputtered helplessly, unable to lie, yet unwilling to tell the truth. She couldn't quite meet his eyes, either. After a moment, she reached over and groped for his hand.

He pulled his hand just out of her reach. "Go home, Maddy," he repeated softly.

Because there was nothing left to say, she did just that.

12

Madison was late arriving to her last day of work at the car dealership, but no one noticed; the place was abuzz with the news of Caress Ellingsworth's death.

Madison went straight to her office. She closed the door, put away her purse, and almost jumped out of her skin when a voice whispered loudly, "I thought you would never get here!"

Madison literally squealed. After the night she had, her nerves were frayed. Having people hide in her office and jump out at her didn't improve matters.

"George Gail, what are you doing here?" she demanded, clutching at her chest to keep her heart in place. Any minute now, it might pump its way right out of her body.

"Shh! Don't say my name! No one can know I'm here."

"Why *are* you here?" Madison asked bluntly, staring at the disheveled woman. George Gail's hair was unkempt, her makeup smeared, her clothes crumpled and stale. She looked terrible.

"I had to see you! We have to plan our strategy!" The frantic woman grabbed for Madison's arm with hands that were icy cold and trembling.

"Strategy? What are you talking about, George Gail?"

"Shh!" the woman hissed. In a loud whisper, she spoke frantically. "I told you, don't say my name. Do you think anyone heard you?"

"There are only three people out there, and they're all too busy talking about Caress to notice anything else."

Her head bobbed up and down. "Good, that gives us time to develop a plan."

"What on earth are you talking about? What strategy? Why do we need a plan?"

"To throw the police off track!"

Madison eyed her cautiously. "George Gail, is there something you need to tell me?" On second thought, she didn't want to hear a confession. She threw up her palm. "Stop. Never mind. If you have something to say, say it to Brash. Or to a lawyer. Leave me out of it."

"But you're working for me! You're already involved!"

"I've told you a dozen times, I am not a private investigator."

"You've been doing investigative work for me, in private," George Gail Burton pointed out.

"I'm not licensed. What I find is strictly on amateur status. We've been through this."

"But you were the one to discover that my husband was having an affair with—with *her.*"

Madison sighed heavily. "That still doesn't explain why we need a plan and why you are hiding behind the door."

"I told you, no one can know I'm here."

"The walls are solid, George Gail. You can have a seat in the chair, no one will see you." Madison tried to keep exasperation out of her voice as she seated herself behind the desk. The other woman was genuinely distraught.

George Gail slumped into the nearest chair with gratitude. "What a night!" She blew out the words on a whimpered breath. "Tell me everything you know about Caress' murder."

"I was thinking *you* could tell *me* what you know."

"Nothing! I can't find out a thing! Cleo Bishop called all hysterical, saying she was dead. That's all I know. I rushed over here as soon as I could!"

"Who is Cleo Bishop?"

"She makes all the costumes for the church Christmas play."

Madison's face puckered in confusion. "So, what's her connection to Caress? Why was she so hysterical?"

"Because Caress directs our play!" George Gail's incredulous tone suggested Madison should already know this. "She has a role in it, too. Usually Mary, but one year she portrayed an angel. You should have seen the outfit Cleo made for her that year. Absolutely stunning. Yards and yards of—"

Before George Gail could go into full detail, complete with hand gestures, Madison interrupted her. "I remember you saying you were in the play, as well. Meaning you worked with Caress on them?"

"Of course. Like I said, she was our director. I admit, I only had a small part each year. This past year, I was one of the wise men." Seeing Madison's quizzical eyebrows, she went on to explain, "Not many men participate in the play. I managed to wrangle Curtis into playing Joseph, and your

Uncle Joe Bert was a wise man, along with me and Darla Mullins. They were the only two men willing to help out." As a new thought crossed her mind, George Gail gasped and made a scandalized expression. What was left of her blue eye shadow appeared like a stormy streak beneath her tussled bangs as she threw a hand to her generous bosom. "What if *that* was when it happened?" she breathed in horror. "What if I pushed him into her arms? What if their sordid affair started when they were playing parents to Baby Jesus?"

"From everything I have heard about your husband, George Gail, I sincerely doubt that," Madison assured her. *Then again, according to those very same people, he would also never cheat on you.* "Someone mentioned Darla Mullins last night. Who is she?"

"She and Caress are best friends. They do everything together, just like your Aunt Trudy and me. You rarely see one without the other."

Madison imagined how horrible it would be to lose her own dear Genny. The thought was unbearable. "Poor Mrs. Mullins," she murmured with empathy. "I can't imagine what she must be going through."

"I'm sure she's desolate," George Gail agreed. "They were practically inseparable."

Madison drummed her fingers as she thought aloud, "She probably knew whether or not Caress was having an affair with your husband." Too bad she hadn't known about her earlier. Talking to the friend would have been so much more pleasant than practically witnessing the actress' death.

George Gail's audible gasp drew her attention back on task. "We'll have to tell her not to say a word!"

You should be the one in Hollywood. Madison grunted the thought to herself. Definitely a drama queen.

Schooling her voice to mask the irritation she felt, she asked, "George Gail, was there something I could do for you?"

"You have to help me. I need an alibi!" Her hysterical voice rose higher than she intended. Her widened eyes swallowed all traces of blue shadow and she clamped both hands across her mouth. As if the belated action somehow recalled the hurled words, she repeated them in a loud whisper, "I need an alibi."

Dread welled in Madison's chest. Not wanting to get involved—yet knowing she already was—Madison had to ask. "Why do you need an alibi?"

George Gail stood from her seat and paced the small office, wringing her hands. Madison didn't pressure her. A few more tortured paces, and the distraught woman fell back into the chair with a heavy admission. "I can't remember what happened last night."

"Do you remember calling me?"

"I think so. Yes. Yes, I called you and told you Curtis left the house."

"You wanted me to go to the sale barn and see if he was there."

"Was he?"

"No. You called again later, saying he called home. Something about a trailer breaking down. You insisted I go home and go back to bed."

George Gail gave her an apologetic look. "I have been disturbing your sleep lately, haven't I?"

Madison hated to bring the subject up, but she had five hundred dollars at stake. "Do you remember offering to pay me extra for all the sleep I was losing?"

After a slight hesitation, she nodded slowly. "I think so. Overtime. Five hundred dollars."

"Yes, that's right. But I didn't feel right about taking that much money for just driving around the barn a few times, so I decided to drive over to Caress' house."

"Was he—was he there?" The other woman's chin quivered as she awaited the answer.

Madison's heart went out to her. Her voice was kind as she assured the worried older woman, "No, George Gail, he wasn't."

She perked up considerably, until a new thought occurred to her. "Was—Was I there?"

The image of Trench Coat flashed through Madison's mind. The image offered the right size, the right shape, but she had difficulty believing this vulnerable woman before her could commit such a vile and vicious crime. George Gail was melodramatic and perhaps a bit scatter-brained, but those were hardly the traits of a murderer. Still, the thought had entered her mind last night. Instead of giving a direct answer, she asked with curiosity, "Why would you ask that?"

George Gail's hand trembled as she rubbed her fingers across her forehead. "I—I drank too much wine last night. I don't remember what happened. I know I called you a couple of times, called Curtis and kept getting his voice mail. I remember thinking I ought to go over there and give Caress a piece of my mind, but I—I remember having trouble getting the door open."

Madison frowned. "It sounded like you were outside the last time you called me."

"It was the car door I couldn't open," George Gail confessed. "And I couldn't open it because I couldn't find my keys.

I remember going back inside and lying down. The room was spinning. That's the last thing I remember until the phone rang this morning, when Cleo called to tell me about Caress."

"Then why do you think you may have gone to Caress' last night?"

"Shh!" She looked over her shoulders with a frantic motion. "Don't say that so loud!"

Madison matched her loud whisper with her own. "Why do you think you need an alibi, George Gail, if you were passed out at home all night?"

She peered back over her shoulder, assuring herself that the door was closed and they were alone. "You're bound by client confidentiality, right?"

"I—I don't know," Madison said with an uncertain frown. "You are my client, yes, and there's an implied and explicit trust between us. But it's not like I'm a doctor or lawyer and legally bound to secrecy."

"But you won't run to the police, will you, with what I'm about to tell you?"

"Of course not. But please know if *they* come to *me*, I'll have to tell them what I know. And this may be a good time to tell you that I am considered a key witness to Caress' murder."

"You *saw* her being murdered?" George Gail gasped.

"Not exactly. I saw her fighting with her attacker, and they fell to the ground. I didn't exactly witness the stabbing, thank goodness, but I knew something was wrong when she never got up. I was the one to call 911."

"Then you can be my alibi! If you saw her killer, then you know it wasn't me!" The relief in her voice was palpable.

Madison made no comment.

After a conspicuous moment of silence, George Gail noticed the tiny lines that appeared between Madison's puckered brows. "Wh—What? It—It wasn't me, was it?" she squeaked.

"I don't know," Madison told her honestly. "I don't think so. All I saw was the killer's back. Do you happen to own a trench coat?"

"No." Madison's relief was short-lived when she added, "But Curtis does. I sometimes borrow his. Why?"

"Uhm, you might want to check it out when you get home," Madison suggested.

"Why?"

"The killer wore a trench coat, which would probably be covered in blood."

George Gail made a small choking sound, something between a gasp and a cry. The color drained from her face.

"What is it? Are you all right?" Madison asked in concern.

"This—This is confidential, right?" She glanced back over her shoulder to ensure there was still no audience.

Madison agreed with a sigh. "Yes."

"Wh—Wh—When I woke up this morning," she managed to choke out, "there were car keys in my hand and blood on the sheets!"

13

Madison stumbled through the rest of the day, tired and groggy and more than a little out of sorts. She didn't want to be in the middle of a murder investigation. She didn't want to withhold knowledge from the police. She didn't want to be torn between Brash and her client. Both ties—this new and tender relationship with the chief of police and her professional obligation to George Gail—were tentative and undefined. Most of all, she didn't want George Gail to be guilty.

Her best tactic, she determined, was to ignore the entire situation in the hopes that it might go away. Impossible, of course, but worth her best try.

She was in no mood for guests, but when she drove up at home that evening, a familiar white van occupied the driveway. With all the commotion of witnessing Caress' attack and finding George Gail in her office, she had all but forgotten about Nick Vilardi and *Home Again.*

On the plus side, there were only five gawkers gathered round the van today. She noted that fact with forced appreciation as she pushed past them and let herself in the house.

"Well, there she is now," Granny Bert said brightly as Madison opened the front door. No doubt, the trio had been talking about her.

"Hello." Madison offered a cautious smile to the television star and his producer. Part of her worried what Granny Bert had been telling them, while the other part of her worried how she must look in her oversized sweater and jeans. Why hadn't she worn something more flattering today? Oh, yes, that's right; after practically witnessing a murder, she had only slept about fifteen minutes last night. Her wardrobe had been the least of her worries when getting dressed.

"Madison, how lovely to see you again!" Amanda Hooper beamed at her from behind a half-empty juice glass. "Your grandmother was gracious enough to make us power shakes."

Half-empty? They were more than likely still half-full, Madison mused, eying the mostly green concoction with a suspicious eye. She would have offered an apology, but Granny Bert looked quite proud of herself. Her glass, Madison noted, was empty.

Nick Vilardi stood from his place on the couch and motioned for Madison to have a seat beside him. "How are you today, Madison?" His eyes skipped over her with a subtle but warm sweep.

"I'm fine, thank you," she murmured. Fully aware of the warmth in his gaze, a slight blush stained her cheeks as she settled on the far end of the sofa, nearest the chair her grandmother occupied. She folded her hands into her lap and fiddled with them nervously.

"We met your children earlier," Amanda continued. "They are both delightful, and so well mannered. Lovely teenagers."

"Thank you." This time, Madison's smile was genuine. They were discussing her favorite people, after all. Clearing her throat, she reluctantly addressed a new subject. "I—I want to apologize for leaving so abruptly yesterday."

"Don't think a thing of it!" Amanda gushed. "We know it was a lot for you to process. And apparently, we took you by surprise, merely by showing up." She slid a reproachful eye to Granny Bert, who still beamed happily from her recliner.

"Definitely," Madison agreed.

Nick was eager to get down to business. "I brought over a preliminary first draft of the renovations I'm proposing." He handed her a sketchpad as he spoke.

"I—I don't understand. I told you yesterday that I cannot afford this project."

"I'm working on some options to get you financing." There was a hint of excitement in his voice, suggesting he had good news.

Or what he thinks is good news. Madison hated to dull the attractive spark that echoed in his eyes, but there was no need in prolonging the inevitable. No lender would agree to finance anything with her name on it, not after the way Gray had destroyed their credit. "I'm afraid getting a loan is out of the question."

"I'm not talking about a loan."

Madison's eyes immediately flew to her grandmother. In light of a recent conversation in which Granny Bert offered to use her influence to get Bethani on the cheerleading squad, Madison wouldn't put it past the old dear to pull a few strings on her behalf. "Granny, did you—"

Bertha Cessna stopped her before she could finish the thought. She thrust up a deeply lined palm. “Don’t be looking at me with that tone of voice,” the old woman warned. “I have nothing to do with this.”

Madison arched her brow. “You and Genny were the ones to instigate this whole charade to begin with.”

She conceded with a shrug of her bony shoulders. “Other than that.”

Nick motioned to the sketchpad she had yet to open. “Please, have a look. And let’s not worry about the financial details right now.”

“Easy for you to say,” Madison muttered. Fifty thousand dollars was hardly a detail to be ignored, but she did as he asked. She glanced down at a detailed rendition of the Big House’s exterior. “It’s a good drawing, but it looks the same.”

“Ah… but look at this.” His finger traced the pointed roofline of an additional turret added to the rear of the house. “I propose adding a turret back here that will house new bathrooms on all three levels. It is the best way to work in new plumbing, while keeping with the integrity and architect of the house.”

“You’re right. I didn’t even realize that was a new feature.” She was duly impressed. She was also impressed by his cologne, which floated out to caress her senses as he bent his head near her own.

Nick flipped to another page. “This would be the newly designed kitchen. It would allow for maximum counter space, plenty of cabinets for storage, and an efficient footprint. No more walking halfway around the room to access the stove.” He pointed out a dozen features that left her mouth salivating. His sketch made even her kitchen in Dallas look rugged in comparison, and it had been professionally designed and decorated. This design, complete with new appliances, granite, and the painted white cabinets she adored, blended a traditional turn-of-the-century farmhouse look with all the modern amenities she could ever need or want.

"There's more," he grinned, turning the page. He showed her the plans to relocate and enlarge the laundry room, along with adding a second bathroom to the ground floor. The next page in his sketchbook detailed the spacious new bath for the second floor. The old bath would be remodeled and turned into part of the master suite. By the time he finished explaining his vision for her private sanctuary and the added bathroom for the third level, Madison was drooling. The house was everything and more than she could ever want.

When she closed the pad at last, he sat back with an expectant smile. "So?" he asked. "Do you approve?"

"It's—It's amazing."

Amanda was the one to comment. "Then why don't you look more pleased?"

"These plans are absolutely stunning. If money weren't an issue, I would have you start immediately."

"As Nick said, don't worry about the money for now."

"How can I *not* worry?" Madison said in exasperation. She looked at Nick with accusation in her eyes. "I know what you're doing. You think that if you dangle just the right carrot in front of me, I'll find a way to make this happen. But you aren't listening. I can't afford the renovations."

Nick jumped to his feet, his face registering frustration. "I'm offering you the deal of the decade, and you're *still* trying to drive a better bargain?"

Angered by his assumption that she was playing a game, Madison flew to her feet and practically yelled. "I'm not trying to drive a bargain. I'm trying to get it through to your thick skull that I. Have. No. Money. Get it? I'm broke! No matter how great of a deal you offer me, I cannot afford it!"

They stood staring at one another, both their chests heaving with raw emotion. Madison tried to read the thoughts flashing in his stormy-blue eyes, but she refused to be distracted by the sheer beauty of them. No matter how charming and magnetic the man might be, she still had no money.

Amanda was the one to break into the terse silence in the room. "Nick," she began softly.

Nick ignored his producer. Shaking off whatever she might have to say, he spoke out, his words practically a growl. "I want this house."

"Get the numbers down," Madison challenged smartly.

"Not going to happen."

The footstool on Granny Bert's recliner came down with a loud *thump*. "Now hold on, you two. No need in squaring off like a couple of old gunslingers. Young man, I like what you've drawn up for the house. Now you go on back to the city and find a way to make it happen. When you get those numbers down, you come on back and we'll talk business."

Nick stared at the old woman in shock. "Down? Get the numbers *down*? This is over a one-hundred-thousand-dollar renovation. Close to two hundred thousand, with these extras I've thrown in. I'm offering it to you for the rock-bottom price of fifty thousand. It can't get much lower than that."

Granny Bert gave a sudden weary sigh. "He's right, Madison. He's offering you a wonderful deal. All of those bells and whistles for a mere fifty thousand." She shook her wrinkled head with just the right amount of awe.

Madison stared at her grandmother in dismay. Whose side was she on, anyway? "I can't afford the bells and whistles, Granny," she practically hissed. "Or the house."

"Of course you can't." Her grandmother reached out a bony hand and patted her arm. "So you'll just have to live without the bells and whistles. The house needs a few walls knocked out here and there, but don't worry, Hank Adams is a fairly decent handy man. He has a nice little crew of rag-tags and misfits, most of them trained right here locally at the high school shop class." She slid a sly glance at Madison the others couldn't see. "True, Billy Blackburn is as clumsy as an ox on ice, but he means well. Verna Bishop had a fireplace like the one at the Big House and he dropped a hammer on it, busting that marble all to pieces, but do you know what he did? He took all those little bits and pieces and made her a walkway out to her pool. She says the gas insert is so much more efficient, anyway. We could do that with all the fireplaces, don't you think? They have some nice ones at Home Depot that look like little pot belly stoves."

While Nick Vilardi visibly blanched, the old woman continued, "And no need to worry about re-doing any of the wood floors. We'll just slap down some carpet. Or those laminate planks they have these days. Almost look real." She marveled at the wonders of modern technology as she slid an eye to Nick's face. It was growing paler by the moment.

Knowing exactly what her grandmother was doing, Madison chewed on her lips to bite back a smile. To their guests, it appeared she was contemplating her grandmother's suggestions.

"Now, about that drawing on the dining room wall," Bertha Cessna clucked, tucking her arm through her granddaughter's. "I was thinking a nice thick coat of paint should cover it right up. Maybe—"

"No!"

The word was torn from Amanda Hooper. "You can't paint over that mural!" she cried in horror. Actual tears welled in her eyes.

"Sure you can," Granny Bert responded, her tone chipper. "I've seen it done a dozen times. All you need is—"

"But that's a Seymour Addison original! Nick! *Do* something!" the television producer wailed in beseech.

"Ladies," he said hastily, a rare nervous quality in his voice, "I'll need a little time to put something together, but I need your promise that you won't start on any renovations until you hear from me."

"I don't know," Granny Bert said uncertainly. "How long are we talking? Do you have any idea what it's like sharing this little old house with three extra people?" Never mind that her family of six had lived here comfortably for years. "Having teenagers in the house can wear on the nerves something awful. All that noise and loud music and parties late into the night. No offense to you, dear"—this, thrown Madison's way—"but I can hardly wait for you and those noisy teens to have your own place."

"None taken," she assured her grandmother. She knew it was all a show; the twins were extremely well behaved and were always the first to bed each night.

"I'll need to talk to the network brass and some of our sponsors," Nick said. "Two weeks, tops. Can you give me that long?"

"I really don't see the point," Madison said. "At the risk of sounding like a broken record, I have no money to invest in this project."

Granny Bert agreed. "That pot-filler do-hicky was nice, but you can carry your pots and pans back and forth to the faucet like you've always done. And even though Nick here talked about how nice that butcher block island is—top quality workmanship and fine wood grain and all—we could just rip it out to put in a dishwasher. Much more useful, if you ask me." She added a smart little nod that allowed her to cut her eyes again toward Nick Vilardi's panicked expression.

"Again, let's not be hasty," the man pleaded. "Let me see what I can do about getting those numbers down."

All but ignoring him, the old woman offered more advice to her granddaughter. "They have those nice big pieces of remnant carpet you can buy down at Carpet Barn. All the rooms might not match, but it beats that scratched-up wood floor. You could even get enough to do the stairs."

The veiled threat to the staircase sent Nick over the edge. He snatched up his sketchpad and, with a jerk of his arm, motioned for his producer to stand. "Come on, Amanda, we have work to do."

The blond woman scrambled to her feet as he directed, allowing Nick to pull her toward the door where he whirled around and faced Madison with a look that could only be described as a glare. "I'll be back," he declared. "I'm not about to let some two-bit carpenter lay a finger on that house. You two have no idea what kind of treasure you have on your hands, and what damage one of your local yokels could do with a hammer and a bucket of paint!"

"Again, I have no—"

He cut her off before she could finish her tired old mantra. "I'll find the money to restore your house—*properly*—even if I have to sell my soul to the devil to finance it. When I want something, I make it happen." He all but shook the sketchpad at her. "And I want this house."

Madison stood in the middle of the living room, her mouth agape at his vehement parting.

Granny Bert trailed their guests to the door, waving in farewell and issuing a friendly invitation to return. Once the duo passed the growing number of fans in the driveway and crawled into the van, the old woman closed the door and gave a satisfied little cackle.

"And that, my dear," she announced smugly, "is how you skin a polecat."

14

Granny Bert was still crowing with delight while she and Madison made supper. Madison indulged the older woman, allowing her to gloat over her cunning negotiation skills. She added the appropriate murmurs of agreement in all the right places, but her mind raced with possibilities. What if Nick actually did find a way to remodel the Big House for a fraction of the cost? Would that make buying the old mansion feasible?

She was still debating the issue in her mind when Bethani came blazing through the door, long blond hair trailing behind her. "Mom! Mom, where are you?"

"Refrigerator." She popped her head out as she searched for a decent head of lettuce. Either Granny Bert's refrigerator was on the blink, or Moe's Market stocked inferior produce these days.

"Oh. I didn't see you there. What are you doing?" Without waiting for an answer, the fifteen-year-old went on to gush, "I have the most unbelievable news! You'll never guess what happened! Go on, guess!"

"Well—"

"He asked me out! The cutest boy in school asked me to the Valentine's Day Dance! Can I go, Mom, please? I know Daddy always told me I had to wait until my sixteenth birthday, when he could take me out and show me how a real man should treat a lady on a date. But Daddy…" Her bright voice faltered and tears swam in her eyes before she forged on through "… Daddy can't… So can I go, Mom, please? It's really more like a group of us going, not an actual date. And Blake is going!" She flung the last part out in challenge.

Madison waded through the flood of emotions and errant thoughts that accompanied her daughter's rushed words. What did Grayson know about how to treat a lady, anyway? She'd rather Bethani not be subjected to his version of a 'real man.' But the tears in the young girl's voice broke through Madison's hardened heart and made her own eyes water. She was thankful that her daughter was happy and fitting in so well at school. Bethani's enthusiasm was contagious, right up until reality set in. Where on earth would she find the money to buy the teenager a dress for the dance?

The teen gave her all of five seconds to respond before wailing, "You're not saying anything, Mom! You're not going to let me go, are you? *Granny*, do something!" She turned beseeching blue eyes to her great grandmother.

"Whoa, whoa, whoa," Madison broke in. "I never said you couldn't go."

"Then can I?" Hope gurgled in her baby blue eyes.

"I assume we're talking about Drew Baines?" He was a junior and president of the Future Farmers of America. Until a few weeks ago, Bethani made fun of his organization. *Funny how a handsome face can make a girl do an about-face,* Madison mused. Visions of two other handsome faces floated through her mind. This wasn't about Brash and Nick, however. Madison brought her attention back to her daughter, just in time to see her frown.

"Drew? He's taking Teryl Perez. She wanted to go with Blake, until they found out we were like fourth cousins or something. So now Drew is taking Teryl and Blake is taking Danni Jo Combs, since she and Shawn Bealls just broke up. Jeff Adams is taking Megan, so we're all going together in a limo that Mama Matt is renting us." Bethani tossed her blond head as she explained the intricacies of high school dating. "Please, Mom, can I go? You just have to say yes!"

Megan deCordova was Bethani's newly made best friend and happened to be Brash's daughter. The teen lived with her mother and stepfather, who were, respectfully, Madison's former arch nemesis and high school boyfriend. As it turned out, Shannon Wynn Aikman wasn't nearly as horrible as Madison had imagined all those years, and Matt, a.k.a. Mama Matt, seemed intent on playing matchmaker between her and Brash.

"I still don't know who asked you!" Flabbergasted, Madison managed to squeeze the words out between her daughter's rant.

"Mo-om! Who am I always saying has the dreamiest green eyes? Josiah Burton!"

"Burton? Is his grandmother George Gail Burton?"

"I don't know, maybe. His grandfather is partners with your uncle at the sale barn. Josiah works there on weekends and during the summers. He's saving up to buy a truck, so he wanted to know if you could get him a good deal at the car dealership."

"As of today, I no longer work there. Uncle Glenn is back from his cruise, so I'm done with that job. But I can put in a good word for him," she offered.

"So I can go?" The teen bounced up and down, taking the offer as a sign of general good will and approval.

"I want to meet him first."

Bethani squealed in delight. "You're the best, Mom!" she said, throwing her arms around her mother and kissing her cheek. "I'll go text him right now!"

As the blond whirlwind swept from the room, Madison mumbled, "What ever happened to calling?"

"What ever happened to coming to the door and asking to meet the parents before you asked a girl out on a date?" Granny Bert countered with a grumble.

Madison sighed. "I guess we're old school. And I guess she's going to need a dress."

Bethani needed a dress, Blake needed a new shirt, and they all could use a dinner date.

After their shopping excursion at the College Station mall, they gathered for a late dinner the next evening at a favorite restaurant. It was the perfect time to tell the twins about her newest embroilment in yet another murder case.

"Seriously, Mom, this has got to stop," Blake chastised her. "Nothing like this ever happened in Dallas. Yet we move to the country where things are supposed to be nice and quiet, and this is the second murder you've gotten tangled up with! What gives?"

"Just an unfortunate case of being in the wrong place at the wrong time," Madison assured her son.

"And you actually *saw* the killer?" Bethani questioned with eyes big and wide.

"Just their back. I can't identify him. Or her, whichever the case may be."

"But they can identify you." Blake made it a statement, not a question. There was a crinkle of worry between his blue eyes.

"I—I don't think so. Not really. It was dark that night, and very foggy. I'm sure we have nothing to worry about."

"And this lady was a TV star? To be such a little town, there sure are a lot of famous people," Bethani said with an amazed shake of her head. "Glitter Thompson is a former Las Vegas dancer, Tug Montgomery is the former Heisman trophy winner, Brash deCordova a former NFL player, and now this Caress person, former daytime soap star. Go figure."

Her brother piped in, his worry already forgotten. "And soon we'll have Blake Reynolds, baseball superstar and home-run king!" With a grin, the tall youth took an imaginary bow.

"Yeah, you're a legend in your own mind," his sister quipped.

But Madison wasn't really listening to their banter. She was thinking about what Blake said.

Could the killer identify her?

And, more importantly, what would he—or she—do about it?

Two nights had passed without interruption from George Gail, but that hardly meant Madison could sleep well. New worries plagued her. What if the killer came after her? Would her children be safe? Had that black car been following her today? What if Nick Vilardi came through with a deal on renovating the house? Then she would be forced to decide whether or not to buy it. And why hadn't she heard from Brash? Was he still angry at her? It had been three days since Caress was killed.

Three days, but no funeral. Due to the criminal circumstances of Caress' death, an autopsy was ordered. Next of kin had to be notified; the actress' family, what little there was, was scattered around the country. And John-Paul Noble had to arrange to fly in from Paris.

With the arrival of Valentine's Day, Madison had no time to worry about funerals, eccentric clients, or exasperating men. Her babies were going on their first dates. A quadruple date as it were, which at fifteen was the best kind. Madison took a ton of pictures, shed a few melancholy tears she tried to hide from the twins, then stood back and watched as her babies, looking excited and all grown up, took those first gigantic steps away from her.

Madison lingered on the porch as she watched the limo pull away. Where had the time gone? Just last week, they were toddlers, getting into everything, times two. Wasn't it just last night that Blake lost his first tooth? The Tooth Fairy tiptoed into his room and slid a handful of change beneath his pillow. And wasn't it only yesterday Bethani learned to whistle? She had been so proud, even if the resulting shrill tones drove her and Gray nuts that first week.

Time, Madison determined, had no sympathy for a mother's tender heart.

By the time she finally collected herself, Madison had few moments to spare. *At least there are no ruffles,* she noted with approval as she slid into her own dress.

It was gorgeous, but impractical; she could hardly wear it to church, or even to a wedding. It was strictly a party dress, and heaven knew how seldom she went to those. *Maybe I can wear it again at Christmas,* she mused. The deep red was right for the season, but the neckline was lower than she preferred and the skirt a bit tight. Very sophisticated, the dress was something like she would have worn in Dallas.

For the first time, Madison realized how much she had always hated dressing up for one of Gray's events. And they had definitely been his: his friends, his colleagues, his desired lifestyle. She would have been just as happy staying in most evenings, cuddled up with the twins or a good book.

Determined not to think of Grayson tonight, Madison shook off memories of prior Valentine's spent with the man she once loved. It didn't bother her to be spending this 'holiday' alone; there was too much happening in her life right now to be worried about romance. Once again, she would be content to stay home with a good book and a glass of wine, but tonight was important to her friend.

With that thought in mind, she slipped on a pair of black pumps, spritzed on perfume, and braced herself for the evening ahead.

15

"Genny, this place looks amazing!"

Despite her having spent most of the day helping her friend decorate, the place looked different by the time she returned two hours later. Genny had added the finishing touches to make the atmosphere absolutely perfect.

Twinkling white lights crisscrossed the room, interspersed here and there with strands of red luminance. Antique paper hearts, strands of crystal beads, and photocopies of old love letters, edged in glitter, gave the room a nostalgic air. Dubbed a mixer, tonight was more about friends than lovers. A few intimate tables were set up in the back for an aura of romance, but most of the tables—all topped with white linen cloths, flickering candlelight, and scattered rose petals—were set for parties of six or more. Instead of hushed romantic notes, a live band played upbeat tunes and the center of the room was cleared for spontaneous dancing. In lieu of a menu, a long buffet stretched down one side of the restaurant, overflowing with delightful creations and fancy offerings usually reserved for weddings.

"This is incredible," Madison proclaimed. "And look at you! You look gorgeous!"

"Thanks," Genesis beamed.

Where Madison was tall and straight, her friend was shorter and curvier; not exactly plump, but shapely with generous contours. Her short blond hair tended to curl around her heart-shaped face and, she often lamented, called attention to the sharp point of her chin. Few others ever noticed the chin; her twinkling blue eyes and charming dimples were showstoppers. Although she was seldom mistaken for a beauty queen, when Genny Baker flashed her smile, her face lit up with an inner radiance that made her truly beautiful.

"Do you like your dress?" Genny worried.

"I have to admit, you did a great job picking it out. And yours is gorgeous."

While Maddy's dress stretched sleekly down her long frame, Genny's was short and flared. The full skirt rustled when she moved, swishing around a layer of red petticoats. The dresses were totally opposite, but perfect for each of the women who wore them.

"I did good, even if I do say so myself!"

Madison laughed at her friend's cheeky reply that lacked an ounce of modesty. "Okay, so what do you need me to do? People will be arriving soon."

"Here, take this tray. I have to check on one last detail in the kitchen."

Thirty minutes later, the café filled up quickly.

"People are going to go crazy when they find out all of this is free," Madison murmured to her friend. She spoke out of the corner of her mouth as they stood near the door, greeting guests as they arrived.

"I love my new career. This is as much a gift to myself, as it is to the community." Waving at the couple stepping through the door, she called out a warm greeting. "Matt! Shannon! I'm so glad you could come."

"We wouldn't have missed it for the world! This is absolutely fabulous. And you two look amazing!" Shannon all but squealed, grasping first Genny's hands, then Madison's.

As the couple moved on, a deep voice spoke near Genny's ear. "I'll second that. You look… I can't even find the right word, you look so beautiful."

"Aw, Cutter, what a nice thing to say." In spite of herself, Genesis blushed. It did wonders for a woman's soul to hear such heartfelt praise from any man, especially one as ruggedly handsome as Cutter Montgomery. Even though he was several years younger than she was, Genny wasn't as immune to his charm as she liked to pretend. He looked particularly handsome tonight. The red western shirt set off his dark-blond hair and year-round tan. Black jeans and a black tooled leather vest gave his sexy cowboy look an added edge. "And you clean up quite nicely yourself, I might add." Her eyes twinkled as she took a pointed glance behind him. "Where's Callie Beth? Is she meeting you here later?"

His open scowl made her regret her words. "I've told you a dozen times, she's not my girlfriend!"

"I don't think she got the memo," Genny said softly.

"I don't mean to sound rude, but that's her problem, not mine. We've gone out a couple times, mostly with a group, but she's hardly my Valentine."

"Well, that's what tonight is all about," she beamed. "Mingling and mixing among friends." She waved a hand toward the quickly filling room. "Have a seat wherever you like.

We'll open the buffet line in about ten minutes. And thank you for coming."

There was a line forming behind him, but he seemed not to notice. "There will be dancing later, right?"

"Absolutely."

"Then I'll save a dance for you." He gave her a flirtatious wink before ambling off toward a group of friends.

Genny laughed at her own foolishness as she felt another blush stain her cheeks. What a shame he was too young for her, too old for Bethani. Then again, he was just about right for Shilo Dawne....

She gave the crowd another fifteen minutes to get settled. Then she called for their attention and made a brief speech, thanking the townspeople for welcoming her and making her business so successful. Because of them, her dreams of owning her own restaurant and bakery had come true, and tonight was her way of giving back. This was a party, she announced, free of charge. Madison and Shilo Dawne would be around soon with flutes of champagne. Over the excited murmur of the crowd, she gave a flourishing hand movement to the table behind her and proclaimed that the buffet line was now open.

As people were re-seated, Madison and Shilo Dawne delivered the sparkling wine. Madison moved among the tables with her tray and a warm smile, until a woman stopped her with the simple words, "You're her, aren't you?"

"I beg your pardon?" Madison didn't recognize the other woman, but her squat, stocky figure did seem vaguely familiar. "You're the one who ... saw... Caress, aren't you?" When she faltered over the words, Madison knew this must be Caress' best friend. Her heart went out to the other woman's palpable sorrow.

"Yes," she nodded gently.

The other woman thrust out her hand. "Darla Mullins," she confirmed. "Could we talk?"

Madison glanced first at her empty tray, then at the people around them. Most had already been served. "Sure," she shrugged.

Even when Darla Mullins shoved to her feet, Madison still towered over her. Darla was short and thick. There was little definition to her shape; she was like a solid chunk from her thick neck down to her thick thighs. Her hair was cut short and severe. Dressed in a dark pantsuit, the light coat of mascara and large hoop earrings were her only nod to fashion. Like she and Genesis, this other duo of friends were exact opposites.

"I keep thinking we have met before," Madison said.

"You're probably thinking of my sister, Myrna Lewis."

"Oh." For a moment, she could think of nothing else to say. Myrna Lewis was hardly her favorite person. After making a terrible scene with Bethani here in this very restaurant, the woman had tried to tarnish the teenager's credibility and Madison's business reputation with vindictive verbal attacks. Few people in town even liked the woman, but there were some who listened to her bitter lies.

"Dean told me what a wonderful job you did filling in for him and Myrna at the insurance agency," the sister said as she led the way to a less populated area of the room.

"Thank you." As irony would have it, and much to Myrna's dismay, Dean Lewis had hired *In a Pinch* to fill in while they were out of town for a few days.

They came to a stop in a dimly lit corner. "As you may have heard, Caress was my best friend."

"Yes, and I am so sorry for your loss."

"I still can't believe she's gone. We were inseparable. We had just talked on the phone an hour before… before…" Darla Mullins put a chubby hand over her mouth as if to hold the horrible words inside. Collecting herself, she asked, "What did you see, Mrs. Reynolds? I need to know what her last minutes were like."

"I—I really didn't see… the end."

"I thought you were an eyewitness!"

"I saw her arguing with someone, yes, but I didn't see her actually be… I didn't see it happen."

"Do you—Do you think she was in pain?"

Madison couldn't help but frown. She was brutally stabbed to death, numerous times. Of course she was in pain!

The words, of course, were never spoken aloud. She smoothed the frown from her forehead and went with a well-meaning lie. "I think it was very quick. Hopefully she didn't have time to feel much pain."

The other woman slumped in relief. "Thank the Lord," she breathed, making the sign of the cross across her saggy bosom. *At least she had that in common with her friend.*

Appalled at her thoughts, Madison cleared her throat uncomfortably.

"So you saw who did this?" Darla asked, gripping Madison's arm with a surprisingly strong hold.

"Not really. I never saw a face."

"Oh? Then you're really no eyewitness at all."

In deference to her sorrow, Madison allowed the snarky tone in her words to slide. "Mrs. Mullins, do you know if Caress was seeing anyone romantically?" she asked instead.

The other woman bristled. "Why would you ask that? And what business is it of yours, anyway?"

"I—I heard she was seeing someone here. I just wondered what local man could compete with her long-time boyfriend, John-Paul Noble." She flashed a smile, hoping to look appropriately star-struck.

"Well, you heard wrong, on both accounts," Darla Mullins snapped. "She and John-Paul were over years ago."

"So, she didn't have a current boyfriend? She was such an attractive woman, I'm a bit surprised by that."

"I can assure you, she wasn'*t* involved with any man from here."

"Oh?" Madison pressed. "I heard she was seeing… a married man."

"Who?" Darla demanded. "Who was she supposedly seeing?"

"Uhm, I'm not sure I should repeat gossip."

A light of suspicion sparked in the other woman's eyes before she swelled with indignation. "Well, I can assure you, that isn'*t* true! Caress was far too classy to be involved with any redneck hillbilly from around here!"

Grief was one thing; open hostility was another. Taking an immediate dislike to the woman, Madison gave her a false smile. "Yes, I see the resemblance now. You and your sister are remarkably alike."

"So I've heard." She apparently didn't detect the insult in Madison's words and kept right on talking. While doing a mental shrug, Madison almost missed the words, "I'd like to hire you."

"Hire me?"

Even Madison heard the squeak of surprise in her voice.

"Yes. You do own a temporary agency, do you not?" Darla demanded.

"Yes, I do."

"Good. Then be at *Boundaries* first thing Monday morning."

"But —"

Darla looked her directly in the eye, challenging her to lie. "Do you have another job lined up for Monday morning?"

"Uh, well… no."

The other woman fairly smirked. "Good. Then I'll see you sharply at eight o'clock. The corner of Third and Juniper. Don't be late." She walked away before Madison could come up with a reply. Apparently done with the party, Darla Mullins kept walking, right out the front door.

Madison had no idea how long she stood there, staring after the strange woman. She was finally aware of someone approaching. A familiar voice spoke near her ear, flavored with concern. "Maddy?"

Snapping out of her trance, she looked up into Brash's dark eyes. "H—Hi," she stammered.

"Are you all right?"

"I'm not sure." She relayed the odd conversation and the way Darla practically ordered her to work at *Boundaries.*

"They are an odd lot, she and her sister. Yankees," he said by way of explanation.

"I'm of half a mind not to show up Monday morning."

"The other half?"

"Lucky for me, that's the sensible half, the one that keeps track of my finances." A rueful smile played along the lines of her pouted mouth.

His dark eyes zeroed in on her lips. A new energy charged the air as he came a step closer. "Happy Valentine's Day, Maddy."

"Happy Valentine's to you, too." Why was her voice suddenly so husky? She didn't care a thing in the world about celebrating this day.

"You look gorgeous. Red is definitely your color."

That was good, because it appeared in both of her cheeks. "Thank you," she murmured. Her eyes fell to the starched shirt of his uniform. "Working?" It was a needless question, but it kept her from saying something foolish, like how good he looked, as well.

"Yeah, but I thought I'd run by and take a chance at my luck."

She gave him a quizzical look.

In response, Brash held out his hand. "Dance with me, Maddy?" he asked lowly.

She moved into his arms more eagerly than was proper. When he laughed, the sound did warm and wicked things to her fragile libido. *It's the stupid holiday,* she told herself. A made-up holiday at that. It made even sane people behave foolishly, all in the name of love and romance. *Not that I want either,* she assured herself. *I've done without it for the past two and a half years, I can do without it for another two and a half. By then, the twins will be out of school and I'll have time for myself again. I'm good till then.*

"Maddy?" Brash scrutinized her with a slight frown. "Where did you go? I lost you for a second."

She tried to push off her foolishness with a laugh. He tucked her hand deeper into his, curling it close against his very warm, very broad chest. Not that she noticed or anything. She said the first thing that came to mind. "I was just thinking working nights all the time must be murder on your love life." *Lordy, where had that come from?*

"I don't always work nights," he assured her, his voice sounding amused.

Since she had already brought the subject up…. "So, you never remarried after you and Shannon split up?"

"Nope."

"Why not?"

"Never met the right woman."

She loved the way his deep voice rumbled within his chest. Madison allowed herself to sink into his warmth as she rested her head against his shoulder. Her arm tightened around his waist and she could have sworn she heard him give a very manly purr.

"Any serious girlfriends?" she pressed.

"There was one long-term girlfriend, but I wouldn't call it serious," he said. They were still in the darkened corner, swaying to the music more than actually dancing. Both knew it was a thinly veiled excuse to be close to the other. "It ended when I moved back here."

"Waco isn't that far. You could have kept seeing one another."

"To be honest, I was glad for the break."

"What about once you came back here? Surely you've dated."

Muscles flexed beneath her cheek when he shrugged. "A little," he admitted. "There was a female deputy in Navasota, but our schedules kept getting in the way. A substitute music teacher who was here only for a semester. I went out once or twice with Lana Kopetsky, a few more times than that with Margaret Chatham. All in all, a pretty pathetic showing for a single man in the prime of his life."

Lulled by the deep cadence of his voice and the warm vibrations rumbling off his chest, Madison felt completely content within his arms. Her limbs felt deliciously heavy and languid. She could stay right here forever, just like this…

With a bit of a delay, she roused herself enough to murmur, “Lana Kopetsky, huh?” She recalled what Granny Bert had to say about the woman.

“Not one of my better choices,” he admitted. “But in my own defense, I was new back in town and didn’t know she had a reputation. By the second and final date, I was fully aware of her notoriety and how she got it. The woman was like a barracuda.” He shuddered for effect.

Madison chuckled. “I’m sure you were fully capable of taking care of yourself.”

“Barely.”

“And Margaret Chatham? Why is that name familiar?”

“School nurse.”

“That’s right. Oh, she’s a beauty.” Just thinking of the shapely and petite woman with the gorgeous dark complexion, Madison felt clumsy and awkward.

Brash’s arm tightened around her once more, tugging her ever closer. She no longer felt languid; she felt very much alive. He dipped his head to purr against her ear. “She’s nowhere nearly as beautiful as you, Maddy. And she looks terrible in red.” He maneuvered them into a slight spin that presented his back to the crowd for more privacy. He continued to press against her as he whispered, “Red is definitely my favorite color.”

“Is it—Is it hot in here to you?” She knew her face was flaming.

The look he gave her was surely illegal in the southern portion of the United States and half of Kansas. It was certainly doing crazy things to her, making her think the wildest thoughts. "Very hot," he practically growled.

They stared at one another for a long moment. Madison finally managed a deep gulp. "Uhm, Brash?"

"Yeah?"

"The music stopped," she whispered.

"I still hear it." He thumped their clasped hands against his chest, right over his heart.

She nodded ever so slightly as she breathed out an admission. "So do I."

They continued to sway to a melody only they could hear. Halfway into the next song, this one a lively toe-stomping tune, they came out of their shared trance and realized they were making a spectacle of themselves in front of half the town. They moved apart with a minimum of fuss and cleared throats.

"Thanks for the dance, Maddy. I guess I'd better get back to duty."

"But you just got here," she protested.

He gave her the smile that had starred in all her high-school fantasies and far too many of her current ones. "I got what I came for," he assured her. He tipped his fingers to the brim of his hat. "Night, Maddy. Happy Valentine's."

"Happy Valentine's to you, too, Brash." She knew she was grinning like a fool, but this was the best Valentine's Day she could remember in recent history.

16

Standing beside the buffet table, Genesis' face glowed with happiness. Her party was a resounding success. The fliers she handed out and posted around town made no mention of the price for tonight's festivities. They merely dubbed the event as a Valentine Mixer, with great food, live music, and the promise of a good time. Those who came were expecting to pay for their meal, which made giving it away free all the more exciting. For the past two hours, someone was constantly at Genny's side, thanking her for her generosity, telling her how much they appreciated her, and what a wonderful time they were having. Although she planned for tonight to be merely a party, it quickly became a promotional event. Several people asked about booking private parties and if she catered.

She watched the crowd as they milled about, visiting and laughing and dancing. The atmosphere reminded her of a wedding reception, which probably explained why two people had already asked to have theirs here. Not many children were here tonight, but the few who attended were on the dance floor, doing silly imitations of their favorite dance routines.

As with any local gathering, a group of old farmers stood off to one side, discussing the latest weather conditions and the price of hay and cattle and how their crops were doing. Their wives were scattered about the room, visiting with old friends, having another bite of this or that dish with musings of '*what is in this? I must get the recipe,*' and exchanging tidbits of gossip. Tucked into the far corner of the room, a handful of couples sat at the smaller tables with eyes only for one another. It was refreshing to see one of those couples was Darrell and Tammy Hamilton, married for almost thirty years. Even more endearing, Hank and Sadie Bealls, both easily in their eighties, had dominated the dance floor all evening long. Genesis hoped that if she ever found her one true love, they would be as happy and devoted to one another as these couples were.

Her eyes followed the dancers, enjoying the fancy footwork and the flash of colors as couples swirled and twirled. Spotting Cutter and Shilo Dawne, she was surprised the rugged fireman knew the moves to the trendy dance step; she thought two-steps and line dances were more his style.

Her gaze traveled among the crowd, until a couple against the far wall caught her eye. She smiled as she recognized Brash and Maddy swaying in the shadows. His head dipped low as he murmured something near her ear, their hands clasped together over his heart. *Mmm, looks interesting,* she thought. *No one deserves happiness more than Maddy.*

The song ended, and couples slowly left the dance floor, drifting back to their tables. Shilo Dawne headed toward Genesis, her green eyes bright and excited. She looked particularly lovely tonight in her fashionable outfit, part of which she had crocheted herself. It occurred to Genesis that she could never pull off such a look herself, but on the dark-haired beauty, it worked, and worked well. *Youth,* she mused. *And skinny genes.*

"Miss Genny, this is the best party, EVER!" the young woman gushed. Keeping her hands hidden from Cutter's view, she gave an exaggerated thumb's up and an excited smile.

Genesis laughed aloud, amused by her obvious crush on the fireman. Cutter stepped around the younger woman and extended a hand toward Genny. "I believe you owe me a dance," he reminded her.

"Oh, you kids go on and have fun. I'll cover for Shilo Dawne."

The young woman was about to accept the generous offer, but Cutter spoke first. "Not a chance. You deserve to have a little fun tonight, too. Have you danced at all tonight?"

"I've been busy."

"Then I insist." Cutter took her hand and placed it on his arm as he tossed Shilo Dawne a wink. "Shilo Dawne, take over from here. Me and this little lady in red are going to dance."

Genesis couldn't resist the giggle that bubbled out as he led her to the dance floor. "Who left you in charge?" she teased.

"Guess I appointed myself." A self-satisfied smile hovered around the corners of his generous mouth. "Come on, if anyone deserves to let their hair down and have a little fun, it's you."

She ran her fingers through the ends of her short blond hair. "Can't really let it down too much," she brooded. "Little too short for that."

"I like your hair."

"I thought men liked long hair. Like Shilo Dawne's." This tune was slower than previous ones, allowing for a nice flow of conversation as they moved to the music.

"She's got pretty hair, that's for sure. But I can't imagine you with anything but short hair. It suits you." He gave her a warm smile, the kind that engaged his entire face. His eyes sparkled with appreciation as he told her once again, "You look so beautiful tonight, there's really not an adequate word to describe it."

Genesis ducked her head so that he couldn't see her blush. "Thank you," she murmured. Embarrassed, she tried to deflect the attention from herself. "You and Shilo Dawne seemed to be having a wonderful time. Maybe it's a good thing Callie Beth didn't come."

"Oh, she came," he said in a weary voice. "She's over there sulking in the corner as we speak."

Not for the first time, Genesis told him, "You shouldn't be so irresistible, Cutter. You seem to be having trouble selecting just one special lady from your little harem of eager admirers."

He scowled. "It's not like that," he insisted. "I don't encourage them. And I don't use them."

"I'm sorry. I didn't mean to offend you. Poor choice of words on my part. But, for what it's worth, my vote is on Shilo Dawne. She's really a very nice girl."

Cutter looked down at the woman in his arms. There was a troubled expression in his eyes. "Can I ask you something?"

"Anything."

"Why do you always try to play matchmaker?"

Genny laughed at her own foolishness. "Just a romantic at heart, I guess."

"Yet you have no husband or boyfriend of your own." As an afterthought, he added, "Do you?"

"No, definitely not."

"And why not? I can't imagine how a wonderful woman like you has managed to stay single all these years." With a fancy little legwork, Cutter twirled her effortlessly around the floor and switched their positions. A vertical line puckered between his eyes as he studied the expression on her face. "You've been married before?" His voice reflected his surprise.

Did a twelve-hour marriage even count? Long ago, Genesis discovered it was easier to reply with a simple 'no' than to explain the truth, but she heard herself giving Cutter Montgomery an honest answer. "When I was very young and very foolish, I had a very brief marriage to my high-school sweetheart. We ran away one summer morning and found a justice of the peace. The marriage was annulled by nightfall."

"What happened?"

Her single sigh revealed a wealth of long ago sorrow. "Long story."

"I'd like to hear it sometime."

"Maybe sometime," she agreed. "It's ancient history by now. And I'd rather focus on the future."

"And what does your future look like, Genesis Baker? What do you see in your stars?"

She peered over his shoulder, to the room crowded with friends and customers. "To be honest, my present is so full of unexpected surprises that I haven't even thought about the future. I'm perfectly content for now."

"'Content' and 'happy' aren't necessarily the same thing," he noted with a philosophical air. "Are you happy?"

Genesis considered his words. She darted a glance back at the crowd, then up at his intent hazel gaze. A ripple of something warm wiggled through her heart. Excitement? Sheer happiness? She had everything she had ever dreamed of. *Well, except for a man in my life,* she acknowledged, but there was still time for that. She was only thirty-nine years young, after all.

With a confident smile, she unconsciously tightened her fingers around his. "Yes," she said softly. "Right now, I am perfectly happy with my life."

His thumb rubbed across her fingers. There was no denying how much he admired the woman. She was a true asset to their small town. Her business was booming and, although he would never admit as much to his mother, she was the finest cook he had ever known. He idly wondered what it would be like to marry such a cook; he would definitely need new jeans and bunker gear, at least one size larger. He smiled at the image he had of himself, bloated from too many meals at her table. "You, of all people, deserve happiness," he proclaimed as the song drifted on its last notes.

Their feet wound slowly down to a stop, but his arms were still wrapped loosely around her as the lead singer spoke into the mic.

"We have a very special lady out on the dance floor, ladies and gentleman. Let's give a big hand to the hostess of tonight's party and the owner of this fine establishment. Miss Genesis, I know everyone here agrees with me when we say you are the best thing to happen to The Sisters in a very long time. So this next song is for you. Happy Valentine's Day to the pretty little lady in red."

As the band began to play the song by the same name, Genesis blushed. The crowd responded with enthusiastic applause, whistles, and even a few cheerful catcalls. The other dancers melted away, leaving only her and Cutter on the floor.

"Shall we?" he murmured, tugging her in close for the slow dance.

The craziest sensations flooded through Genny's body. It was being in the spotlight, she told herself. That had to be the explanation for this sudden rash of nerves that assuaged her. She didn't want to make a fool of herself with all eyes upon her. Surely it had nothing to do with the firm young body she was pressed against. Nothing at all to do with the strength in the arms that held her, the warmth of his breath as it fluttered against her ear. Nothing to do with the sexy undercurrent of his cologne, or dancing with this particular man. He was almost young enough to be her son, after all. Much too young for her.

"Relax, Genny." His voice was a warm, reassuring rumble as she tensed in his arms.

"But they're all looking at us."

"Because they've never seen you look so beautiful. Just like the song says, they've never seen you shine so bright." His voice fell an octave. "And every man in the room wishes he was me right now, holding you close. Touching you."

Genesis drew in a sharp breath at his provocative words. He was a natural-born flirt, she reminded herself. Yet a part of her knew that wasn't so. She had always suspected that, deep down, he was a bit shy around women.

He seemed fully confident now, however, as he dipped his handsome head to hers, cheek to cheek, even as the singer crooned those very words. "Relax, Genny. Forget about them.

It's just you and me and the music," he murmured. "Just me and the lady in red."

Letting the warm timbre of his voice wash over her, Genesis released the breath she unwittingly held and relaxed against him. She felt his smile against her cheek. Tugging her a little closer, Cutter tucked their joined hands between them. Surely it was a sleight of the hand when his fingers brushed against her breast. Then again, feeling his body's immediate response, maybe not.

This is insane, she told herself. He's young enough to be my little brother. It's just the music and the song. Some silly, sexy song. And when did he stop calling me 'Miss' Genny?

Once she relaxed, Genesis found they moved in perfect unity. Their steps could have been choreographed. Cutter Montgomery, the welder turned volunteer fireman, danced as well as any man she had ever known. Her previous career had taken her to many fancy balls in cities all across the nation and even abroad, but this small-town country boy had as much grace and confidence as any ballroom dancer. Her eyes glittered with appreciation as he spun her out for a fancy twirl.

"Wanna try a dip?" he asked as he reeled her back in.

"What if I fall?"

He pressed his face against her hair and whispered a mysterious, "I already have." Then he pulled back and told her with earnest eyes, "I'll always catch you, Genny. You're safe with me."

Even though their feet continued to shuffle, the moment between them stood still. There was only the beat of the music and the clamor of their hearts. Then a slow, sexy smile broke out across Cutter's face.

Thinking she had surely lost her mind, Genesis allowed him to slowly dip her backwards. She felt herself sweep low to the ground, but she felt no fear. His strong arms were beneath her, his handsome face was above her. "Trust me, Genny," she thought she heard him say, but it was difficult to make out the words over the clatter of their audience. Apparently, the crowd was impressed with their dance moves. Cutter pulled her up with ease, even though she knew she weighed more than was vogue. He hauled her in close, tucking her body up tight against his own.

This time, there was no denying it. The air around them sizzled. If there had been space for air between them, it would have evaporated into steam. The wild pulse of awareness drowned out the sound of applause. Their quickened breath hummed in tune to the sexy beat of the song. Genny could tell herself the pounding hearts and the short breaths were the result of a strenuous dance, but that was no explanation for the way their feet forgot to move. Tangled in the other's gaze, they swayed to the dying strands of the music, the tension between them building.

"Genny?" Cutter's whispered voice was hoarse. He was obviously as surprised as she was.

Genesis gulped in a breath of air. He still held her so tightly it was difficult to breathe. With large, uncertain eyes, her bewildered shake of the head was almost imperceptible. She wasn't sure what she would have said at that moment, but she never had the chance to utter a word. The applause had died away and the crowd was oddly quiet, watching in confusion as the couple on the dance floor simply stared at one another.

When Cutter's fire radio went off from where it sat on the table, the tone-out was clearly audible, right along with the dispatcher's words.

"River County Sheriff's Office to The Sisters Fire Department. We need you in route to The Sisters Sale Barn for a structure fire. Repeat, the sale barn is on fire."

17

The crowd thinned out immediately, right behind the three firefighters attending the mixer. Most followed along to the fire, some to offer help, some just to be nosy.

Allen Wynn, who left his wife behind at the café, soon called back to say the fire was under control. The fire department contained the damage to some of the cattle pens out back, leaving the main structure unscathed. The few pens of cattle still at the barn awaiting pickup had scattered and were running scared through the streets of Naomi; some even ventured out onto the highway. A group of volunteers mounted horses and four wheelers, going out to gather the herd.

Within an hour of the call, the party was over and there was nothing left to do but clean up.

"You can go on home, Maddy," Genesis told her friend. "I've got this."

"Are you kidding? You let your staff go; I'm not about to leave you with all of this!"

"You need to be home when the kids get there. Find out how their first dates went."

"I'm trying to block the words 'first date' from my mind. I still have a couple hours left before I have to acknowledge them. All the kids are going back to Shannon and Matt's after the dance. We parents pitched in for late-night pizza."

"The expense of having teenagers is never-ending, huh?" Genny offered a sympathetic smile as she fell into a nearby chair and slipped off her high heels. Her sigh of relief was audible as she wiggled her toes.

"I hear it lets up in another twenty years or so. And I am so glad you just did that. I've been dying to get out of these shoes since about ten minutes after I arrived!"

"Any more of that champagne you were toting around all evening? I could go for a bottle or two right now."

"Don't we need to clean up first?" Madison suggested. She spotted a large opened bottle in an ice bucket and went to fetch it. "Of course, it's already opened, and it would be a shame to let all that fizz go to waste..."

"My thoughts, exactly. Besides, the staff will be back in the morning to clean. I let them go tonight to celebrate what was left of Valentine's." She held out a flute, flashing her dimpled grin as Madison filled it. "My, you pour that with such flair, my dear."

"Champagne was never my wine of choice, but Gray always insisted on serving it to our guests. Apparently, he thought it showed class." She wrinkled her nose in distaste as she filled both glasses. It was unclear whether the expression was for the beverage or for the opinions of her late husband.

Judging from her healthy gulp of the effervescent wine, Genny guessed the latter. "Thank you for all your help tonight," she said. "I couldn't have done it without you."

"You had everything totally under control. All I did was smile and pour champagne. You did the hard stuff."

They discussed the evening in detail, reliving the highlights and discussing conversations had or overheard. Madison told her friend about the odd encounter with Darla Mullins.

"It appears I have a new client," she concluded uncertainly. "We never discussed money or terms or what I'm supposed to do, other than to be there 'sharply at eight and not be late.'" She lowered her voice to do a stern and fierce imitation of the other woman.

"With Darla Mullins, it's hard to say. She's an odd duck."

"That's what Brash said."

"Hmm. I saw you dancing. So what's it like, dancing a slow dance with Mr. deCordova?" Genny's grin had a conspiratorial air as she held out her glass for seconds. Or was it thirds? Her hand seemed a bit unsteady.

"To be honest, I don't even know. Were my feet even touching the ground? My head was floating up somewhere in the clouds." She poured herself more champagne with decidedly less finesse than earlier. Definitely their third round.

Madison swished the clear liquid around in her glass, watching as it sparkled and swirled. "Am I pathetic, or what? Almost forty years old, acting like a silly schoolgirl."

Genesis took a big gulp from her own glass before admitting on a raw whisper, "I'm even worse."

"How so?"

"I think I have a crush on a man half my age." Her words were only slightly slurred.

"A nineteen-year-old? Seriously?"

"He might as well be," Genesis moped. "What's another five or six years, when I'm already old enough to be his cousin?"

Even to her sluggish brain, the words didn't make sense. "There's no age restrictions on cousins."

"I know, but it sounds better than admitting the truth, that I'm old enough to be his sister." One look at Madison's confused expression, and Genny conceded, "Okay, okay, so I'm old enough to be his mother!"

The champagne made her mind fuzzy. Narrowing her eyes to focus on her thoughts, Madison ventured a guess. "Does this have anything to do with that X-rated dance you had with Cutter Montgomery?"

"You saw that, huh?"

"I was sitting behind old Mrs. Crowder and Gladys Peavey. They were practically drooling. And I think I may have gotten third-degree burns from the ricochet of Callie Beth Irwin's searing glare as she watched you two."

"My name is going to be dragged through the gutter," Genesis predicted with gloom.

"Why? Every female in town has a crush on Cutter Montgomery, from Dolly Mac Crowder and my Great-Aunt Lerlene, to Callie Beth and Shilo Dawne. I even heard the youngest little Hadley girl—who's probably not even in kindergarten yet—tell someone he was her boyfriend."

Genesis brightened somewhat. "That's true, isn't it? I'm not just some pathetic old woman, right, trying to cling to my youth? I'm simply taken in by his charms, just like every other woman in town."

"The man is a hunk, that's for sure." Madison held her glass up toward the light, surprised to find it empty once again. A frown curled her lips downward. "Do they even use that word anymore?"

"Nowadays I think you say the man is hot." Draining her own glass, Genny mumbled, "And, Lord, is that man hot! Well equipped, too."

"Genny!"

"Well? He was holding me tight. And certain things... happened." A silly giggle escaped along with the admission.

"So, this isn't a one-sided crush," Madison observed as she tried to recall something Granny Bert recently said, something about older women and younger men. More specifically, something about Cutter Montgomery and if she herself were thirty years younger... What was it her grandmother said?

What Madison thought was a light bulb suddenly flashed in her mind. Her champagne-besotted mind. "I know what this is!" she said brightly. "This is one of those tiger things!"

Genesis gave her a blank stare, finding it difficult to focus on only one image of her friend; several floated before her eyes.

"You know," Madison explained, "when a sexy older woman takes on a boy-toy. A tiger." Madison was quite pleased with herself for being so hip. *And Bethani complains I'm behind the times. Pffft.*

"Grrr. I'm a tiger." Genny made a claw motion with her hand, then dissolved into giggles. She tried to say something else, but soon the giggles turned into outright laughter.

The sound was contagious, drawing Madison under with its rolling current. Excessive champagne had a tendency to make everything funny. Soon tears rolled down both women's cheeks. Every time one of them would attempt a straight face, another wave of hilarity would hit and the laughter started all over again.

Her sides ached by the time Madison managed to say, "I—I forget. Why are we laughing?"

Her question earned a hoot of mirth, but Genesis finally wheezed out her reply. "Because—Because—Because the word is 'cougar' not 'tiger!'"

The blunder created another gale of laughter. Eventually Madison called for relief. "St—Stop! I can't do this anymore! I—I hurt from laughing so much."

"And I've got to pee! Thing is, I don't remember where the bathroom is!" Genesis slapped the table as if she had told the world's funniest joke.

Still snickering, Madison staggered to her feet and tugged on her friend's arm. "C—Come on. I'll show you."

Genny's face puckered with sudden melancholy. "Thank you, Maddy. You're the best friend I've ever had."

"That's why we're spending Valentine's together, Genny. Just you and me."

The thought was instantly sobering.

18

Madison knew it was too good to last. Almost midnight on Sunday night, her phone rang.

She didn't bother with looking at the screen. "What do you want, George Gail?" she mumbled groggily.

"I have to talk to you!" the other woman hissed frantically.

"What is it?"

"I think someone is outside!"

Madison stifled a yawn. "So wake your husband."

"He's not here. The fire flared back up at the barn. I'm scared, Madison!"

"Then call the police."

"I can't! They might start asking questions." As Madison reluctantly slid from her nice warm bed and headed toward the closet, quietly grumbling the entire way, George Gail continued, "And they might see the blood."

"What blood?"

"The blood that was on the sheets last week!"

"Surely you've washed them by now."

"Well, of course, but they might use one of those purple light thingamajiggies. I watch TV, you know. I know how they can still detect blood, even after you've used bleach and painted over it a time or so. You can't cover up blood."

George Gail made even less sense than usual. Madison rubbed her eye and tried to follow the other woman's babble. "You painted your sheets?" she asked in confusion.

"No, of course not. I'm just pointing out that they have ways of finding out about the blood. So you can see why I can't call the police."

"No, George Gail, I can't." Madison tried very hard to keep the exasperation out of her voice. "If you're calling to report a possible break in, the police aren't going to come into your house and search for blood stains."

The woman gasped. "You think they're trying to break in?" she squeaked in terror.

"I thought *you* said that." Madison pinched the bridge of her nose with two fingers, silently counted to ten, and started over. "George Gail, why did you call me?"

"I want you to come over here."

"No. It's late and I'm already in bed. And you still owe me five hundred dollars from before."

"Come over and I'll pay you."

"If someone is outside, call the police," Madison advised in a sharp voice. "I'm going back to bed."

"What if someone tries to kill me, too? What if they set another fire here at the house?"

"Fire?"

"You don't think these fires are an accident, do you? Someone knew about Curtis and Caress, and they set the fire at the sale barn to send us a message."

As much as she would like to hang up the phone, Madison found herself listening to the ludicrous claim. What if the fire really had been intentionally set? "What kind of message?" she ventured to ask.

"Come over and we can discuss it."

"You're just trying to trick me into coming over there."

"All you have to do is drive by. You could pull up in the driveway and shine a flashlight around. If someone's out there, you'll scare them away."

"I have a better idea."

"I'm listening."

"First of all, turn on all your outside lights."

"I can do that." Madison heard movement on the other end of the line as George Gail bustled about. "I'm flipping on the back-porch light right now," she confirmed, sounding relieved to have a solid plan.

"Perfect. Now when I give you the signal, I want you to hang up the phone."

"What are you going to do? Are you on your way over?"

"No, I'm calling the police, and then I'm going back to bed. Here's your signal. Good night, George Gail."

Sharply at eight o'clock the next morning, Madison parked in front of the large old building with its newly painted sign. The name '*Boundaries*' was neatly centered amid a border resembling a barbed-wire fence. Checking to see that the contract was still snuggled inside its manila folder, Madison finger-combed the ends of her hair one last time and crawled from her car, into morning air frosty and sharp.

Darla Mullins greeted her with two snapped words. "You're late."

Madison checked the clock on her cell phone. "It's two minutes after eight."

"Precisely. I told you to be here sharply at eight o'clock, so that makes you two minutes late."

Resisting the urge to call the whole thing off—she needed the money, after all—Madison plastered on a smile and asked, "What is it I can do for you, Mrs. Mullins? I'm afraid we never discussed the nature of the job."

"Obviously, I'm a licensed surveyor," the woman sniffed. Madison glanced around, wondering what made that fact so 'obvious.' Other than the large drafting board off to one side of the room, an oversized copier, and the long, shallow drawers of a few built-in cabinets, it seemed to be an ordinary office. A receptionist's desk stopped guests just past the front door, standard pot plants filled all corners of the room, photographs of nature adorned the walls, and unmarked doors led to rooms unknown.

"We provide surveys," Darla Mullins continued, "and all the legal documents and paperwork associated with them. We make numerous trips to county court houses, confirming plats and deeds and providing current information. You may be required to make such a trip, look up information on the internet, type documentation, draw up contracts, and accompany me in the field, as well as answer the telephone. Can you manage all that?"

"Yes."

"You'll be filling in for Natalie, who is out with a broken arm. My son also works here. I will be in and out this week, attending to details of the funeral. Expect to work long hours."

Without asking for Madison's customary rate, Darla Mullins informed her of the hourly wage she was willing to pay. Since it was two dollars more an hour than she normally charged, Madison let the bossy attitude slide as she whipped out the contract and secured a signature.

"The breakroom is behind that door, down the hall, first door on the right." Darla stabbed a stubby finger at the middle doorway. "I take my coffee black."

So I'm to be your gopher, Madison thought, but she offered her best fake smile as she stood her ground. "Shall I get us both a cup, while you make out a check?"

The surveyor balked at the notion of paying half the fee up front, but Madison referred to the newly signed contract. As the squatty woman grumbled and disappeared behind the first door, Madison went in search of the breakroom.

Hidden behind the middle door was a long, dark hall that dissected the rear of the building in half. Madison couldn't help but suppress a shiver; she hoped she was never sent to the nether ends of the hallway, which faded mysteriously away into the shadows.

There must be a light switch around here somewhere, Madison thought, groping for one along the paneled walls. She reached the breakroom before finding one, but at least she found its switch easily enough. Incandescent light flooded out from the bulbs, spilling into the darkened hallway and making Madison feel a bit foolish.

She found a Keurig coffee maker in the breakroom and studied the selection of pods at her disposal. Which kind would Darla Mullins prefer? Instinct urged her to select the bold styling of Sumatra roast.

Now for the cup. Three stoneware mugs stood upside-down on a drying mat beside the sink. Madison determined Darla's personal mug by the process of elimination. She couldn't imagine the other woman sipping from the rim of bright pink; this one, she decided, belonged to the absent Natalie. She would re-wash it and use the pink mug for herself. The brown and tan mug with 'Texas' emblazoned upon its side had a western feel. The son's cup, no doubt. Which left the unmarked dark green mug, plain, simple, and surprisingly heavy, as Darla's. The stark simplicity somehow suited the woman.

With two cups of coffee in tow, Madison returned to the front office. Darla was waiting with a check in hand. "Make sure I get my money's worth," she snapped. She didn't thank Madison for the coffee, simply snatched it from her hand.

The sharp movement caused the dark liquid to splash over the edge. Just missing either woman's hand, it dribbled down to the floor. Darla watched it fall, then said, "You'll find paper towels in the breakroom." She turned and retreated to her office without another word, effectively adding the title of *Janitor* to Madison's duties.

Madison was wiping up the mess when the hallway door opened and a man stepped into the room. His expression registered the same sense of surprise she knew was written upon her face.

So this is the son, she presumed. He had a great body, toned and well proportioned, but the scale was slight for a man. In a smaller setting—a child's playhouse, for instance—his petite frame would be unnoticeable. But silhouetted in the doorway, the dark hall looming behind him like a yawning hole, the difference was pronounced.

Madison thought of the rumors about John Wayne, and how camera shots were angled and stage props set to make him appear taller than he actually was. Hollywood lore claimed he was often silhouetted through smaller-than-normal doorways to give the illusion of being a big and powerful man. *This man,* she mused, *could use a similar prop.*

He was strikingly handsome, with blond hair cut short and fashionable, and friendly blue eyes. His wardrobe, however, struck her as odd, especially here in The Sisters, where jeans and pearl snap shirts were standard attire. The crisp collar of a white button-up shirt pushed from the neck of his burgundy sweater. Beige chinos hugged his legs with their skinny cut. His flat-soled shoes were some sort of sheepskin-lined suede and had the expensive look of a European designer. Except for the maturity she saw in his face, he could easily pass for a preppy teenager, dressed for a day on his father's yacht.

"Mom didn't tell me she had a new rug," he said, the edges of his blue eyes crinkling with humor. "I approve."

The waggled eyebrows made it impossible not to return his smile. Madison gave a final swipe of the floor and stood. She could feel his blue eyes flickering over her. She idly wondered if he approved of her simple but understated wardrobe: black slacks with tailored white shirt.

"Derron Mullins," he said, coming forward to extend his hand. "You must be filling in for Natalie, poor old girl. Tough break, pun intended."

"Madison Reynolds," she smiled, returning his firm handshake. Unlike his mother, there was something about the young man she immediately liked.

He eyed the bright pink mug in her hand and pretended a deep scowl. "You're using my mug," he informed her with a whine.

Derron took great pleasure in watching the surprise on Madison's face. With a broad smile, he wagged his blond eyebrows again and answered her un-asked question. "Yep, gayer than a rainbow flag on a windy day." He dropped his voice to a stage whisper. "But don't tell the neighbors. I don't think they know."

Madison laughed aloud as he prissy-walked his way to the desk. He fell into the chair, crossed his leg at the knee with excess motion, then dangled his foot as he batted his eyes and drawled, "Any questions?"

"Yes. Would you like some coffee in your pretty pink mug?"

"I'll let it pass this once, dollface, but don't let it happen again." He winked as he uncrossed his legs and rolled his chair up to the desk. "Besides, we're all perfectly capable of getting our own coffee around here, Dragon Lady included. Don't let my mom bully you."

Madison made a meek admission. "It's rather hard not to."

"The only way she'll ever respect you is if you stand up to her. Deep down, buried far, far beneath the rough layers, is another rough layer. Twenty layers beneath that, she's a bit of a softy. But don't tell her I said so."

"I wouldn't dream of it," Madison said, eyes twinkling.

Derron Mullins voiced the thought running through her own mind. "I think we're going to get along fine, you and me."

"I think so, too. So tell me. What am I supposed to do around here? Is that my desk?" She pointed to the one where he sat. If she were guessing, she would say Natalie was the receptionist, while Derron worked one on one with his mother.

The telephone rang and Derron held up a 'hold that thought' finger in her direction. With a surprisingly professional air, he answered the phone, "*Boundaries Surveying.* This is Derron. How may I help you today?"

By the time he finished the call, Madison knew she had guessed wrong. Derron Mullins was a knowledgeable and efficient receptionist. Given his mother's disposition, he was, she decided, the personality behind the business, the PR man. Derron drew the clients in, Darla performed the surveys, and Natalie did something in between. But what?

"Sorry, where were we? Oh, yes, you were hoping you were the receptionist." The blond man flashed her a sunny smile. "Sorry, sweetie, this job belongs to yours truly. You, my dear, get the pleasure of working directly with Dragon Lady."

Madison bit her lip, unsure if it was a grimace or a smile she suppressed. "Do you always call your mother that?"

"Only on her good days. Sometimes she can be outright nasty." Derron's slim shoulders shivered in mock terror. "Let me show you to your office."

As luck would have it, Natalie's office was down the dark hallway, almost to the very end. Even with the lights on—the switch was on the *other* side of the door, in the front room—the passage was dimly lit and downright spooky. It was an old building with wooden floors that creaked and groaned, and fourteen-foot ceilings that allowed the wind to chase itself through the empty space, whistling and moaning, taunting and teasing as it rattled anything within its reach.

"Sure you don't want to trade spots?" Madison was only half-teasing as she followed him down the lonely path.

"Sorry, I'm afraid of ghosts. But I hear they're remotely friendly back here, as long as you play Springsteen."

"Will Bryan Adams do?"

He shrugged, reaching around the doorway to flip a switch. "Worth a try." With a flourishing hand, he motioned for Madison to precede him into the small office.

As she squeezed past the desk, she realized why he stayed in the hall; there was only room for one person inside the crammed office. A large table stood in the middle of the room, leaving only enough clearance for the row of custom-made lateral filing cabinets that lined the far wall. The table, she presumed, was to unfurl oversized plats and renderings. The heavy oak chair shoved beneath it was one of those handy creations that unfolded into a stepladder, presumably to reach the top drawers. Weak light filtered in from horizontal casement windows slung high on the walls. Judging from the chill in the room, cold air seeped in around the windows.

Dual stacks of cardboard boxes climbed high behind the door, threatening to topple over at any moment. Wedged into the front left corner of the room were a green metal desk and a rolling chair.

"This will be your domain while Natalie is out," Derron explained. "Bathrooms are across the hall."

"What do I need to do?"

"I'm sure Dragon Lady will be back here soon, breathing fire down your neck. Till then, make yourself comfy, get acquainted with our ghosts, holler if you need me. I'm extension three." He grinned and ducked out of the doorway, leaving Madison alone in the gloomy office.

She heard the 'ghosts' within minutes of his departure. They howled their way through the cracks of the windows and sang a low, sad melody against the dropped tin ceiling of the old building. The lonesome sounds were more irritating than they were intimidating. It didn't take Madison long to locate the small stereo system behind Natalie's desk and to drown the noisy ghosts with her own choice of music.

As predicted, Madison soon heard Darla's brisk movements in the hall. Polyester swished between her full thighs, loud enough to be heard over the music and the ghosts. Her feet tapped out the sound of impatience as she neared.

"File these," she said without preamble, holding a stack of folders in one hand. She waved a sheet of paper in the other. "And pull these. I have to be at the funeral home in an hour, so be quick about it." She dropped the files onto the table and was gone before Madison could untangle her feet from the chair's rollers quickly enough to stand.

It took several minutes to understand the filing system. Once the new files were nestled among the others, she began the arduous task of finding the two files Darla requested. She found one, then resorted to calling Derron to locate the other.

"There's another file room across the hall. You should find it in there."

If she thought Natalie's office was cramped and gloomy, it was nothing compared to the file room. It took her almost as long to reach the file cabinets as it did to locate the needed file within them. She waded through more boxes and stacks of old newspapers, skirted around a dusty exercise bike and a broken chair that never quite made it to the dumpster, sidestepped a trash can sitting in the middle of the room to catch a leak when it rained, and cringed when she saw the rat trap, baited and waiting. The quicker she was in and out of the room, the better.

She rushed up to Darla Mullin's front office and rapped on the closed door, entering after she heard the terse, "Come in."

"Here are the files you needed. What would you like me to do while you're gone?"

"Familiarize yourself with our standard forms. Derron will bring you the appropriate paperwork."

"Anything else?"

"The forms are rather lengthy."

"Okay. Well, if you think of something I can do, you know where to find me."

"There is one other thing...."

"Yes?"

Madison was surprised by the look of venom upon Darla's pinched face. "I'll not have you spreading vicious rumors about Caress. Her death, I'm sure, was an accident. As far as we know, the other person stumbled and accidentally stabbed her."

A dozen times? Madison's mind screamed in protest.

That fact, however, might not be for public consumption. And she wasn't so heartless as to point out the gory details of the actress' death.

"I'll not have my dear friend's name sullied with rumors of elicit affairs and some alleged brawl. She isn't here to defend herself."

Tamping down her anger, reminding herself that Darla Mullins was hurting, Madison managed to keep her voice relatively calm. "First of all, I have not been spreading rumors about your friend, vicious or otherwise. Second of all, there was no 'alleged' brawl. I witnessed a fight between Caress and her attacker. I have no idea what instigated it or why they were fighting, but I do know Caress was holding her own, right up until the end."

Darla's answer was a disdainful sniff.

"What? You don't believe me?"

"It was hardly Caress' style to engage in common fist fights."

"I don't think there was anything 'common' about this fight, Mrs. Mullins. It resulted in your friend's death."

Fury appeared in Darla's fleshy cheeks, the dull red color of river-bottom dirt. "I don't need the likes of *you* reminding me that my friend has died!" she spat.

Madison drew in a sharp breath and quickly counted to five; ten was too long to hold her tongue. "Perhaps this arrangement was a bad idea. I think it would be best if I tore up our agreement and called it a day."

Darla Mullins was obviously torn. She clearly didn't like her temporary employee. For whatever reason, she treated Madison with open antagonism. Yet she noticeably stalled, reluctant to dissolve their contract.

"No," she finally decided, her voice tart.

"Why on earth not? I can't see this being a pleasant experience, for either one of us."

"Since when did work become a pleasant experience? I need someone to fill in for Natalie this week and for myself while I am busy with funeral details. You need a job. This has nothing to do with bonding or nominating the other for 'Best Boss/Best Worker' of the month. This is strictly business." Again, a contemptuous sniff. "I thought you were at least professional enough to distinguish the two."

Out of sheer stubbornness, Madison raised her chin. "Oh, I am. And as such, I insist you treat me with professional courtesy. We don't have to like one another, but we do have to treat one another with a certain amount of respect."

Fire flashed in Darla Mullin's bugged eyes. Her nostrils flared. After engaging in a heated staring match that neither woman was willing to look away from, the surveyor finally dropped her gaze. "That will be all," she said in dismissal.

Just as Madison reached the door, Darla issued a final warning. "No playing on the computer. None of that Spacebook foolishness."

With a demur smile, Madison murmured, "No, of course not."

Madison stopped by Derron's desk and found him openly cruising through his own social network account.

"You have some paperwork for me?" she asked, still seething from the ordeal with his mother.

"Not that I'm aware of. Have you seen this video of the cat on a skateboard? Hilarious."

"Your mother wanted me to look over some of the standard forms, whatever those are. She said you had them."

"She'll be coming out of the office in about two minutes. I'll pretend to be looking them up for you."

Derron busied himself rifling through desk drawers, chattering about how to fill out a form in general. He paused long enough to tell his mother goodbye, kept up the banter until she had time to make it down the back hallway and out the door, then slammed the desk drawer shut and sat back with an exaggerated, "Whew! Thought she would never leave!"

"But where are the files?" Madison asked in confusion.

"There's no hurry. Have a seat and take a load off." Derron waved a hand casually through the air. "She'll be gone through lunch. You've got plenty of time to study a few forms. Most of it just plugs into a standardized form on the computer anyway. It's not like it's rocket science."

With the raw edge of her anger fading, Madison felt the first few pangs of guilt eating away at her conscience. She could have been more sympathetic; Darla Mullins had just lost her best friend, after all. She had every right to be cantankerous.

"How is your mother handling Caress' death? I understand they were best friends."

"They practically lived in the other one's pocket. She's devastated, even if she pretends it's business as usual."

"Have they been friends long?"

Derron thought about her question for a moment. "For about four years, I guess. We all moved here about the same time, so they had that in common."

"At the risk of sounding rude, that appears to be about the only thing they had in common," Madison ventured to say.

Derron flashed a disarming smile. "I know, right? Caress and I had more in common than she and my mother did. But somehow, they just clicked. Opposites, and all that." He waved his hands in a fluttering motion. "They were practically inseparable, until it came to shopping. Whenever it was time to head to the mall, Caress would call me before she called my mom. The Dragon Lady has no sense of style, after all."

"So you knew Caress well, too, I suppose?" It shouldn't have come as a surprise, but somehow it did. Of course, he would know his mother's best friend.

Tears welled in his bright blue eyes. "I still can't believe she's gone. She taught me so much about fashion and the ins and outs of dressing for society. She was like a second mother to me, filling in all the gaps my own mother so sadly lacks."

"I'm so sorry for your loss," she purred the appropriate words, even as her mind raced ahead. She knew very little about Claudette 'Caress' Ellingsworth, but obviously Derron had known her quite well. The man might be an invaluable source of information.

"It just doesn't make sense," he was saying. "Everyone loved Caress. She was an absolute angel. Why would anyone want to k—kill her?" His chin quivered as he stumbled over the word.

"I don't know. Sometimes these things don't make sense."

"I know she doesn't show it, but my mother is crushed. I heard her crying last night, late into the night."

"You live with her?" Madison asked in surprise.

He bobbed his head in affirmation. "It's always been just the two of us."

"Your father....?"

"Divorced my mother when I was like six. For almost twenty years, it's just been us. I've thought about moving out a time or two, but she always begs me to stay. She's really rather clingy."

"Your mother?" Madison failed to control the astonishment in her voice.

"I know she puts on a tough front, but like I said, she's a softy at heart."

Madison remained dubious. "I'll take your word on it."

"People just don't understand my mother. Caress had a way of seeing through all the bullshit and understanding there was a real person beneath the bluff. I'm afraid to know what she'll be like now, without Caress' steadying hand."

"I heard rumors that Caress had a boyfriend."

"She and John-Paul Noble were over years ago, but the tabloids couldn't let it go. Don't get me wrong, they're still great friends, but the romance died long ago." Derron's eyes glazed over as he breathed dreamily, "But what a dreamboat. Six feet, one inches of absolute divine manhood. Uhm, uhm, uhm. That. Man. Is. *Fine*!"

"You'll get no argument from me." Madison chuckled, even though she wasn't accustomed to having such a conversation with a member of the opposite sex. She hesitated before pressing on. "But I heard Caress was seeing someone local. More than one man, in fact." It wasn't true, but she needed to know if there was anyone else with a possible grudge against the former actress. If she prove George Gail's innocence, she needed to find another suspect. "I heard she was a bit of a … flirt."

"Of course she was. She was a gorgeous woman and was used to all that fame and attention. Flirting just came naturally to her, but it never meant anything."

"Really? I heard there was a long list of lovers in her past." Again, a total lie.

Derron darted an involuntary glance toward his mother's empty office. He knew something, Madison was certain of it.

But he shook his head in disagreement. "No, I'm pretty sure you heard wrong."

"It was probably something she wouldn't want to talk about," Madison pushed. "Are you sure she never talked about old boyfriends?"

"Like I said, she and my mother were practically inseparable, and I never heard a word about a boyfriend, past tense or otherwise."

"Surely she had other men over the years, other than John-Paul."

Derron lifted a delicate shoulder. "None that I ever heard about."

"You're sure?"

Derron pursed his lips, obviously debating on how best to answer. "There weren't many people in The Sisters that met her... requirements," he finally said in diplomatic fashion. "Caress wasn't like most people around here, if you know what I mean."

Madison thought about the dainty and elegant woman she had followed from the *Bumble Bee* that day. Her wardrobe, alone, set her apart from most residents of the sister cities; her star status rocketed her light years ahead. There probably were few men, indeed, that measured up to her standards.

So how did Curtis Burton make the cut?

The thought haunted her, even as she droned a noncommittal, "Hmm."

19

Madison made a point to arrive early the next morning. As instructed the day before, she parked along the side of the building and used the back entrance. The side entrance was every bit as dark and dismal as the hallway; more so, in fact, for the doorway was tucked into a poorly lit and slightly damp nook. The air itself was musty and stale.

Madison hurried inside, forgoing the coat rack waiting to take her jacket. She found the light switch on that end of the hall and waited for the dim light to guide her way toward her office. Her footsteps echoed in the quietness of the old building. Even the ghosts were silent this morning.

"Darla?" she called. "I'm here!"

Hearing no reply, she stopped inside her little office long enough to deposit her jacket. Secretly glad for the excuse to go to the front of the building, she made short work of the long hallway. She reached the door leading into the reception area and bumped it open with her shoulder.

She promptly bounced right off it. The door was locked.

Fighting down a ridiculous sense of panic, Madison tried the handle again. Nothing. She knocked on the wood panel. "Darla? The door's locked." She waited a few moments, then tried again. "Darla, I was letting you know I was here, but the door seems to be locked."

Hearing no movement from the other side of the door, she concluded that Darla had stepped out for a moment. It was five till eight and the office wasn't officially open yet. Turning back down the hall, she was just past the breakroom when the lights suddenly went out, plunging her into darkness.

Her feet stalled and she stifled a frightened gasp. Faulty lighting, she was sure. Or perhaps Darla thought she was turning the light on instead of off.

"Darla?" she called over her shoulder. "Could you turn the lights back on, please?"

No answer. And no light.

Biting into her lip and wondering why, oh why, she hadn't turned the light on inside her office when she threw her jacket inside, Madison sucked in a deep breath and trudged on down the hallway. She thrust out a hand toward the wall to guide her path. Halfway down the long passage, her eyes grew accustomed to the darkness and she could see where she was going.

The ghosts, noisy once more, cheered her along her way.

Once in the relative security of her office—it was difficult to think of the tiny, dismal room as a sanctuary—Madison flipped on the light switch and reached for the phone. She pressed extension 3 and heard exactly what she expected: nothing but endless ringing. Then she pressed "1," Darla's extension.

"What is it?" Her barked greeting was as hostile today as it had been yesterday.

"Oh, you are in," Madison said in surprise.

"Of course I'm in. I'm always here by seven thirty."

"I tried the door to the reception area, but it was locked. I guess you didn't hear me knocking?"

Instead of answering, Darla asked coolly, "Did you need something?"

Taken aback by her rude manner—and wondering why it even surprised her—Madison stuttered, "I—I was just letting you know I was here."

"Fine. I'm leaving today at lunch, so you'll be the one going to the courthouse this afternoon. You know where it is, I presume?"

Riverton, the county seat of River County, was hardly bigger than The Sisters. It would be difficult to miss the huge old courthouse that dominated the center of town. "Yes, of course."

"Good. I left some files in your office. Put them away." With that order, Darla hung up the phone.

Madison wrinkled her nose in distaste as she dropped the receiver back into its cradle. Apparently, office etiquette differed from social etiquette, which dictated that the caller be the one to signal the end of the conversation. That, or Darla had just hung up on her.

Turning her eyes to the table in the middle of the room, she saw a huge, sloppy pile of papers and manila folders. She half-suspected Darla had upended one of the cardboard boxes and dumped its contents onto the table, just so Madison would have to file them away. She sorted through them and dividing them into smaller, more manageable stacks.

About fifteen minutes later, she heard Derron come in the back door. He flipped on the hall light and popped his blond head in to say hello. He glanced at a few of the files she handled and frowned.

"Why do you have those in here?"

"Your mother left them here. She told me to file them."

"Those belong in the file room. Anything dated five years ago or earlier is stored in there."

"But… almost all of these are old files!"

Derron wagged his blond brows. "You'll get your exercise today, dollface. That's a lot of files to carry."

"I think that was the whole idea," Madison muttered. Darla had gone to extra effort so that Madison would be banished to the dark dimensions of hell, otherwise known as the file room.

But, Madison gloated silently, *the joke's on her*. Darla was the one footing the bill for the dirty little trick. If she wanted to pay her to do non-existent busy work, Madison was more than happy to cash the check.

By the time Madison sorted all the files and returned them to their proper home, it was almost noon. With Derron's blessings, she gathered the forms she needed to fill out at the courthouse and left *Boundaries* early enough to drop by the house. A quick bite to eat, and she was on the road headed to Riverton.

She took the shortest route, even though it led down a series of twisting farm-to-market blacktop roads. The scenery was prettier out here than on the major highway that connected the towns. At least this route was illustrated. Oat fields on her right were dotted with Howard Evans' herd of registered Brangus cattle. On the far horizon of Clem Johnson's land, oil field crews scurried to take down a workover rig. Across the road, two pump jacks rocked in steady rhythm, earning their nickname of a metal rocking horse. She slowed as she turned onto the county road that took her past the Gleason Poultry Farm. Ignoring the bad memories that still haunted her in the middle of the night, she concentrated on something positive. Don Ngyen had probably taken over by now, finally owning the farm promised to him for so long.

Madison cranked up the radio, determined to drown out the unpleasant memories of being kidnapped and almost burned to death. She sped past the farm, pressing on the accelerator as she entered a straight stretch of road. There was no one else on the remote section of blacktop, allowing her a sense of freedom and spontaneity.

Bopping her head in time to the music, Madison sang along with the familiar tune. She was a bit off key, but what did it matter? There was no one around to cringe at the sour notes. What she lacked in musical ability, she made up for with enthusiasm. She belted out the song, complete with facial gestures and body movements. Aretha Franklin might even owe her a little respect for this fully animated rendition.

Caught up in her dual roles as lead singer and drummer, Madison almost missed her turn. The last-minute maneuver required both hands, destroying her beat against the dash. She hit 'rewind' on the satellite radio service that came free with the car for the first three months. By summer, she would have to give up the handy features to avoid another bill, but she might as well enjoy it while she could.

She was doing the final roll-down of the word when a flash caught her eye. Sunlight glinted off the shiny grill of a car approaching from behind. A car coming up fast and hard on her bumper. Madison instinctively punched her foot onto the gas pedal, shooting ahead of the speeding car. She was surprised when it kept pace.

"Geesh, if you're in that big of a hurry, go around me," she grumbled aloud.

The car kept steady behind her, prompting her to grumble louder. "What are you waiting on? You have plenty of room. The road is perfectly straight."

When the car made no effort to pass her, she went so far as to motion to the driver to come around. By now, she was traveling faster than she liked down a road pitted with holes and known to have active deer crossings. If she slowed the slightest of speeds, the car would tap her bumper. How would she ever explain *that* to the insurance company?

The car finally decided to pass. Grateful for the small favor, Madison pulled her foot from the pedal as the white vehicle came up beside her. Her gratitude lasted only until she got a glimpse of the driver. She couldn't see a face, but the fedora and the trench coat were all too familiar. And, she realized, so was the car: it belonged to Caress.

Determined not to panic, Madison took a quick inventory of the situation. She was still going a breezy 68 on a road designed for 55. Trench Coat kept pace with her, not even attempting to pass. Coming up sharply ahead was a damaged guardrail, still mangled from the pickup truck that skidded into it last month and went facedown into the gully below. Even if she tried to swerve off the road before the ravine, the ground was still soft from a recent rain. More than likely, she would be stuck in the mud and at the mercy of the relentless Lincoln.

Her only hope was to speed up and outrun the car, sailing past the guardrail before the other driver could push her into it. The only problem with that plan was that the road curved just beyond the gully. Madison wasn't sure she could make the bend at anything faster than 45.

She only had a few seconds to make her decision. Madison decided to risk it. As she moved her foot in place, a large green tractor lumbered around the bend. The white Lincoln, still in the passing lane, was directly in its path. Trench Coat had no choice but to speed up and shoot in front of Madison, squeezing into the right lane between the tractor and the guardrail.

A driver less skilled would have never made the curve, but Trench Coach managed the road with ease. But with a witness around, Trench Coat had no interest in terrorizing Madison. The white car sailed on down the road and quickly disappeared. Madison slowed down to little more than a crawl as her knees knocked together. She pulled over into the first available driveway, sat there long enough to collect her senses, and then headed back in the direction in which she came. No way was she proceeding down the road so that Trench Coat could ambush her.

The re-routed trip into Riverton was blessedly dull. Madison collected the information she needed and came home by way of the highway. She made a mental note not to travel the backroads, at least not unless someone knew where she was. And on the way home, she called Brash. She pretended the only reason was to report the use of Caress' car and the would-be plot to run her off the road, but the real reason was that she simply needed to hear his voice. The deep timbre of his concern made her feel somewhat protected and gave her a sense of security as she continued the drive home.

After a quick dinner with the kids, Madison squeezed in a few hours to work on the case she had accepted from the private detective in Houston.

Donny Howell claimed he suffered a debilitating injury while working in the oil field industry. His employer was fighting the Worker's Compensation claim he filed and wanted proof that his injury wasn't severe enough to warrant the back brace he wore. Her new job, via the private detective, was to follow Donny and catch him engaged in any sort of physical activity.

Madison found it ironic that the man lived on the same street as Caress, and that he, too, didn't believe in closing his curtains at night. After three boring hours of waiting outside his house, she knew for a fact he did nothing that evening but sit on his couch and drink a six-pack of beer in front of the television.

It must be some sort of prerequisite for living on North River Oaks, Madison mused. The homeowner's association must clearly state that anyone living on this street must do so with their curtains wide open. That way, there's no secrets from their neighbors. And it's so much more efficient than gossip.

From where she sat, she had a clear view into Caress' kitchen window. A light was on beneath the overhead microwave, offering just enough light to see beyond the kitchen, into the doorway of the dining room. The room where Caress had been murdered at the hands of Trench Coat.

A chill moved through Madison, but it had nothing to do with the frosty February air. Trench Coat knew who she was. Trench Coat made the threat clear today: back off. Do not talk to the police.

Somehow, Trench Coat had known she was on that road today. The only explanation was that she was being followed. Trench Coat knew enough about her life and her schedule to know where she was and when she would be alone.

Trench Coat, it seemed, knew quite a bit about her.

She, on the other hand, had no idea who hid behind the hat and coat. And that lack of knowledge made her vulnerable.

Could Trench Coat possibly be George Gail? Her gut said 'no.' Then again, Maddy's own husband had lied to her and deceived her for months, and her gut never once put up an argument, suggesting that perhaps her gut was no judge of character.

If not George Gail, then who? Who else had reason to want Caress dead? According to Darla and Derron, everyone loved their friend.

In fact, most everyone she had spoken to agreed on that fact. Caress Ellingsworth was a valuable and well-respected member of the community. She was famous. According to some, the star brought a touch of dignity and class to their community, not to mention a fair share of business. Tourists, though few and far between here in The Sisters, often drove by her house, in hopes of seeing the well-loved soap star. People from neighboring towns attended the Christmas play each year, eager to see not only her performance, but also her vision for directing the story. Visitors meant revenue. Revenue meant the towns of Naomi and Juliet profited from the aged actress. So why kill the main attraction?

Because, Madison knew firsthand, this had been a crime of passion, not premeditated murder. Trench Coat and Caress had gotten into a heated argument and somehow, Caress had wound up dead. Caress, in fact, had been the first to strike.

So, the question still remained: who knew Caress well enough, or was angry enough with her, to fight with her in her own home?

Madison quickly discarded the idea of it being an intruder. When she first glimpsed them through the window, they were engaged in a conversation, not yet an argument. And Caress was clearly not frightened of the other person, judging from the way she had shoved and slapped. She hadn't cowered. Obviously, she knew her killer well enough to let him or her into her home.

A lover, perhaps? It had to be someone other than Curtis Burton; Trench Coat's size and shape was all wrong for the lanky cowman. And just because neither Derron nor his mother knew of a lover, didn't mean there wasn't one. Somehow, Madison needed to find out whom else the actress had been involved with.

Madison's imagination fizzled out after that. She could think of no one other than an intruder or a spurned lover who could have done this.

She would not—could not—allow herself to consider another possibility, no matter how obvious: a lover's jealous wife would have perfect motive for wanting Caress dead. But that category would include George Gail, and she wasn't ready to give up on the thought of her innocence, not yet.

As Madison stashed away her camera and acknowledged that tonight was a bust as far as catching Donny Howell was concerned, she made another realization. If Brash discovered the affair between Caress and Curtis, he would naturally consider George Gail as a suspect.

Which might mean it would be up to Madison to help prove her client's innocence.

20

"What was so urgent that you had to call me at the light of dawn and insist we meet?" Madison asked as she slid into the booth at *New Beginnings* across from George Gail.

Unfazed by the harsh tone in her companion's voice, George Gail pushed a plate of sticky buns toward her. Sparkly blue eye shadow winked in the morning light. "I know how early you go to bed at night, so I figured you must get up first thing. I wanted to catch you before you left the house."

"At 5:47? Where else would I be?"

George Gail offered an innocent shrug.

"Don't you ever sleep?" Madison grumbled.

"Not much, not since this whole ordeal with Caress began." Wringing her hands with a sudden bout of nerves, George Gail fretted, "How could I sleep these past few weeks, knowing my husband was having an affair right under my nose? And how can I sleep now, knowing I might have..." she darted a glance around the room, then lowered her voice to a whisper "...killed someone?"

"George Gail, I don't think you killed anyone."

"Shh! Keep your voice down!"

"Look, there's no evidence that points to you."

"Then how do you explain the blood?" she hissed.

"You probably cut your finger that night and just don't remember."

George Gail visibly brightened. "Say, that sounds good. I think that's what I'll tell the police when they come to arrest me."

Madison frowned. "The police aren't coming to arrest you."

"Then why did the chief ask to stop by the house today?"

"Maybe to talk about the fire at the sale barn? The intruder at your house Sunday night? Maybe he's collecting for a food drive. I don't know, George Gail, and it's too early in the morning for me to have to think about it. I need coffee."

"To be such an early riser, you're not much of a morning person, are you?" the heavy woman smirked.

"I'm not an early riser! You woke me up and insisted I meet you here!" Madison pressed her fingers to her temples, feeling the beginnings of a headache coming on.

After a daunting first two days at *Boundaries,* then sitting for three hours last night on a failed stakeout, she was in no mood to face George Gail's needy wheedle before her first crucial cup of morning coffee. So far, it wasn't lining up to be a good day.

Or perhaps she was wrong.

"Here's the five hundred dollars I owe you," George Gail said, slipping an envelope her way.

"Oh. Okay. Thanks."

"You sound surprised. Did you really think I would stiff you?" The blue shadow didn't look so sparkly when George Gail frowned.

"No, of course not. Not exactly." Madison fidgeted in her seat. "I mean, that was the night you were a little… fuzzy. I thought you might not remember."

"Like I can't remember whether or not I stabbed a woman to death?" she asked in a mope.

"Please don't start that again. You know as well as I do, you are not capable of murder." Much to her relief, she saw Genesis headed her way with a mug of steaming coffee. "Bring the whole pot," she told her friend before she even reached her.

Genesis arched a graceful brow and shot a discreet glance toward George Gail. "Having that bad of a morning, are we?" she grinned.

"You know, that's one of your major character flaws. You're always so disgustingly chipper in the morning." Madison grabbed the coffee mug and took a large gulp of the steaming liquid, welcoming the burn that slid down her throat.

George Gail put a chubby hand to her mouth and spoke aside to Genny in a poorly disguised whisper. "She's just as grumpy at night. I thought I was doing a good thing, calling her this morning."

"You two go ahead," Madison mumbled. "Have your fun at my expense. I'm the one who's sleep deprived."

Genesis merely laughed. "Give the caffeine time to kick in," she advised George Gail. "She'll be almost human by the second cup."

Madison wrinkled her nose at her friend's departing back, resisting the childish urge to stick her tongue out. Pulling her bleary gaze back to her client, she said, "Tell me again, why you dragged me here?"

"We have to come up with my statement, the one I'll give to the police. Did you bring paper? Write that down about cutting my finger. I liked that."

Madison ignored the directive. "What exactly did Brash say when he asked to drop by?"

"Just that he wanted to come by and talk to us this afternoon."

"And you think that means he's coming to arrest you?"

"I can't imagine why else he would come over."

"If he was coming to arrest you, I doubt he would call and make an appointment first. They tend to spring that sort of thing on you, trying to catch you unaware."

"Maybe." She sounded doubtful as she plucked another sticky bun apart. She was stuffing it into her mouth when she suddenly froze. Her eyes widened, and she practically choked on the mouthful of glazed yeasty bread.

"George Gail? Are you all right? What's wrong?" Madison asked in alarm.

Her companion clamped one hand over the mouth, while with the other she pointed a chubby finger toward the door. "Him," she squeaked.

Madison followed her gaze. She heard the excited buzz of other patrons as John-Paul Noble stepped inside the restaurant.

In spite of herself, her own heart rate sped up at the sight of the famous actor. Exactly as Derron Mullins claimed, the man was a prime specimen of manhood. Just over six feet, he stood tall and straight, a fascinating blend of toned muscle and good bone structure. Even if his hair was a bit too black to be natural and his tan a little too dark to be authentic, he wore the look with finesse. Who cared about the fine details? The man was beautiful. Bright blue eyes and a row of white, even teeth set off his tan to perfection. He wore a tailored suit of pale gray and a blue tie that highlighted his eyes. A cream-colored cashmere coat was thrown casually over his shoulders.

Madison tried not to drool.

"That is most definitely not the trench coat I saw," she muttered to herself. Even though he wore a fedora atop his head, there was no mistaking John-Paul Noble's powerful physique with the squatty image she had seen through the window. She couldn't resist a star-struck, "Mmm-mmm," before turning back around in her seat.

"What a dreamboat." George Gail propped her elbows on the table, her chin into her hands, and stared unabashedly as the actor made his way into the restaurant. Her eyes traced his every move as he gave the staff a charming smile and ordered coffee. All three waitresses rushed to his side, until Genesis pulled them away with a soft reprimand to allow the man some space.

"It's just not fair," George Gail pouted. "Why did Caress have to be so greedy? Wasn't it enough that she had John-Paul? Why did she have to go after my husband, too?"

"I don't know, why don't you ask him? Isn't that him coming inside right now?"

George Gail was obviously flustered. "What on earth is he doing here? He said he'd fix his own breakfast this morning! And how on earth am I going to explain sitting here with you? I told him I had a hair appointment."

"At six thirty in the morning?"

"He's a man," George Gail said with a shrug. "His eyes glaze over when I mention anything that has to do with beauty products. He has no idea what they even do in a salon, much less what time they open!"

After stealing another wistful look at John-Paul, Madison turned her attention to Curtis Burton. She knew the exact moment he spotted his wife. A look of genuine pleasure stole over his face, and a smile lifted the corners of his handlebar mustache.

His long stride made short work of crossing to the back booth. "Well, this is a pleasant surprise. I get to have breakfast with my beautiful bride, after all." He swooped down to kiss his wife on the mouth. "Mmm," he purred in appreciation. "Sticky buns." He kissed her again, licking her lips in the process.

Giggling like a schoolgirl, George Gail scooted over and made room for her husband. As he tucked his arm around her round shoulders and dipped his head for another kiss, she swatted him away and pointed to Madison. "I have company."

"Well, so you do." The rugged rancher offered Madison a lazy smile. "No offense, but even after thirty-nine blessed years of marriage, when George Gail is in the room, she's the only woman I can see."

It took Madison all of five minutes to know what Granny Bert had claimed all along: Curtis Burton wasn'*t* having an affair with Caress Ellingsworth. The man was clearly smitten with his wife. He hung on her every word. When he looked at her—which was practically the entire time he sat there—his eyes had a gentle glow that could only come from his soul. He touched her constantly. Before his breakfast came, he entwined his fingers with hers. While he ate, he sat close enough that their thighs touched. As they lingered over a last cup of coffee and the couple shared another sticky bun, he kept his arm loosely around her shoulders. His devotion to his wife was so touching and so sincere, Madison found herself growing misty eyed. *That* was the sort of marriage she wanted. *That* was the kind of love and devotion missing from her own union with Gray.

"It was nice to finally meet you, Curtis, but I really must be going," Madison said. She was surprised to see almost an hour had slipped by. Curtis Burton was a good conversationalist and she had actually enjoyed visiting with the couple, even George Gail. With her husband around, the woman didn't act nearly as ditzy.

"Come by the house any time," he invited, standing up as she slid from the booth. He tipped the brim of his cowboy hat in gentlemanly style. "Any friend of George Gail's is a friend of mine. And of course, I practically grew up as a Cessna. Tell Granny Bert I said hello."

"I will. And George Gail?" Madison paused to send the woman a pointed look. "That little problem we discussed? The first one? Believe me, you had to have been mistaken."

On her way toward the door, Madison allowed herself one last lingering perusal of the handsome John-Paul Noble.

Mmm, mmm, indeed.

Caress' funeral was set for Thursday morning.

Darla brought a black wreath to hang on the door of *Boundaries.* Since Caress was family, she said, it was only proper to close during the services. Although she and Derron would take all of Thursday off, she expected Madison to open the office in the afternoon.

Alone in the big old building, Madison found it to be more than a bit spooky. Howling 'ghosts' aside, the place was dark and depressing. She spent the afternoon at Derron's desk, thankful not to be stuck in her own office in the back.

The afternoon was long and boring. The phone rang exactly twice, and one of those calls was a telemarketer. Just to hear another voice, Madison let the man go through his entire spiel and even pretended interest, right up until the part when he asked for her credit card.

At five minutes before five, Madison began turning off lights and computers. She made sure the breakroom was tidy, the furthest she had ventured into the dark hallway today. She had even avoided going to the restroom to save herself the long walk among the ghosts.

As she was about to leave, the telephone rang. Without caller ID, she had to rely on her sixth sense to predict it was Darla calling.

"*Boundaries Surveying*," she said cheerfully into the receiver, deciding to end the day with a little fun. "And no, Darla, I didn't leave early."

She heard the disdainful sniff on the other end of the line. "What if I had been a customer and you answered in such an undignified way?"

"But you're not."

"You didn't know that."

"Sure I did. That's why I answered that way."

Another sniff. "Enough foolishness. I need you to retrieve a file for me."

"Right now?" Madison's playfulness turned to dismay. All the file cabinets were in the back, in either Natalie's office, or the dreaded file room.

"Yes, right now. You're still on the clock."

"For another thirty seconds or so. Can't this wait until morning?"

"No. I need you to review the file before we leave in the morning."

"You'll be out of the office tomorrow?" Try though she may, she couldn't hide the hopefulness in her voice.

"*We* will be out of the office," her sour employer corrected. "Dress appropriately for the outdoors."

"Oh."

"I need you to pull the survey on Allen Wynn. He and Hank Adams are in an ongoing boundary dispute and we will be re-surveying the properties. You may leave the file on your desk and I will stop by and pick it up this evening when I leave. We're still at Caress' house."

"How—How was the funeral?" Madison tried to inject concern into her voice. In spite of the fact she disliked Darla Mullins, she felt compassion for the other woman's loss.

"Very nice and very sad. Thank you for asking." Her tone remained brisk and businesslike, but Madison detected a slight crack in the clipped words.

"Again, I'm very sorry for your loss," Madison murmured. She offered a small olive branch. "I'll leave the file on the table so you'll easily see it."

"Very well. I'll see you at eight."

With a reluctant sigh, Madison locked the front door, stuffed her keyring into her pants pocket, and decided to exit out the back, after retrieving the file. No need in walking that hall twice. Flipping on the light to the hallway, she hurried down the dismal path to the back office and made quick work of finding the file. The ghosts cheered her on, wailing and moaning as she pushed the drawer closed with her hip and dropped the folder onto the table behind her.

A draft sneaked its way around the windowsills, howling a lonesome tune. An unusually strong draft of air slammed the door of her office shut, causing her to jump.

Chiding herself for being so jumpy, Madison went to the door and tugged on it, only to find it stuck. She tried to twist the knob, but it refused to turn. She shoved her shoulder against the solid panels of the door, complaining about the old building and jambs that swelled.

After several failed attempts at getting the door to budge, she realized she would have to call for help. She could just imagine Darla's reaction when she disturbed her. Maybe, she decided, she should call Derron first.

But what was his phone number? Come to think of it, she didn't even know how to reach Darla outside the office. A quick punch of *69 was of no help; apparently that feature was unavailable on the phones, as well.

She could always call Genny. With a sigh, Madison punched the familiar number into the office phone and was greeted by silence. *That's odd,* she thought, staring down at the receiver with a frown.

She belatedly realized there was no dial tone. She jabbed the hook up and down several times, trying to get a connection. Still nothing.

As Madison fished her cell phone from her purse, she thought she heard a noise in the hall. Had someone come in through the back? Maybe Derron opened the door and created a cross draft that sucked her office door shut.

"Derron? Is that you?" she called against the closed door. She jiggled the handle one more time. "Derron? … Darla? … Anyone?" She kept trying the handle, even as she dialed her cell phone with the other hand.

Distracted by her efforts to open the door and the noisy wail of the wind, it took a few moments for her to realize her call hadn't gone through.

"Hello?" Madison spoke into the cell phone, hearing her own voice echoing back into her ear. "Genny? Are you there?" Still her own voice.

This is really strange, she thought with a frown. She punched 'end' and tried again, with the same results. Beginning to get uneasy, she dialed her home number. The same empty echo greeted her.

"Okay, calm down," she said aloud to herself. "There's nothing to be alarmed about, just a lost signal. It will be back in a minute or so."

She waited a good five seconds before trying again.

Another bump from the hallway had her heart lodged in her throat. "D-Derron?" she called again, her voice not quite as strong as before.

Without warning, the lights went out; not only in the office, but in the entire building, plunging Madison into darkness. She found her voice, strong and loud, as she called out for help.

"Derron! Darla! I'm in here! The door's stuck! Open up!" She rattled the door on its hinges, but there was only silence on the other side.

Instinctively, Madison pulled away from the door. Something wasn't right. The phones weren't working and the lights were out. A power failure? That hardly explained the noise in the hall.

She heard it again. To her overactive imagination, it sounded like feet shuffling. She tried her cell phone again, then one more time. The light from her screen lit up the room, enough to see the outline of the door. Had the handle just turned?

By now, Madison was more than uneasy; she was flat-out frightened. Keeping her eye on the door handle, she inched her way backwards, her hand groping for the chair she knew was there. Without making a sound, she eased the heavy piece toward the door and wedged it beneath the doorknob. Between the wailing of the ghosts and the heavy thud of her heart, she could no longer hear the noise from the hall, but this time she was certain she saw the handle twist.

She tried the phone one last time, dialing 911. Not even the emergency number worked. Fear flooded through her body as she realized her cell signal had more than likely been jammed.

There was only one person who would have reason to trap her in the empty office, cut the power and the phone lines, and jam her cell signal—Trench Coat!

21

Madison searched the darkness for some way to defend herself. She did a mental survey of the room, reluctant to use the light from her phone in the irrational fear of being seen; the door and walls were solid, but Trench Coat was on the other side. She wasn't taking any chances.

She knew the only windows in the room were high above the oversized filing cabinets. As her eyes grew accustomed to the darkness, she could detect the faint glow of waning daylight beyond their dusty panes. Another half hour or less, and the sky outside would be dark.

Did the windows even open? For all she knew, they were painted shut. Even if she could reach them and they functioned correctly, could she shimmy her way through their narrow openings?

The doorknob moved again, this time with a distinct rattle. Trench Coat made no secret of trying to get in.

Spurred into motion, Madison pulled open the bottom file drawer of the middle cabinet. Normally, she used the ladder chair to reach the top drawers of the custom-made file cabinets, but the chair provided a far more valuable service at the moment by keeping Trench Coat at bay. Testing the sturdiness of the metal slides that held the drawer in place, she gingerly stepped onto the thin rails, balancing her weight on either side. When she didn't crash to the floor, she took it as encouragement to try the next drawer.

On the third drawer, her foot slipped. She felt the files crush beneath her shoe and give way, allowing her foot to sink to the bottom of the drawer with a slight twist of her ankle. Trying to steady herself, she grabbed for the only thing in her reach. As her hands curled around the edge of the top drawer, she inadvertently tugged too hard. The drawer slid out almost to its full extension, pushing her out with it. As she dangled in the air, feet flailing and grappling for traction, she heard the door jostle behind her.

In retrospect, Madison realized it would have been easier to drop to the floor; her feet were within twenty inches of the ground. But she was operating on fear, and fear seldom factored in rational thought. So instead of dropping to the floor and starting the climb over, Madison shoved her body forward, trying to urge the drawer in. She misjudged the momentum needed and used too much force with her body slam. The drawer smacked forward, catching her fingers in the process.

Crying out in anguish, Madison managed to hold on through the pain, long enough to disengage one hand at a time. She hauled herself up and managed to get first one arm onto the top of the cabinet, then the other. Her fingers screamed in pain, her elbows scraped against the cold metal, and her shoulders protested the hanging weight of her body. Still, she clung to the side of the cabinet with determination.

She lost a shoe in her attempt to scale the side of the cabinet and find a foothold among the drawer pulls, but Madison finally managed to crawl her way to the top of the monstrous cabinets.

She rested for a moment, panting from her efforts as she lay on her back. *So this is where the ghosts hang out.* Wisps of cold air howled in around the windows, finding the tiniest of cracks to whistle their way through. *Another five minutes and I'll be good to go.*

Above the ghostly wail of the wind, she heard the door rattle again within seconds. It was the only motivation she needed to get moving.

The windows were not painted shut, but they might as well have been. Years of dust and rust and grime made the hinges stiff and stubborn.

The old casement windows hinged on the bottom and opened from the top. Even though she could reach the hasps, she didn't have enough leverage to force them free. When Trench Coat banged against the door, Madison jerked files from the drawers to form a haphazard step. The extra inches were all she needed to work the ancient fasteners open.

She yanked on the window with all her might, but it refused to budge. Crying out in pain, Madison used both bruised hands and every ounce of strength to tug the rusty hinges into motion. The window finally swung down and free, just as her makeshift step gave way. Her ankle turned again and she fell to her knees, banging her chin against the window in the fall. Stars exploded before her eyes and blood spurted in her mouth when she bit her tongue, but cold air rushed in through the opened window. At last, the ghosts were silent.

The same couldn't be said for Trench Coat. Knowing the rattling door might give way at any moment, Madison mustered the energy to push off her knees and scramble through the narrow opening. She was halfway through the window, pushing forward, when she faced the next battle: getting down from the lofty height.

Madison paused to study the buildings in the fading daylight. Miss Juliet insisted on a pretty town, which included buildings with ornamental brick patterns, faux gables with false facades, stylish window ledges, and architectural stars. From the sidewalks, all six buildings within the block appeared to be the same height, but from this vantage, she could see the truth: the flat tops of the back-to-back buildings were staggered.

Her temporary office was on the interior wall of *Boundaries*, so the windows opened to the inside of the block. Getting onto the lower pebbled roof of *Juliet Title Company* wasn't the problem; getting off it would be the problem. The title company was the shortest of the buildings, flanked on three sides by its towering neighbors.

Craning her neck upward, she could tell the roofline of *Boundaries* was another eight feet over her head. The empty building to the rear was only slightly shorter. Her best option would be City Hall.

Balancing herself on the windowsill, Madison threw her remaining shoe off, then dangled long legs in the air as she gathered the courage to continue. She instinctively knew the jump would hurt, not to mention the journey up. Her ankle was already twisted, her hands were bruised and bloody, and her muscles ached from climbing. But she had gotten herself into this mess, and now she had to get herself out.

So here goes.

She plopped onto the roof with a sad lack of grace. Her ankle protested by refusing to hold her. After a few staggering steps, she hobbled the rest of the way, until she collapsed against the wall of City Hall. She tried her phone again, but the signal was still jammed.

If Trench Coat somehow managed to get to the windows, Madison knew she would be a sitting duck. There was nothing on the roof to hide behind, nothing to protect herself with. She had a brief vision of her cold, dead body left up here to wither, hidden from the world below. How long would it take for someone to discover her remains?

Her only choice was to keep moving. She lumbered to her feet, balanced best she could on her tiptoes, and stretched as far as humanly possible. *Still not tall enough! Stretch, Madison, str-ret-tch.*

She sank back down in exhaustion. Drawing in a deep breath, she tried something else; she would have to climb.

She found a tiny crevice in the mortar between two bricks and dug her fingers inside. Another stretch of unnatural limits, and her right hand grazed the edge of an architectural star. The socks she wore offered traction as she began the arduous task of climbing the wall.

After slipping and falling, and starting over a half dozen times, she eventually got the hang of it. It was a grueling process, but she made slow and painful progress. She cried out in relief when her fingers scraped the fancy brickwork at the apex of the building. Thank goodness for the ornamental details of old buildings! She would no longer think of their elaborate stylings as pretty but useless; the staggered depths of the masonry were quite useful as she gripped a protruding brick with her scraped hands and hauled herself up the final distance.

With a loud groan, Madison propelled over the edge and hurled herself onto the flat graveled roof of City Hall. She ignored the tiny pebbles biting into her flesh; for now, at least, she was safe.

Madison contemplated her choices as she lay there panting. She could hurry down and hope she beat Trench Coat into the street and to relative safety, or she could stay where she was and wait him out.

But how long would that take? Surely, Trench Coat would realize his mission had failed and he would be eager to escape without detection. And sooner or later, Darla Mullins would return to *Boundaries* and see that something was amiss. But which would it be... sooner, or later?

She was down the rickety old fire escape in no time, skipping steps and stumbling a time or two in her haste for freedom. It was after five o'clock and the only business still open was Moe's Market, directly across from *Boundaries*. She didn't dare take the chance of Trench Coat catching her before she made it there. Instead, Madison ran across Main Street toward the florist. With any luck, someone might still be there.

She was out of luck.

With Valentine's Day and Caress' funeral behind them, the flower shop and nursery were locked up tight. Undeterred, Madison slipped behind the house turned business and made her way through the backyard. She could surely find refuge at the Big House.

It was dark enough now that the streetlights had flickered on, throwing a peculiar glow into a night still hovering in twilight. Staying out of the bulb's glow, Madison moved in the shadows of gathering darkness as she scurried across Third Street. She crossed to the corner lot near the back of the property.

With still no sign of Trench Coat, she blended with the shadows of the trees and shrubs until she found the gate she was looking for. She unfastened the latch, slipped inside, and ran toward the safety of the house. From there, she could call for help and wait until it arrived.

Her first two attempts to call were unsuccessful. Her cell signal was still jammed. The night air was cold as she sat in the shadows of the porch, so she drew her long legs up close to her chest and hugged her knees for warmth. By now, she was shivering, as much from fright and spent energy as from actual cold.

Huddled on the porch, Madison surveyed the street for any sign of her stalker. She was feeling optimistic when something across the street caught her eye. It was the most difficult time of day to see, but was that a person beneath the bank's awning? Wasn't that the hem of a coat she saw... a khaki-colored trench coat? Her eyes had trouble focusing in the darkening twilight.

Madison pushed her way further into the shadows and slowly stood, keeping her back flat against the wall. Her eyes never wavered from the dark shadow beneath the awning across the street. Cars zipped back and forth between her and the object she focused on, but she barely blinked. She inched toward the front entrance of the Big House, pulled open the screen door, and poised her hand over the doorknob, all without taking her eyes off the shadows. She glanced down only long enough to search for the key on her keyring, the one she added after Genesis hijacked her and the *Home Again* duo.

Even as she jabbed the key into place, her eyes flew back to the shadows across the street. She caught another movement out of the corner of her eye, this one much closer. She jerked her head around to examine the wrought-iron fence around the Big House. Beneath the weak glow of the streetlight, she saw the eerie glimmer of a skeleton mask as Trench Coat squeezed his bulk through the gate out front.

Swallowing the squeak that sprang up in her throat, Madison slipped inside the house. Her hands trembled as she locked first the doorknob, then the deadbolt. She had a sinking feeling neither would deter her stalker for long.

As she hurried through the house making certain all the doors were locked, she tried her cell phone again. Madison dialed 911 and heard a blessed two rings before the line went silent. She frantically redialed. After three more attempts, her call went through.

"Finally!" she cried in triumph. "I'm inside the Big House in Juliet and I need help." She spoke quickly, talking over the operator's calm request for more information. "Yes, yes, yes. Just listen. Call Brash deCordova and tell him Maddy needs his help. I'm at the Big House and Trench Coat is chasing me. He'll know what I mean."

"Ma'am—"

"Just do it!" Madison barked as she hung up the phone. She hit the 'silent' button, stuffed the phone back into her pocket, and searched for a place to hide. As she passed through the kitchen, she saw a shadow slither outside along the window. Trench Coat would no doubt find a way inside soon.

Shutting the door between the kitchen and butler's pantry, she found a rolling teacart to prop against it. Trench Coat might choose another route inside the house, but if he came through the kitchen, she could at least make his exit a bit more difficult.

Granny Bert said the house was filled with hidden passages, but Madison had no clue where they were. It was dark inside the house, with only the palest of light filtering through the windows. Occasionally, she would use the glow from her cell screen to light the way, to save from stumbling over furniture and unfamiliar paths. She ran frantic hands over doorframes and tried to twist sconces on the wall, pushed on built-in bookcases and patted down solid walls, hoping to trigger a secret panel. Nothing.

By the time she reached the library, she knew Trench Coat had found a way inside the house. She heard a loud thud as the kitchen door swung into the teacart and rattled the silver service. There was a savage curse, the clatter of dishes falling to the floor, the squeak of old wheels as the wooden cart was shoved aside. Then there was silence.

The fireplace! Granny Bert said she once hid in a secret passage behind the library fireplace!

With renewed hope, Madison tried a dozen things, tapping as quietly as possible on the paneled walls, twisting and turning anything she could feel in the darkness, praying she would find the passage before Trench Coat found her.

Over her shoulder, she saw the beam of a flashlight slicing through the darkness in the next room. Her time was running out. She shoved on the wall and felt a slight give. Not more than two feet wide, a burled walnut panel filled the gap between a built-in bookcase and the fireplace.

Madison instinctively slid her hands across the panel with pressure and felt the wood slip, tucking discreetly behind the bookcase.

She opened the panel just enough to wedge her body inside. It was a tight fit, but she sucked in her stomach and tugged on the wood to close it. The panel hung on some unseen obstacle and refused to slide back in place.

Using her stockinged feet to feel along the bottom of the panel, she detected a piece of cloth hung in the track. Pinching her toes together, she managed to pick the cloth up with her lower digits and free the path. She slid the panel in front of her face, nearly clipping her own nose, as she watched the beam of the flashlight bob ever closer.

She stilled as Trench Coat stepped through the threshold into the library. Madison shrank back into the narrow passage as far as the walls would allow. The panel didn't close completely, but she dared not take the chance of moving it again. Fearing the light might detect the white of her eyes or the buttons on her blouse, she hovered just beyond the opening. She couldn't see a thing through the slim crack, other than the sweep of the flashlight crisscrossing the room.

The light bounced around the wall she stood behind. Tiny pricks of white stabbed through crevices of the bookcase. Madison didn't dare to even breathe. If only her heart wouldn't clamber so loudly! Surely Trench Coat could hear the racket inside her chest; the erratic pace echoed noisily inside the small confines of the secret passage.

When the flashlight swung the other direction, Madison dared to take a deep breath. She pushed herself further into the shadows, behind the bookcase. The passageway led along the wall and connected to some other part of the house… but where? Did she dare press her luck and find out? What if it led her straight into Trench Coat's path?

Brash would be here soon. She could hold on until he came. As long as she was perfectly still, perfectly silent, there was no reason she wouldn't be safe here in the secret passage. Trench Coat was six feet away but had no idea where she hid.

The tickle began in her throat. Madison tried ignoring it as she watched the flashlight's beam travel around the room once more. She swallowed frantically, trying to drown the itching sensation that grew worse by the moment. She put a hand to her throat and tapped. She tried massaging it. The scratch clawed at her windpipe, morphing into a burn. Her eyes watered and her breath weakened, but she didn't cough.

Just as she conquered that crisis, her nose began to itch. Madison hastily rubbed the end of her appendage. She blew a stream of air up from her mouth, trying to chase away loose particles of dust. She wiggled her nose again, trying desperately to ward off a sneeze. The harder she tried to ignore it, the worse it got.

The light was finally retreating. With any luck, Trench Coat would be out the door and on to the next room before her sneeze erupted. Because try as she might to hold it in, she knew she was going to sneeze. She buried her face inside her shirt, pinched her nostrils closed, and gave in to the urge.

To her ears, the sneeze sounded like a cannon going off. Madison held perfectly still, willing Trench Coat to keep going. With any luck, he hadn't heard the muffled sound.

Judging from the swing of light bouncing back into the room, luck wasn't going her way. A bright beam of light spilled into the tiny sliver of space along the panel's edge. Pinpoints of light fell across her face and chest, tiny pricks of white that worked their way through nail holes and minute cracks. Madison instinctively shrank back, wedging herself into the tight quarters of darkness.

Another sneeze burst forth, unannounced. It gave no warning as the sound tore from her body and echoed in the small space. Her secret location was no longer a secret.

The light came closer, bouncing around in a frantic motion as Trench Coat tried to find the secret panel. No longer having a choice, Madison knew it was only a matter of time before he found her. She would have to go down the dark passage and see where it took her.

Madison slid to her right, pushing her way into thick cobwebs and dark, empty space. She managed to bite back the next sneeze, but the twisting motion brought her shoulders forward. When she tried to straighten, she found she was stuck.

This can't be happening! she inwardly wailed. She tugged and pulled and strained, but there was no doubt about it; she was wedged inside the narrow space, with no means of escape.

No longer worried about being stealthy, Trench Coat banged around on the other side of the panel, trying to find a lever to reveal the secret passage. Between his banging and the frantic tempo of her heart, Madison almost didn't hear the sirens.

The sirens grew louder. Trench Coat switched off the flashlight and quietened. Madison strained to hear what was happening on the other side of the panel. The rustle of cloth told her he was still in the room, more than likely hiding.

The sound was faint, but she heard Brash's voice call her name. She willed him inside, imagining him drawing his gun as he slowly approached through the darkened house. He was probably through the foyer now, trying to decide whether to go left or right. *Right, Brash, right.* She willed the thought into his head.

She heard his voice getting stronger. "This is the police! Who's there? Identify yourself now." His voice came closer. "Maddy, where are you?"

Deciding to risk it, she screamed out as loudly as she could. "The library! The library, Brash! But be careful, Trench Coat is in here!"

She heard the rustle of more clothes, more movement. The sounds were too clumsy to be attributed to Brash. Madison strained to listen, but she never knew when Brash stepped into the room. For long moments, silence reigned.

The next thing she heard was a loud whack, Brash's muttered curse, and a series of bumps and bangs and thuds. Then there was silence once again.

It seemed an eternity before she heard Brash's voice. It sounded muffled. Groggy. "Maddy? Where are you, Maddy?"

"In the wall! Behind the bookcase. I'm—I'm stuck."

She heard bumbling and a few more curses.

"Turn on the lights," she called. "There's a panel that slides by the fireplace."

After an eternity, light seeped in around the edges of the panel. The bright swatch grew larger as the wood slid slowly aside. She could turn her head only enough to see Brash struggling with the board.

"Ouch! That's me!" she said as he gave the panel a final shove and it banged into her knee.

"Where the heck are you?"

"Behind the bookcase, far side. Hurry up. It's hard to breathe back here."

"Yeah, well it's hard to stand up out here," he grumbled. She could see that he kept putting his hand to the back of his neck. With the other hand, he reached into the dark recess of the passage and groped for her. "Take my hand. I'll pull you out."

Madison tried to do as he instructed, but she was wedged firmly between the two walls. "I'm stuck really tight. Where's Trench Coat? Did you catch him?"

"No, he hit me over the head and got away."

"Are you all right?"

"Just shut up and pull," he said testily. "Keep coming, that's right. Now heave."

"I'm trying!" She sucked in a deep breath and strained with all her might. "It's. No. Use. I'm stuck."

"Am I going to have to tear down this wall to get you out?"

"Heavens, Nick Vilardi would have a fit. Okay, one more time."

Brash heaved and pulled as Madison struggled to push herself free. It was a slow process, but she felt the tiniest shift. Her skin scraped against wood, gathering splinters in the process. With a loud rip of fabric, Madison broke free and tumbled out of the narrow space, smacking into Brash. With a single swoop of his arm, he hauled her out of the passage and jerked her up against the warm, solid wall of his chest.

The bright light of the room blinded Madison and curled her eyes into a squint. When she unfurled her lashes, she saw the blood.

"Brash! What happened to you? You're bleeding!"

"Told you, Trench Coat got the drop on me. Hit me over the head with that vase." He nodded to the broken pottery on the floor as he continued to hold the back of his neck with one hand, her waist with the other. Once his eyes slowly focused, he surveyed her. "What about you? You have a bruise on your cheek, bloody knuckles, and no shoes."

She gave him the condensed version. Though she was hurting in more places than she cared to admit and there seemed to be a definite draft in the general area of her derriere, she was more worried about him than she was herself. "Are you sure you're all right?"

"Never said that." His words became more slurred. It occurred to Madison that he held her so tightly to keep his own body upright. He was leaning into her as much as he was supporting her.

His blue eyes shuttered closed and he sagged against her, just as Officer Schimanski burst through the door. Together, Maddy and the other officer managed to get Brash's bulky form into a nearby chair until the paramedics arrived.

"Brash. Brash, wake up. You need to stay awake." Madison rattled his arm as he drifted in and out of consciousness.

"Hard to," he mumbled.

"You have to, Brash. Talk to me. Did you see Trench Coat? Did you get a look at his face?"

"Yeah," he said groggily. "Looked like hell. White face, all bones."

"That was a mask, Brash."

His eyes were closed again. "Not Halloween."

What on earth was taking the ambulance so long? "No, it's not Halloween," she agreed. She shook him by the arm to keep him awake. "Do you know what month it is? What day?"

"Valentine's," he murmured. "You were wearing a red dress."

"Yes, that's right. We danced together at the Valentine's Mixer. Do you remember that, Brash?"

"Course I do." He reached out to clumsily pull her into his arms. "Dance with me, Maddy."

She chuckled as she patted his chest. "Easy there, Tiger. Neither one of us is in any shape for that right now."

"You okay?" He peeled open one blue eye to look at her.

"I'm fine. It's you I'm worried about. That's a nasty bump you have there."

He gave her a goofy grin. Even when only half-conscious, the man had the power to render her knees into Jell-O. "Kiss it and make it better."

The paramedics banged their way into the room at that moment. Waving them toward Brash, Madison stepped out of their way. Despite his weak protests, the crew wasted no time in loading the police chief onto the gurney.

"Maddy." His voice was weak but determined as he held out a hand and insisted the paramedics not take him yet.

"I'm here, Brash," she said, stepping up to his side and taking his hand.

He was too weary to open his eyes. "Sure you're okay?"

"I'm fine, Brash. You're the one who needs to go to the hospital. Now be good and let them take you there."

"…Owe me a kiss," he murmured.

Madison blushed and glanced around at their audience. One paramedic grinned, the other looked irritated. Officer Schimanski bit back a snicker and the two firemen on scene pretended a great sudden interest in the room's decor.

Bending over him to whisper in his ear, Madison brushed a kiss across his cheek. "Yes, Brash, I owe you a kiss."

"Soon, Maddy." There was an edge of impatience in his voice. His eyes popped open for him to stare at her intently.

Madison understood, for she felt that same yearning. The waiting just made it worse. Each time she thought a kiss might finally happen, something interfered, just like now. The tender moment was lost as the paramedics all but pushed her aside. Her hand trailed out of his as they carried him to the waiting ambulance.

Biting her lip in worry, Madison tasted dried blood and was reminded of her own injuries. She was taking stock of all her ailments when two more medics arrived.

"I can walk," Madison insisted, but she crawled onto the gurney anyway. Now that the adrenaline was fading, she realized how exhausted she was. Had they not already turned to mush, her abused muscles would surely scream in protest. "I don't need the hospital. The Tuesday/Thursday Clinic here in town will be fine."

"We normally transfer to the hospital, ma'am," one of the paramedics said.

"Please, I'm too tired to argue. Just take me to the clinic. And where's my phone? I need to call my family."

22

The Sisters Health Clinic was a multi-service facility that shared not only office space, but office days. On Mondays and Wednesdays, chiropractor and acupuncturist Trong Ngo served the citizens of their small community. On Tuesdays and Thursdays, the space functioned as a family clinic. And on Wednesdays, old Doc Menger opened his scaled-down dentistry practice.

Luckily for Madison, it was Thursday and the clinic was open for another thirty minutes. Other than a little girl being treated for a rash, she was the only patient that late in the day.

"We'll get you cleaned up and out of here in no time," the nurse assured her with a smile.

"Aren't you the school nurse?" Madison asked in confusion. She even checked the nametag to make certain: Margaret Chatham.

The pretty brunette looked up from her task of cleaning Madison's knuckles. The solution she used stung like the devil, but at least her manner was gentle.

With a nod of her dark head, the nurse smiled. "Yes, that's right. But I pick up a few hours here and there. Anything to make ends meet." With a slight shrug of her slim shoulders, she offered a weak explanation. "I'm a single mother."

Madison felt an immediate bond with the other woman. They were both around the same age, both with the responsibility of raising their children alone. That, however, was where the similarities ended. Margaret Chatham looked small and dainty next to Madison's tall, lanky form. She wore her auburn-kissed brown hair long and curly, held out of the way with a simple silver clasp. Next to Madison's peachy skin tones, the nurse's skin had a healthy olive glow, the kind Maddy had always envied. With her coffee-brown eyes and full lips, the woman was a true beauty. *And no matter what Brash tried to tell me, I know she looks gorgeous in red*, Madison thought. Still, she decided she liked this Margaret Chatham.

"Ah, say no more," Madison commiserated. "I'm a single mother, myself. Teenage twins."

"Yes, I know. Bethani and Blake. And you've done a wonderful job with them, by the way. They are both very polite and well mannered."

Liking the nurse even more, Madison gave her a sincere smile. "Why, thank you. That's always nice to hear."

"I know, right? We try to raise them right, teach them their manners and to respect their elders, but we never know how they actually behave when we're not around. It's a bit like the tree that falls in the forest, don't you think?" She offered a light laugh as she swiped Madison's knuckles once more. Seeing her patient flinch, she said, "Sorry, I know this stings. Almost done."

"So how many children do you have?" It helped to keep her attention focused on something other than the antiseptic's bitter bite.

"Just one. Samantha. She's fourteen and the light of my life."

"Does she go to school here?"

"Oh yes. She's president of the freshman class, honor roll, newspaper staff, UIL contestant, a Girl Scout Senior." She stopped with a self-conscious laugh. "Sorry. Proud parent-itis. Sometimes I don't know when to stop."

"Why ever would you apologize? She sounds like a very bright and lively girl."

"Definitely lively! I have a bit of trouble keeping up with her at times. We love to go camping and hiking, but there are days when she can run circles around me."

"We used to camp some," Madison recalled with a touch of melancholy. "Back in the day."

"Why did you stop?" Margaret finished with the knuckles and turned her attention to Madison's tender cheek. "That's going to be a beauty in the morning," she predicted. "Hope you don't have a hot date this weekend." Her dark eyes twinkled, revealing little flecks of gold.

Madison harrumphed. "Hardly!"

"Have you been divorced for long?"

"Not divorced. Widowed."

"Oh, I'm so sorry!" She was truly contrite for the blunder.

"I'm managing," Madison assured her. She was a bit surprised to realize she spoke the truth. In spite of the difficulties she faced, she *was* managing. And rather well, if she did say so herself.

"It's always been just Samantha and me," the other woman confessed. "I'm already dreading the day when she goes away to college."

"I know what you mean. The twins went on their first date Saturday night. I cried like a baby, seeing my babies all grown up like that. Think they'd mind if I went away to college with them?"

Margaret Chatham laughed. "I say it's worth a try!"

The women chatted as the nurse attended to Madison's injuries. There was even mention of getting together for lunch one day. Madison was quite pleased with herself, making a new friend without the help of the vivacious Genesis. Genny had a natural way of drawing people to her. Without her friend at her side, Madison tended to be more of a loner. She suspected Margaret Chatham might have the same tendencies.

"Well, I think that should about do it," the pretty nurse concluded. "You need to watch for infection in all your scrapes and cuts."

Madison held up a recently scarred palm and nodded. "I just got over a recent injury. I know all about keeping the wounds clean and dry." She had worn a bandage on her hand for a week after the ordeal at the Gleason Poultry Farm, and still it had become infected.

"So be a good patient and keep an eye on these." When she lightly patted the gauze circling Madison's knuckles, the clasp of her bracelet snagged in the fibers. "Oops, sorry about that."

"No problem. And that's a lovely bracelet, by the way."

"Thanks. My friend Brash gave it to me for Christmas."

"Br—Brash?"

"Yes, you know him? Oh, of course you do," she chided herself. She didn't notice the sudden pallor of Madison's skin. "He's chief of police, former football star, and the most eligible bachelor in all of The Sisters. Or for our generation, anyway; Cutter Montgomery claims the spotlight for the younger ladies." She flashed a smile as she collected wrappings from the gauze and threw away the trash.

"*This* Christmas?" Madison clarified on a squeak.

"Yes, that's right." Margaret smiled and paused at the door. "The doctor will be in to give you your walking papers. Sit back and relax for now. I'll check in with you in a few minutes."

Madison stared after her newly made friend: Brash's *girlfriend*, so it seemed! How dare he flirt with her… hold her so close… promise to kiss her… talk about Margaret so casually, as if she were part of his distant past… when he was still buying her Christmas presents!

Seething with fury, Madison didn't bother checking the caller ID when her phone rang. She jerked the phone to her ear, her mind still on the two-timing police chief. If he thought he had a headache now, just wait until she was through with him!

"Hello," she snapped.

"I want to know what the meaning of this is!" The bellowed words on the other end matched her own mood. It took a moment for Madison to recognize Darla Mullin's voice.

She struggled to shift gears. "What—What do you mean?"

"This office is a disaster! What on earth happened in here?"

Given the fact that Caress had been Darla's best friend and there was still an on-going investigation into her murder, Madison was reluctant to mention Trench Coat. Instead, she went with general details. "There was an intruder at the office today. I was trapped in my office without lights or phone. I had to escape out the windows."

"An intruder? Why, I've never had an intruder in all my years of business!"

Madison noted the lack of concern for her own well-being. She made no comment, but it didn't stop Darla from further rantings.

"I don't know what kind of people you are associated with, young woman, but they aren't welcome in my establishment! And I expect you to come down here immediately and clean this mess up."

"I'm sorry, but at the moment I'm a little pre-occupied. I'm in the ER."

She could hear Darla's chest puffing out with indignation. "If you think, for one minute, that I am going to pay your ER bill, you are sadly mistaken!"

"Please, don't worry about me." Madison's voice dripped with sarcasm at her employer's blatant lack of concern. "I'm fine, really."

Darla Mullins sniffed. "I trust, then, that you're well enough to be here early in the morning. You can clean this mess up before we leave for the field."

Madison sighed. "I may be sporting a pair of crutches in the morning. I have a sprained ankle."

"Then I hope you can juggle, because your job is to carry the equipment."

23

Madison groaned as daylight filtered through the blinds and pierced her eyelids. She snuggled deeper into the covers, idly wondering why every muscle in her body ached. Despite the crazy dreams she kept having all night, she wanted nothing more than to go back to sleep. The dreams themselves had been exhausting—climbing around on cabinets, scaling brick walls, running through shadows and hiding in dark, tiny places—but with any luck at all, she could fall back into a dreamless slumber. It was definitely worth a try.

Her cheek was tender as she buried it against the pillow. When she gingerly probed it with a questioning touch, she found her fingers were stiff and swollen. Reluctantly prying one eye open, she saw the gauze wrapped around her knuckles.

An anguished cry tore from her as she struggled to sit up in bed. Her legs felt like she had run an uphill marathon. Her arms and shoulders felt like she had bench-pressed an elephant. All points between ached and burned. Her tongue felt three times its normal size and she was pretty sure she was dizzy, but the pain made her nauseous and unable to concentrate. She fell back into bed with another whimper.

"Ah, so you finally woke up."

She saw Granny Bert's wrinkled face floating above hers when she opened her eyes again.

"I—I've got to go to work," Madison mumbled. In her mind, she threw back the covers and swung her legs over the side of the bed. In reality, her fingers picked at the covers and found them too heavy to lift.

"Already took care of that," Granny Bert informed her. "You've got the day off."

"Wh—What? I can't..."

"You can't go to work, that's for sure. You can't even lift your head. What I want to know is, what in tarnation gave you the idea that you were Spider-Man?"

"I had to get away from Trench Coat." With her tongue swollen from having bitten it the night before, her words came out thick and fuzzy.

Her grandmother scowled. "They must have given you some powerful pain pills at that clinic. That's the same thing you kept saying last night. Between the thick tongue and the drugs, I can't make head nor tails of what you're saying. Something about trench coats and George Gail and bracelets and kissing Brash deCordova."

Madison attempted to scrunch down into the covers and bury her face. The effort was too painful. "Argh!" she moaned instead. "Just cover me up and smother me."

Instead, her grandmother laughed merrily. "The part about kissing Brash I understood perfectly, but what's this about coats and George Gail? You weren't making a lick of sense."

"Whoever killed Caress thinks I can identify them. They wear a trench coat and are stalking me."

"Time to get yourself a gun. I carry a sweet little .25 that fits in the palm of my hand."

The thought of her feisty little grandmother armed with a gun almost made Madison feel sorry for anyone foolish enough to be on the other end of that barrel. "Don't like guns," she muttered through her swollen tongue.

"Well, you're in luck then, because this Trench Coat fella prefers to kill people with knives."

Point taken. She made the acknowledgment silently, knowing how much Granny Bert loved to gloat.

"So what does any of this have to do with George Gail?" her grandmother persisted.

Madison explained how George Gail had motive and no clear recollection of events for the night of Caress' murder. Even before she finished talking, she felt herself withering under Granny Bert's searing glare.

"I'm going to assume that's your thick tongue talking, and not your thick head. Otherwise, I might just bite it off myself!" Granny Bert propped her hands onto her hips and gave Madison a look mean enough to wither a bulldog. "I know I didn't just hear you accuse George Gail Burton of murder!"

"She can't remember, Granny. She woke up with keys in her hand and blood on the sheets. She told me herself that she'd like to give 'that back-stabbing hussy' a taste of her own medicine."

"Don't mean she went and stabbed a woman to death," Granny Bert insisted. "And I've said it once and I'll say it again, Curtis Burton was not doing the nasty with Caress Ellingsworth!"

She had to agree, but that still didn't clear George Gail; at the time, the woman thought her husband was cheating on her. Rather than argue the point, Madison changed the subject. "What did Dragon Lady have to say about me not coming in to work today?"

"Between alternating threats of firing you and suing you for breach of contract? Not a lot."

"Great," Madison moped. "Now she'll go all around town bad-mouthing me. Between her and her sister, my poor little business doesn't stand a chance."

"Of course it does. I reminded her that it might very well be *you* pressing charges."

"Me?"

"Sure. How can you perform your duties in an unsafe atmosphere? Her lack of a security system and back-up electrical power put your life at risk. Even without some goon on the other side of the door, you could have tripped in the dark and broken your neck. And you seriously have to unfold a chair into a ladder to reach the top filing cabinet? I see all kinds of potential dangers with that. By the time I finished with Darla Mullins, she wasn't only ready to send you a get-well bouquet, but she agreed to pay your doctor bills, to boot."

Madison stared at her grandmother in fascination. "You must be joking."

"The woman is full of hot air and bad manners. And if she thinks she's going to pick on someone in my family, she's going to have to go through me to do it."

With a deep sigh, Madison stared up at the ceiling. She had done it again. Once more, she officially qualified as pathetic. She was thirty-nine years old and her eighty-year-old grandmother was still fighting her battles for her.

Brushing that subject away, Granny Bert changed topics. "Now. Tell me what you meant, blabbering on about bracelets and Christmas presents and kissing Brash deCordova."

Using her thickened tongue to her advantage, Madison feigned innocence. "Wike ooo said. Stwong pain medicine."

Madison could laze around for only so long. Despite her aching muscles, turned ankle, and all her scrapes and bruises, she felt guilty about staying in bed all morning. Soon, she was up and stepping from a hot, steamy shower, ready to *do* something. She started by preparing beef stew for supper, one of Blake's favorites; it should be nice and thick by suppertime.

She also felt guilty about avoiding Brash's phone calls. The truth was, she was worried about him and wanted to know how he was fairing. But she was too confused—and still just a little too hurt and angry—to take his calls right now. She needed to sort through her feelings before she talked to him.

The bracelet he had given to Margaret Chatham bothered her more than she cared to admit. She could rant and rave all she wanted about how Brash had led her on and lied to her. She could make this into all about him and his two-timing ways. But deep down, she knew why it bothered her so much; she was beginning to truly care about Brash deCordova. Somewhere along the way, her schoolgirl crush had turned into something deeper, something based on respect and admiration, not just hormones and fantasies.

Okay, so there's still some of that thrown into the mix, she admitted to herself. She chopped a carrot with more gusto than required. She thought about the jock he had been, and the man he had become. He was still self-assured, still a born leader full of confidence and bravado, but the arrogant edge was gone now. From what she could tell, he was a good lawman, fair and just, and dedicated to his job and community. He adored his daughter and was a good father to her. He worked with the youth at church and rumor had it he conducted two very popular free football camps each summer, one at Texas A&M, the other at Baylor. In addition to being civic minded, charitable—his good traits were numerous, so she skipped to the most obvious—handsome and devilishly sexy, he was so downright *likable.* The plain truth was, Madison liked him as a person; their personalities clicked. She enjoyed talking to him and spending time with him as a friend. And if that friendship deepened into something more, she was okay with that.

Madison frowned in the middle of peeling an onion. Where did that come from? I am NOT ready for a relationship with Brash or anyone else. Men are too much trouble. I don't have time to be falling in love right now, not when I'm trying to pull my life back together.

The fact that the words 'falling in love' even entered her mind scared her silly. That wasn't what she was doing! When and if she ever did give her heart away again, it would be to someone who was worthy, someone who loved her the way Curtis loved George Gail, someone fully dedicated to her, to *them* as a couple. Not someone like Gray, who betrayed her in the worst way possible. And not to someone who had given a piece of jewelry to another woman less than two months ago!

The onions were strong enough to make her eyes water. That had to be the explanation for the sudden tears clouding her vision. Turning on her sauté skillet, Madison concluded that all this had been Brash's fault, after all. He was the one to lead her on with the promise of a kiss. He was the one who called for her to be by his side as he lay on the gurney. He was the one who made her think of crazy things like the future and growing old together. He was the one to talk about music in the heart and dances and that off-handed remark about a 'few' dates with Margaret Chatham. Not once had he mentioned those dates were recent! Not once had he mentioned Christmas presents!

Working herself into a frenzy—it was easier to blame Brash, than to admit the possible truth of caring too much about him already—Madison cranked up the heat on the burner. The skillet sizzled when she dropped the onions in, and it gave her perverse pleasure to watch the edges curl and char. If only some two-timing police chief would curl up and wither that way. She pushed the vegetable around in the skillet, watching as the thin strips became translucent. Too bad men weren't this easy to see through! She tossed in the stew meat, searing the edges the way she would like to sear a certain someone's lying butt. For good measure, she turned down the heat and smothered the skillet with a lid.

"See how you like that, you too-sexy, two-timing, two-bit lawman!" she muttered.

It was still early in the afternoon, but Madison decided to cook with wine. Pouring herself a glass, she thought she might even add some to the food.

24

Still restless, after supper Madison went out for a while. The fact that it was Friday night, less than one week after Valentine's, and that she was spending it alone didn't escape her attention.

She called Genesis, the one person guaranteed to understand her mood and cheer her up.

Genny answered her call with a bright, "Whatcha doin,' girlfriend?"

"Oh, just driving around thinking."

"Uh-oh, sounds dangerous. What's wrong?"

With Genny, there was no need to pretend. She went to the root of the problem. "Why didn't you tell me that Brash and Margaret Chatham were dating?"

"Because I didn't know they were. Are you sure?"

"The bracelet on her wrist—her slim, dainty, nicely tanned wrist, as opposed to my big, bony, lily-white wrist—says they were involved as recently as Christmas. Which, I might point out, was only eight weeks ago."

"About the time you came back to town, and several weeks before you ran into him again."

"Stop clouding the issue with facts," Madison grumbled. "Have you asked him about it?"

"No! I'm avoiding his calls, even though I'm secretly dying to know how he's doing. Have you heard anything?"

Genesis laughed. "Oh, yes, everything from him being in a coma to how he single-handedly pushed a falling beam off his own neck and pulled you to safety, right before the ceiling crashed down and nearly killed you both."

"Funny, that's not the way I remember it happening."

"No, but the rumor mill makes it so much more interesting!"

"Speaking of rumors… guess what Miss Sybille told me when I made a bladder-pad run for her today."

"The new brand leaks?" Genny guessed. "I don't know, what?"

"Two things, actually. Well, three, but you probably don't care that Leroy Huddleston had to get quadruple bifocals. She told me that John-Paul Noble was talking about moving into Caress' house on a semi-permanent basis. Something about he helped her with the down payment and therefore had a quarter interest in the mortgage. Speculation is he wants it as a love nest, one that Carlina Antoine won't know about it. Apparently, they started up hot and heavy while they were making that last movie together."

"Hmm, haven't heard that one yet."

"The next one is even better. Guess who is supposedly in love?"

"Barry Redmond and Angie Jones?"

"What? I thought he was married."

"Technically, yes, but you should see what I do. People forget that when they play footsie under the table—particularly when those feet wander to other places a little further north—that they aren't necessarily hidden from view. I got an eyeful standing at the counter the other day."

"Eeww." Madison shuddered in revulsion. "But, no, that little disgusting tidbit is your secret for now. Miss Sybille told me about Cutter Montgomery, and how apparently he has been struck down by Cupid's arrow."

"Cutter's in love?" Genny snorted skeptically. "I sincerely doubt it, but who's the lucky lady?"

"That's the thing. No one can remember seeing him dance but with a handful of women at the mixer, that handful being Shilo Dawne, old Mrs. Cravey who has to be close to eighty by now, little Tami Sue Hadley who's closer to five, Callie Beth Irwin, his own sister-in-law, and you."

"Who's to say it happened at the dance?"

"According to Miss Sybille, Cutter himself. Wanda Shanks told Miss Sybille that Howard Evans saw him on Sunday morning and said Cutter still had stars in his eyes. Mr. Evans asked him if he had a good time at the dance Saturday night and finally found himself a girl, and Cutter said he not only found a girl, he found the woman of his dreams. According to Miss Wanda, Mr. Evans said he had the look of a man in love, goofy grin and all."

"That's a lot of she said/he said/she said. I wouldn't hold my breath on him finally choosing between Shilo Dawne and Callie Beth."

Even though her friend couldn't see her, Madison waggled her eyebrows mischievously. "Maybe it's neither one of them, ever think of that?"

"No."

"So, have you seen him since the dance?" Madison teased. She noticed her friend's answer was short and curt.

"Of course. He eats in here every day."

"Has he mentioned the dance to you? And the way his—um, how did you put it?—how his *equipment* responded?"

"I haven't really talked to him much," Genesis admitted. "I've let Shilo Dawne wait on him. I don't think her feet have hit the ground since she danced with him!"

"You've been avoiding him!" Madison said in shock.

"Maybe a little. I don't want things to be awkward between us. It was just a dance, no big deal." She fluttered her hands, something Madison couldn't see but was certain of. "And probably just a silly notion on my part. If I believed the rumors about him falling in love—which I don't—my money would be on Shilo Dawne."

"Don't think I don't notice how you're changing the subject."

"Okay, so I'll change it again. I had a phone call tonight. James Callaway called and asked me out."

"That cute professor who teaches dual-credit classes at the high school? Yummy. What did you say?"

"I hedged. I'm not sure I want to go out with him."

"Why not? You said he has a good sense of humor. And in spite of the crazy ties he wears, he's very nice looking."

"I'm just not looking for romance right now. There's too much going on in my life to muddle things up with a man thrown into the mix."

"I understand completely. But should I point out that you've had that same excuse for about ten years now? In fact, I can't even remember the last boyfriend you had." Madison frowned, trying to recall a name or face. She was coming up with a big blank, because her friend never dated.

"There haven't been many," Genesis confessed.

"Maybe this question is a little overdue, like by about twenty years, but you're not—you're not still in love with Tommy, are you?"

"No, of course not. He was my first love, but hardly my soulmate. I gave up dreams of a future with Tommy, long before he was killed in that wreck. The minute our twelve-hour marriage was annulled, I knew it was over between us. I have fond memories of him, but I'm definitely not still in love with him."

"Good. Because you are too young and beautiful to be in love with a ghost. And too vivacious to be an old maid!"

Genesis laughed. "Don't worry, I'll meet my Prince Charming one of these days."

"Then you'd better start kissing some toads."

"Speaking of toads… There were two of them in here today, warts and all. Darla Mullins and her dear sister Myrna graced us with their presence for lunch."

"Ooh, lucky you. I wonder if I'll even have a job come Monday morning."

"Oh, yes, you can bet on it. I overheard Darla plotting her evil scheme to make you carry every piece of equipment she owns out to the nether regions of Allen Wynn's place."

Madison sniffed a few times. "I think I may feel a head cold coming on."

Again, Genny laughed. "Good luck with that one. At least you seem to be in better spirits now."

"Talking to you always does that for me."

"That's what best friends are for!"

Madison drove aimlessly for another ten minutes. When her rambling drive took her down Caress' street, she decided to get in a little reconnaissance on Donny Howell. She parked in the same spot as before, where she had a view of both houses. It didn't hurt that if John-Paul Noble happened to stroll past the window, she might get a glimpse of the handsome actor...

Donny Howell had company. Two burly men sat with him in the living room, drinking beer and laughing. At some point, they all trailed out of the room and she lost sight of them. A few minutes later, a light appeared at the back of the house and, if she used the long-range lens on her camera, she could get glimpses of them throwing darts. She snapped off a few pictures, capturing the wince on Donny's face when he twisted and hurt his back. After that, he sat on the sidelines, cheering his buddies on.

In Madison's opinion, the man's insurance claim was legitimate.

With the camera still up to her eyes, Madison panned over toward Caress' house. Lights shone from numerous windows and there were two extra vehicles under the carport, suggesting John-Paul was still there. As usual, most of the blinds were open.

From where she sat, she had a clear view into the kitchen. With the curtains wide open, it really wasn't peeping, was it? Anyone could see inside, with or without a camera.

Deciding the camera might be a little much, she began to lower it when motion inside caught her eye. Surely one little magnified peek couldn't hurt.

Was that John-Paul? A man had his back to the granite counter. No, the hair was too blond, the build too slight to be the famed actor. Was that... yes, that was Derron. He and his mother were probably there visiting, keeping John-Paul company in the lonesome house.

Like the night she had witnessed Caress' attack, Madison spoke aloud, keeping a running monologue going. She was almost as nervous now as she was then, probably because her conscience ate at her. That night, she had been working; tonight, she was merely being nosy.

"Shame on you, Derron, jumping up on the counter like that," she mumbled to herself. "Granny Bert would have a conniption fit if one of the kids did that at our house. Come to think of it, I'm surprised Darla isn't having a cow right about now. Such behavior isn't proper and dignified, after all." She scrunched her face up and mimicked her temporary boss' superior tone. "What on earth is Derron doing? It looks like he's pulling his shirt off… Hel—lo!"

As Derron whipped off his pullover and tossed it aside, Madison quickly exchanged her camera for her binoculars. They provided more magnified details.

"Why Derron, Derron, Derron. Who knew what you were hiding under those preppy clothes you wear?" Her co-worker's back was finely sculpted with muscles. Muscles that rippled with each move of his arms, especially when they reached forward and his fingers wiggled in a 'come hither' gesture.

"Wait a minute," Madison muttered, not understanding the scene before her. "What is he doing? Why is John-Paul… what is he doing? Is he…. Oh. My. God. He's *nibbling* Derron's neck!"

She dropped the binoculars as surely as if they were on fire. Slapping her fingers to her face, she tried to stop the shocked cry that burst from her lips. It was no use. The sound came out hoarse and troubled.

It was like watching a train wreck. In spite of herself, Madison lifted the binoculars back to her face.

Yep. They were doing what she thought they were doing. Derron was in the process of peeling the shirt off John-Paul's muscular shoulders. John-Paul was working the younger man's belt loose.

Madison was as hip as the next person. She knew Derron was gay and was already quite fond of the man. She had other friends who were attracted to the same sex, and it had never bothered her before.

But John-Paul Noble? The idea was absurd. The man was a legend, a playboy of the highest order. A man-ho, they said. He had romanced women of all ages, all over the world, from Carlina Antoine and Hilary Hyatt to Caress Ellingsworth and, rumors had it, half the women in Hollywood. Had that been all they were… rumors?

Too stunned to move, Madison sat in her car, trying to make sense of what she had just seen.

She didn't even flinch when the passenger door opened and Brash slid into the car seat beside her.

"Maddy?" he asked, catching the look on her face.

"Huh?" She slowly pulled out of her stupor. "Wh—What are you doing here?"

"Looking for you. What on earth are you doing here? And don't give me that song and dance about star gazing again," he warned. "Your star attraction is dead, after all."

"No, I—I'm on a job."

"A job? You're not playing junior detective again, are you?"

"And what if I am?" she snapped. "I can take on whichever clients I see fit. But for your information, this is a legitimate job, sanctioned by an actual private detective. He hired me to gather information for him."

"So Archer took my advice and called you, did he?" To her surprise, Brash looked pleased.

"Huh? How did you—?"

"Who do you think gave him your number?"

"You?"

"Don't sound so shocked."

"But you hate it when I play junior detective!"

"Only when it puts you in danger," he told her. "Which I suspect is the real reason Trench Coat is stalking you. You were playing detective that night, weren't you, Maddy? What I want to know is who hired you. Why were you sitting in front of Caress' house that night?"

Still reluctant to give up her client, Madison remained insistent. "I told you, I was—"

"Star gazing." Brash said the words with her, his tone weary. He watched her face closely. "And tonight?"

"The blue house over there belongs to Donny Howell."

"And yet when I first drove up, you were looking directly into Caress' house."

"John-Paul Noble is still in town. I was star gazing." Her voice held a flat, dejected note.

"For some reason, I actually believe you," he murmured. "So why do you look so glum? Couldn't see anything?" he guessed.

"Oh, I saw plenty."

"Huh?"

Madison sighed. "Do you remember the show 'Hatchet for Hire?'"

"Sure do. It was my favorite TV show, back in the day. Still watch the re-runs sometimes."

"Along with every other girl in America, I had a huge crush on John-Paul Noble. I knew it was impossible—I knew it was just a foolish, impossible dream—but I used to imagine that I might meet him some day, and that he would be so enchanted with my sparkling personality and my wholesome good looks that he would put all those loose Hollywood vixens behind him and fall madly in love with me." She crossed both hands over her heart, her voice filled with just the right touch of melodrama.

"It could happen." His voice, deep and sexy, was much too believable.

She ignored his flirtations. "Some daydreams are so delicious," she told him, "that even when you know they are impossible, it's still fun to hold on to them, somewhere deep in your heart."

"Hey, now's your chance. You have the opportunity to meet him, up close and personal. And he'd be a fool not to choose you over any woman in Hollywood."

She shook her head. "Never going to happen."

"How do you know?" he challenged. "You're a fine-looking woman, Maddy."

"I'm not his type. But he's found someone who is." Without further explanation, she handed him the binoculars.

It took Brash a moment to focus the lens and locate his subject. He finally zoomed in on the kitchen window.

"I can't really see anything... He's leaning down. Has something in his... Good Lord, Maddy, why didn't you warn me!" Brash jumped back, dropping the binoculars in his haste. His eyes were round with shock. "That's—That's... He's with a *man*!"

Her voice was resigned. "Yes, I know."

"They're right there on the kitchen counter! In full view!"

"I know that, too."

Brash scrubbed his hands over his eyes, trying to scour the vision from his mind. He cursed beneath his breath. "You should have warned me!" he accused again.

"I'm still in shock."

"Who—? Do you know who that was?"

"Oh, yes. That's Derron Mullins."

"Little pip-squeak Derron Mullins, the surveyor's son?"

"The one and only."

"How messed up is that? John-Paul was Caress' ex-boyfriend. Now her best friend's son is his... what? Boy-toy? This is straight off one of those soap operas they starred in!"

"John-Paul has a reputation of being a real lady's man. I've never once heard about *this*!" She waved her hand in the vague direction of the house.

Brash shook his head, visibly trying to shake the memory free. The effort drew a moan and he put his hand to his head.

Belatedly, Madison noticed the white bandage peeking from beneath his cowboy hat. "How is your head? What did the doctors say?"

"Concussion. They said it was a good thing I had such a hard head, or they would have kept me overnight. Said I'll be good as new in a couple of days. And you?"

"Sore. Every muscle in my body is in pain. Climbing straight up the side of a brick building will do that to you. Another twenty or so hot baths and I'll probably live," she predicted.

His voice dropped with a serious note that sounded suspiciously like an accusation. "I've tried calling you all day, Maddy."

"Really?"

"Knock off the innocent act. You've been ignoring my calls. Why?" he asked her directly.

"I—I haven't really felt like talking much today. My tongue's still swollen from where I banged my head on the window. I bit it pwetty hawd." To prove her point, she stuck her tongue out at him.

"Funny, never heard it in your voice till just now," he observed dryly. "Come on, Maddy, tell me what's wrong. Why are you avoiding me? I had to come hunt you down. I'm not supposed to be driving yet, you know, but it's the only way I could get you to talk to me."

"Great, so if you pass out behind the wheel and have a wreck, you're going to blame it on me!"

"So drive me home," he suggested. "I'll send someone back for the car. We can go to my house and have a nice, long conversation." He reached out and took her hand. "I might even find a bottle of wine. How about it, Maddy? Drive me home?"

She pulled her hand free, averting her gaze. "Sorry, I'm working."

"Really? I passed Donny in the car with his buddies when I turned down the street."

"Oh? Well, good, I can go home now." She gathered up her equipment, still avoiding eye contact with him.

Brash made no move to get out of the car. "I get the distinct impression that you're mad at me, but for the life of me, I can't imagine why." He studied her for a long moment before making a few guesses. "Is it because I mentioned the kiss you owe me in front of my men? Did you not want people knowing about us?"

"Us? Us, Brash? What us?" She fairly screamed the words at him. *Real smooth, Maddy,* she chided herself. *Way to hide your true feelings.* So much for her plans to remain aloof and unaffected.

His voice remained steady and low, and so beautifully sincere it brought the prick of tears to her eyes. "The us that knows there's something here, Maddy, something real. The us that can't sleep at night, because we keep thinking about that kiss that never seems to happen. The us that's willing to wait for that kiss, because when it finally does happen, we want it to be perfect. We want it perfect because we both know that one kiss is going to change our lives." His voice was pure velvet. "That us, Maddy."

Madison bit her lip, willing herself not to melt, right then and there. Who knew the man was a poet?

"Talk to me," he begged.

"They took me to the clinic." Her voice was small and tight, spoken around the tears gathered in her throat.

His brow puckered in confusion. "And that's why you're mad at me? Because I went to the hospital and you didn't?"

"No, of course not! I insisted they take me there."

"I'm lost here, Maddy. What does that have to do with you and me?"

"The nurse on duty was Margaret Chatham."

He nodded in approval. "Good. I know she took excellent care of you. She's a good nurse."

"Why didn't you tell me, Brash?" she cried, turning an accusing glare upon him.

"Tell you what? That she worked there?"

"No, that you're still dating her!"

His answer was simple. "Because I'm not."

"You were eight weeks ago!"

"No, I wasn't."

"Don't even. Don't you even dare try to sit there and lie to me, Brash deCordova!"

"I'm not lying, Maddy. Margaret and I haven't dated in well over a year. Last I heard, she was seeing a cardiologist from Waco."

"I saw the bracelet, Brash, the one you gave her for Christmas! *This* Christmas, in case it slipped your mind."

"And?"

"And that proves you're lying! Why else would you give her a Christmas present, if you weren't still dating her? Especially something personal like a piece of jewelry!"

Brash rubbed his fingers over his aching forehead. His voice was resigned when he answered, "I didn't think the bracelet was all that personal, since it had some nurse's creed engraved on it and nothing to do with me. And I gave her a gift because I drew her name in our Sunday school class. We all exchanged presents at the church Christmas party, after the play."

Madison was crushed. She felt horrible about having accused him, yet again, of lying to her.

"Oh, Brash. I—I'm so sorry," she breathed in horror. "I'm so embarrassed. I—I—"

"—did it again," he said for her.

"I did, didn't I?"

"Why? Why, Maddy?" He turned to her with sorrow in his blue eyes. "Why do you have such a low opinion of me?"

"I don't!"

"This is a *high* opinion? First you accuse me of being a married man and trying to kiss you behind my wife's back. Now you think I'm lying about dating another woman. If this is a good opinion of a man, I'd hate to see the scoundrels that don't make the mark!"

"I'm sorry, Brash, truly I am. I just... she said... and I thought..." She gave up trying to explain herself. None of it made sense anyway, especially not this terrible pain in her heart.

Silence filled the car's cabin. Tension grew thick and uncomfortable between them. The strain was almost tangible.

"I'm going to make this easy for you, Maddy." When he spoke, Brash's voice was low and raw. "I'm telling you right now, you're the only woman I'm interested in. Yes, there have been women in my past, but right now, I'm only interested in my future. I want a future with you, Maddy. Don't ask me how, but I know we would be good together. And I know it could be forever." He stared at her long enough for her to see the beautiful sincerity in his words. Then he looked away again, and she heard the vulnerability in his voice. "To best honest, the thought scares me a little, but in a good way."

She found her voice, tiny and small. "It scares me, too."

"I don't do halfway, Maddy."

Even though his face was averted, she gave a tiny nod before tucking her head down.

"I know you've had a rough time of it recently. I know your marriage was falling apart, even before your husband died."

Her head jerked up. "How do you—"

"Doesn't matter how I know. All I need to know is that I'm not competing with a dead man's memory."

"You're not."

"Nick Vilardi?"

"What? No! Why would you—why would you even think that?"

"I saw the way you looked at each other." He practically growled. "I felt it in the air. There was something between you."

"Not—Not… this." Nothing had ever been like this, not even with Gray.

"Then I'll wait. I'll give you the time you need to pull your life back together. But there's one thing you need to know, Maddy."

"Wh—What's that?"

"As far as I'm concerned, if a relationship doesn't have trust and respect, then it's no relationship at all. The two go hand in hand, and it's obvious you don't trust me."

"It's not you, Brash," she insisted. On a whisper, she admitted, "It's my own stupidity."

"Doesn't matter. I'll compromise on a lot of things, but not this. Either you trust me, or you don't. You believe in me and respect me, or you don't. Simple as that."

She had never heard such emotion in his voice. Such raw vulnerability. She was humbled, knowing she inspired that level of feeling in the man, but his next words almost broke her heart.

"I can't be with someone who thinks so poorly of me," he continued. "It doesn't matter that it stems from your own insecurities. It reflects on me, on my integrity."

"Brash."

He ignored her whispered cry. "Get your life together, Maddy, and decide how you feel about me. Don't come to me unless you know, without a doubt, that you trust me and respect me."

"I do, Brash. I respect you more than any man I know." If she doubted it before now, his heartfelt speech proved he was a man of integrity, a man worthy of love and respect.

"Like I said, I don't do halfway. If I give you my heart, I give you everything I have, including that same level of respect, that same level of unconditional trust. I don't give those things lightly, Madison."

"Neither—Neither do I."

He faced her then and touched her bruised cheek with a tender caress. "Go home, Maddy. Get your life together. Your head together."

She dropped her eyes. "I'm a mess, Brash," she confessed lowly. "You don't know the half of it."

"When you trust me enough, you can tell me about it."

"I—I don't know..." Some things were too painful to share, even with him.

"Do you believe me when I say you're the only woman I'm interested in?"

"I—I want to..."

She felt him stiffen at the uncertainty that lingered in her words. She suspected the sudden chill in the air deflected from him.

When he put his hand on the door, she cautioned, "You don't need to be driving, remember?"

His voice raked across the ice in his heart, coming out frosty and cold. "You'll never really trust me, Maddy. You still think poorly of me. Surely a car crash couldn't hurt much worse than that."

25

"Mom, we've got to talk." Blake wore a serious expression upon his face as he plunked down into the chair across from his mother the next afternoon.

Madison was at the dining room table, working on her appointment book. She kept thinking if she looked through the calendar enough times, new jobs would miraculously appear within the pages. So far, she wasn't having much luck.

Assuming she even still had the job with *Boundaries* like Genny claimed, it was scheduled to run out in another week; when she was done with surveillance for Murray Archer, she would be down to just the weekly drugstore runs for Miss Sybille.

Shoving aside the dismal book, Madison eyed her children warily. Bethani fell into the other chair and hunched her shoulders into a defensive stance. "Uh-oh. When the two of you gang up on me like this, I know it's not going to be good."

"You know we love Granny Bert," Blake began.

"And she's pretty cool and all, especially for someone her age," his sister was quick to say.

"But something has got to change. Do you know what she did today?"

"I, uh, I'm afraid to even ask."

"To *begin with*"—he made it plain there would be more—"she hung my underwear outside on the clothesline. I didn't even know we had a clothesline, until I saw my whitey-tighties flying high out there on a breeze."

"And my bra, Mom! She hung my *bra* out there, for all the world to see!" Bethani chimed in as she hid her face with her hands.

"Okay, first of all," Madison defended her grandmother, "the backyard is relatively secluded. You can barely even see the yard, what with all the huge old trees and rose bushes and that big motor home parked in the way. And second of all, how many times have I asked you both to do your own laundry? Granny Bert isn't your personal maid."

"There's more," Blake assured his mother. "You know that perfectly delicious stew you fixed for supper last night?"

"The one you ate three bowls of? I vaguely recall seeing it before you slurped it down. I even got a bite or two of it."

Her sarcasm was lost on her son. Food, after all, was a serious subject to a fifteen-year-old boy. "I made sure I left enough for a mid-morning snack. I even hid it in the back of the refrigerator, behind the prune juice. Do you know what she did, Mom? She threw it in the blender and made it into one of her god-awful shakes!"

He looked so stricken, Madison did her best not to laugh. "That's where you made your first mistake," she advised. "Prune juice is the secret ingredient in most of her shakes.

That, or castor oil." No longer so amused, Madison shivered at the memory of one or more of those shakes.

"It gets worse, Mom," Bethani advised. "Tell her, Blake. Tell her what we saw today."

The blond-haired youth put his hand across his chest in a solemn manner. In a voice overly grave, he kept his facial features drawn blank. "Something no teenager should ever be forced to witness."

Madison rolled her eyes. "You're not trying out for the drama club here, Blake. Just tell me what happened."

"It's Saturday. What does Granny Bert like to do on Saturday mornings?"

"She usually goes to her water aerobics class, but I heard the pool was still out of order at the nursing home."

"Right. But since they hated to miss the class two weeks in a row, she and her friends decided to do their aerobics here," Bethani explained.

"So? I doubt they made too much of a ruckus, given all of them are seventy-five or older."

"They came in their exercise clothes, Mom. Their *swimming suits*!"

There was such horror in his voice, such shock in his eyes, that this time she couldn't hold the laughter in. Madison burst out laughing, even as both teens looked at her as if she were crazy.

"The things we saw, Mom," Blake continued, shoulders shuddering. "I may be scarred for life."

"I didn't know it was possible to have so many wrinkles." Bethani's voice was a blend of horror and awe.

"And believe me, Mrs. Shanks should not be wearing a two-piece swimsuit!"

The more her children described the horrors they witnessed, the harder Madison laughed. Just the thought of seeing Wanda Shanks doing leg lifts in a bikini made her stomach curl, and she had no doubt Miss Sybille's wrinkles all but swallowed her bathing suit up whole. But the twins were so comical in their rendition of the geriatric exercise class and what was considered suitable attire for such an occasion. She laughed until she cried, until her sides screamed in protest. Given the week's events, the pain didn't take long to set in. And given last night's heart-crushing conversation with Brash, she deserved the pain as much as she needed the laughter.

"Okay, okay, no more!" she finally insisted. "It—It hurts too much to laugh!"

"Then stop laughing!" Blake grumbled.

"We're serious, Mom. We love Granny Bert, but it's time we find a place of our own."

Bethani's words sobered her right up. Wiping away a lingering tear, Madison peered at the twins to make certain they were serious. Both their young faces were set with determination.

"That's a big step, you know," she said. "Not only financially—"

"I'll get a job, Mom, so I can help out."

"That's sweet of you, Blake, and I appreciate it. And I may have to take you up on it. But more than the financial implications, if we buy a house, we're making a commitment to stay here in Juliet. I know we've had this conversation before, but once we buy a house, there's no backing out."

"What about renting?" Bethani offered.

"Does that mean you're having second thoughts about staying here and graduating from The Sisters High School?" Madison asked her daughter softly.

Until recently, Bethani had been dead set on returning to their old neighborhood in the Dallas suburbs. A new best friend and the opportunity to try out for cheerleader had done wonders for her opinion of the small community, but there were times when the teenager still got homesick. Madison understood all too well; there were times when she missed their old life, as well.

The girl shrugged. "Not really. I mean, it's pretty cool here. I think I can adjust."

It was more of an endorsement than Madison expected. Turning her gaze to her son, she asked, "Blake?"

"You know how I feel. I'm in."

"Then I guess I should tell you that Granny Bert offered to sell me the Big House. I'm actually considering it, in fact, if I can find a way to afford it." She ventured a nervous glance into their faces. "How would you feel about living there?"

"It's a little creepy, but as long as there's no clothesline and no granny aerobics, I'm cool with it," Blake proclaimed.

"I haven't seen the inside," said Bethani, "but the outside looks pretty neat. As long as we paint it. Will I have my own bedroom?"

"You can have two bedrooms, if you like. The place is huge."

"Can we go check it out?"

"Yes, but I need to caution you. It needs some work. Okay, it needs a lot of work, but that's where *Home Again* comes in."

"Can we go over there now?" Bethani asked.

"Well, I guess. Granny's gone this evening, so it's just us."

"I call shotgun!"

Madison laughed at her son. She only hoped she was still able to laugh, after hearing the twin's assessment of the Big House.

Granny Bert brought up the subject of the house the next day after church, asking if Madison had heard from Nick Vilardi yet. Madison allowed her grandmother a good five minutes to relive the glory of 'hoodwinking that Hollywood hunk' into doing her bidding before she answered.

"No, I haven't heard from him yet. I wonder if that's a good sign or a bad one?"

"Be patient, child. It will take him awhile to get all his ducks in a row. Besides, you need the extra time to make sure the house is in your name. Apparently, they're sticklers about remodeling the house only for the family that will live there. I guess it's a safeguard to keep people from profiting from the re-model by selling it the minute the paint has dried."

"I haven't agreed to buy the house yet," Madison reminded her grandmother. "At the risk of having the words engraved into my voice box, I must repeat: I have no money."

"I have the contract all drawn up, you know. All it needs is your signature. Take a look." Granny Bert rummaged around on the table by her chair until she came up with a folder. She barely gave Madison time to look it over. "So? What do you think? Your cousin Larry can be here in thirty minutes to make it official."

"Actually, the twins and I talked about it and I have their blessing to buy the house. But…"

"But?"

"Granny, I don't mean to sound ungrateful. I know it's probably below market value, but there is absolutely no way I can afford a five-hundred-thousand-dollar house." She had known all along that owning the Big House was a pipe dream but seeing the cold reality in black and white stung more than she expected.

"You might need glasses, Maddy girl. Look at those numbers again."

Flipping back through the papers in her hand, Madison concentrated on the zeroes. "Granny!" she gasped. "Have you gone senile on me?"

"No need to get nasty. I know it's a lot, considering the age and condition of the house. We don't even know yet if the foundation is stable or if the roof needs repair."

"But—"

"I know what you're going to say," the old woman interrupted her. "The plumbing is old and rusty, and the electrical wiring is a powder keg just waiting on a fuse. Someone drew all over the walls and the furniture is full of dust mites and spider webs. I know it's a lot to ask for a pile of wood and stone a hundred years old, but I have my eye on adding a retractable awning to the motor home. I need that five thousand dollars I'm asking for the house."

"Granny, you cannot sell me that house for five thousand dollars!" Madison's voice took on a shrill note.

"Now don't try to talk me down," her grandmother warned. "I'm asking a firm five thousand."

"Then you have gone soft in the head. That house is worth five *hundred* thousand, and you know it. You're practically giving it to me!" Oddly enough, her words rung with accusation.

"I have seven grandchildren. I can't be playing favorites, giving a house to one of you and not the others. No, you'll have to buy the house, fair and square. I know it may mean making a few more sacrifices, but anything worth having is worth working for. There's nothing more satisfying than knowing you've spent your hard-earned money on a worthy investment."

Tears welled in Madison's hazel eyes. No matter what she called it and no matter what lesson she was trying to teach, Granny Bert was practically giving her the house.

More than a house, she was giving her a future. Unable to hold the emotions inside any longer, Madison burst out in full-fledge tears.

Pretending not to be moved by Madison's gratitude, Granny Bert huffed, "You really do drive a hard bargain, don't you? I know the house has a lot wrong with it. The kitchen will walk your legs off, the appliances are ancient, and there's not enough bathrooms. Still, it's better than living here with me, all cramped up. The kids need their space. A teenage girl shouldn't have to share her bedroom with her mother, and a teen boy should be able to play his music as loud as he wants. As much as I've enjoyed having you here with me, I can't be selfish. It's time you had a home of your own, and a drafty old mansion seems as good a place as any. So, I'll consider owner financing. How does a hundred dollars a month sound?"

"It—It sounds like I have the best gr-grandmother in the world!" Madison sniffled out the words.

By evening, the papers were signed, and Madison was once again a homeowner.

But when she settled into bed that night, the reality of the situation sank in. Houses came with utility bills. Insurance payments. Taxes. She belatedly wondered what upkeep on a hundred-year-old home must be like.

What on earth had she been thinking?

26

It was difficult to face Derron on Monday morning, knowing what she did about his personal life.

Not that she begrudged the man a little happiness; with a mother like Dragon Lady, he deserved all the love and affection he could get. And if her newly made friend could somehow live out her own foolish schoolgirl fantasies, more power to him.

Still, the images were hard to get out of her mind.

"Word of warning," Derron said, breezing past her in the break-room. "Dragon Lady is on the warpath."

"Great," Madison moaned, taking a swig of hot coffee and immediately wincing. Her tongue was still sensitive. "At least she cleaned up my office."

"Correction. Yours truly took care of that."

"Thank you, Derron," she said with sincerity. "I appreciate it."

"It was the least I could do. You had a terrible ordeal. Are you sure you're up to coming back to work so soon?"

"Can't sit around the house forever."

"Is it true that hunk of a police chief saved you from a burning house? I drove by the Big House, but I didn't see any smoke damage."

"No, that is *not* true!" Madison laughed, shaking her head at the way rumors spread in this town.

"Too bad. I'm sure you wouldn't mind a little mouth to mouth with the chief." He waggled his brows. "I know I wouldn't!"

Madison squeezed her eyes shut, trying to block the image that sprang to mind. *Do not go there. Do not remember that you saw him kissing John-Paul Noble.*

"You okay, dollface?"

"Just a little dizzy still," she glibly lied.

"Again, be warned. I saw the old bat loading the van with lots of heavy equipment. Don't be surprised when she mistakes you for a packhorse."

"Thanks for the heads up."

Forty minutes later, Darla Mullins piled Madison's arms with yet another expandable tripod. When a camera slid from her sagging shoulder, the surveyor slapped it back into place against Madison's back. "There. Just one more transit level and we'll be set."

"You—You really expect me to carry all this?" Madison cried, dipping just in time to catch the tribrach that slid from the haphazard pile she tried to balance.

"Yes and be careful with that. Do you have any idea how much that piece costs? It has an optimal plummet, which makes it more expensive."

"I don't even know what this thing is," Madison admitted.

"It allows for precise plumbing of surveying instruments," she said impatiently. "Now, follow me."

"What are you carrying?"

"Field notes, of course. And flagging tape."

Beneath her breath, Madison muttered darkly, "Don't strain yourself." Of course, she carried the two lightest items.

"Did you say something back there?" Darla asked, turning to give her a condescending glare.

Madison wouldn't give her the satisfaction of knowing she struggled. "Lead on," she said with a falsely bright smile. She shifted the load upon her back and set off after the Dragon Lady.

Darla took the most difficult path. She led the way straight through a narrow gap in a row of brush and undergrowth, instead of going fifteen feet out of the way to avoid the brush altogether. She took them up a hill without stopping, knowing it had to be difficult for Madison when carrying such a load, particularly with a sprained ankle. She marched relentlessly along, even when Madison begged her to stop so she could regroup.

The stubborn little tribrach finally slipped from Madison's hold, bouncing as it hit the ground. Because it was a three-sided object, Madison was fascinated by how easily it rolled. She chased after it, stumbling as she did so. One leg of a tripod dipped low enough to snag a pile of dirt. It was the catalyst that toppled her entire load. Both tripods clattered to the ground, followed by a set of stakes and the surveying rods. The Abney level was next, then the brush ax.

"Darla! Wait!" she cried. She looked around, but the other woman was nowhere to be seen. She had disappeared beyond the next row of trees, leaving Madison alone in the small clearing.

"Since I'm already stopped, I might as well rest for a minute. She'll turn around to boss me sooner or later and discover her packhorse is missing," Madison grumbled aloud. She swung the camera and huge coil of rope off her shoulders but left on the backpack. With only one item to weigh her down, she could almost stand up straight.

Despite it being mid-February with temperatures hovering in the low forties, Madison had already worked up a sweat. She swiped her hand across her forehead and allowed the cool air to blow over her. With her clothes damp with perspiration, it didn't take long to become chilled.

Madison was gathering up her collection, trying to assemble the items with a modicum of care and precision, when she heard the rumble of a motor. Good. Maybe Darla had gone back for the van. There was no reason they couldn't have driven closer. The ground wasn't that soggy, nor the terrain that heavily wooded.

She tried to stack the tripods with their widest points on opposite ends to steady her load, but they kept tangling with the stakes. In frustration, she tugged on one rod and the entire bundle came tumbling down.

"This is like wrestling an octopus!" she wailed. She stood to rest her back, realizing the sound of the vehicle was coming much closer. It gunned its motor, somewhere just beyond that last row of bushes.

Without warning, the bushes parted and an oversized dirt bike leapt from the tangled growth. It sailed through the air with a projected landing of exactly where she stood. Maddy flew out of the way at the last second, feeling the heat of the tailpipe brush against her leg as she flung herself sideways.

She landed hard on her shoulder. Dazed by the impact, she shook her head to clear it. She managed a few ragged breaths before she heard the bike circle and charge again.

Scrambling to her feet, Maddy began to run. Her choices were limited in the small clearing. She couldn't reach the trees before the bike reached her, but she could run in a circle. She yelled for Darla as she took off in a crazy zigzag pattern that left her dizzy and spent.

As the bike kept an uncanny pace with her moves, Madison took in as many details as possible. For a dirt bike, it was huge and heavy. The motor looked particularly menacing, as if it had been beefed-up aftermarket. Naturally the paint color was blood red, just like the helmet the rider wore. The face mask hid his identity, but there was no mistaking the familiar khaki trench coat that he wore.

By now nearing exhaustion, Madison's movements grew clumsy. The air was thick with dust and engine smoke, clouding her vision. She made a miscalculation and stumbled on top of her pile of equipment, falling to her knees. The bike bore down on her, inches away from her face.

She was completely at his mercy. He could take her down right now.

However, slamming into Madison also meant slamming into the pile of equipment, which consisted of jagged edges and assorted metal. At the last possible second, the driver hurled upward into a jump, avoiding the potentially damaging heap by sailing over Madison.

With the momentum of the jump, the bike headed toward the nearby clump of trees. Watching as the driver gunned the motor midair, Madison braced herself for the crash she knew was coming. It would be brutal, given the size of the tree in its path and the speed at which the bike soared through the air.

Madison ducked her head, shying away from the impending crash.

From the corner of her eye, she saw a flash of chrome as Trench Coat did some sort of last-minute maneuver. He twisted his body to one side, just enough to change the bike's trajectory. It hit the tree line with a crash, but it somehow missed the biggest tree. She heard limbs rip and tear as the bike sailed among them and exited on the other side. Madison heard the motor gun once more, then roar off into the distance.

She was still staring into the bushes, trembling in shock, when Darla burst into the opening. She was clearly out of breath and flushed, but her eyes zeroed in on her equipment without missing a beat.

"What on earth happened?" she demanded. "What was that motor? Why are you on the ground? And why is my equipment scattered all over the place?"

Madison tried to explain. She started three times, only to be interrupted by Darla's rantings. The surveyor was more concerned about her equipment than any damage Madison might have suffered.

"What is it with you?" Darla screamed at her. "You invite trouble! I've never had a moment's trouble until you showed up, and now suddenly everything is ruined! Everything you touch is in shambles! You've messed up everything!"

Madison made a snap decision. "You know what, Darla? I quit."

The woman was outraged. Her face turned an unattractive shade of mottled red. Her round eyes bulged and her hands clenched into fists. "You can't quit!" she bellowed. "Who's going to carry all this back to the van?"

"I guess you are, because I'm walking back." Madison was proud of herself for sounding so calm, when inside she was quaking. She turned to walk away and felt the first strike upon her back. She whirled around, eyes flashing. "Did you just *throw* that at me?"

"Yes, just like I'm throwing *this*!" Darla flung a stake directly at her. If her aim had been true, the heavy rod would have hurt. As it was, it fell short of its mark and into the dirt at Madison's feet.

Darla Mullins, however, wasn't a quitter. She tried again. And again and again, until she finally struck Madison on the knee. For the most part, Madison allowed her to play out her anger. The efforts tired her, causing the overweight woman to huff and puff and molder a darker shade of red. When she paused to catch her breath, Madison offered the ultimate insult. She turned her back to her and began to walk away.

"Don't you *dare* walk away from me, you imbecile!"

With renewed ire, the woman hurled everything she could find toward her retreating assistant. It wasn't until she made a lucky shot and hit Madison upside the head with the tribrach that Madison came to a halt.

At almost two pounds, the instrument did its damage. Maddy almost went to her knees, but sheer determination kept her upright. Hand to the back of her head, she turned to stare at the crazed woman in shock.

"Are you insane? You could have killed me!"

"You'll wish you were dead, when I get through with you," she threatened. "I'll sue your skinny ass for breach of contract! You can't just walk out on me like that."

"Watch me."

It was a grand exit, full of dignity and superiority. In actuality, she made it no further than the other side of the trees, but Darla didn't have to know that. The minute she was on the other side of the tree line, Madison fell to her knees and sucked in a deep breath. Her head felt like it was splitting in two. Judging from the blood on her fingers, she decided that might not be too far from the truth.

From her side of the clearing, Darla Mullins screamed obscenities that would put any sailor to shame.

"I'm leaving," she warned. "You don't know the way out. You'll be stuck out here in the woods, with that maniac on the loose… This is your last chance. If you don't come back, this instant, I'm leaving you out here to fend for yourself."

Making her voice sound as if it came from a distance, Madison cupped her hands over her mouth and threw an answer into the wind. "Thanks, but I've already called for a taxi," she yelled. Genny, bless her heart, was already on her way, thanks to a quick text.

She listened as Darla cursed some more and huffed and puffed her way out of the clearing. She stomped noisily away, her heavy footsteps making quite the racket as she retreated down a different trail.

It wasn't until all was silent that Madison began to worry. What if the maniac really did come back? What if Trench Coat was still out there, waiting to run her down? Suddenly not so brave, Madison struggled to her feet. She kept to the tree line, slowly making her way back in the direction she had come. She stopped occasionally, straining to listen for sounds of the dirt bike. She caught enough faint snippets from Darla's angry tirade to know she headed in the right direction.

The longer she walked, the more her ankle throbbed. Her head ached. It was getting harder to focus and she felt light-headed. She was thinking of sitting down and resting when she heard the vague sound of a door slamming. She assumed that was Darla peeling out of the graveled gateway, but there was a sudden rushing noise inside her head. Why was everything so dark? It was still morning… wasn't it?

Madison was no longer sure of anything, not even of where she was. All she knew was that she needed to rest.

She was still there, slumped at the base of a tree, when Genesis and Cutter found her five minutes later.

27

"Do you want to press charges on Darla Mullins?"

"What? No. No, I just want to forget this whole ordeal, including the fact I ever knew her."

Madison was propped up on the couch in the living room, nursing a major headache and a hot cup of coffee. After a fitful night spent in the hospital, she was still every bit as uncomfortable, but at least she was home. Brash sat nearby in a chair, jotting down notes in his ever-faithful pocket-sized spiral.

"Did you find the dirt bike?" she asked.

"Yep. It was registered to Luis Gonzales. He reported it stolen from his garage about a half a mile from the survey site. Said it was taken sometime over the weekend."

"Did you find the coat?"

"Cutter found it stuffed into the bushes, not far from the bike."

"Could you see blood stains on it?"

"Actually, it appeared to be a brand-new coat. Still, I've sent it to the lab in Austin for analysis."

"I guess they can collect DNA and loose fibers and trace evidence to determine Trench Coat's identity."

Brash rolled his eyes. "You watch too many of those television shows, Maddy. It works great on TV, and in record time, too. But it doesn't quite work the same in real life. And there can only be a match if Trench Coat's DNA is already in the system. If he's a law-abiding citizen, chances are we won't catch him that way."

"How can he be a law-abiding citizen and a cold-blooded killer at the same time?"

Brash shrugged. "This was a crime of passion. Who knows what made him crack? Up until he killed Caress, he may have been a pillar of society."

"Her death may not have been premeditated, but he's put quite a bit of thought in trying to kill me."

"Unfortunately, I agree. That's why I want to put you under police protection."

"Do you—Do you really think that's necessary?" she gasped.

"I don't want to take any chances, Maddy. He's tried several times now. He seems to be hell-bent on keeping you silent."

"Maybe we should make some sort of public announcement, admitting that I'm really no eyewitness at all. I didn't see the actual murder take place. And I have no idea what the killer even looked like."

"I'm willing to give it a try," Brash agreed. Then he added, "In addition to protection."

"Brash, you have a police force of exactly three people. You don't have the resources to offer me protection."

"It will take some ingenuity, and I'll have to call in reserve officers and maybe even get some help from the fire department, but I'm not taking any chances, Madison. This is your life we're talking about." The light in his blue eyes warmed her heart, even as the implications behind his words chilled her soul. Someone wanted her dead, and they showed no signs of giving up until they had succeeded or been caught.

"Thank you, Brash. Thank you for wanting to protect me. And thank you for not letting our… differences come between us."

Instead of taking her words as a compliment, he took offense. He jumped from the chair and paced the room.

"Jesus, Madison! Just when I think your opinion of me can't sink any lower, you prove me wrong! What kind of lawman—what kind of *person*?—do you think I am? Do you honestly think I would put our personal problems before your safety? You must think I am a total and complete jerk!"

"No, no, that's not at all what I meant," she tried to assure him. "Please, Brash, sit down and listen to me. Please."

He remained standing. A pained expression filled his eyes. "I have to go back to the station and make a few calls. I asked Cutter to drop by and keep an eye on you while I'm gone."

"Brash, please," she begged.

There was a knock on the door, immediately followed by Genny's voice. "Maddy? Cutter gave me a ride, so I can keep you company this evening. I brought hamburgers." She held up a bag and smiled at Brash. "There's one for you, too, Brash."

"I'll take mine to go. I was just leaving anyway."

Working out the logistics of police protection proved to be harder than Brash expected. One of his reserve officers had the flu; another had thrown his back out after a particularly amorous Valentine's Day. Given the man was over seventy, Brash begged off on hearing more details. By the time he went through the meager resources of The Sisters and half of River County, he realized the job would fall upon him.

But if it meant keeping Maddy safe, he would give up all his sleep and half his meals to see it done. He ignored the little voice inside that said he would give up much more than that. He suspected— no, he *knew*—that if it came down to her life or his, he would take the bullet. He was falling for her and falling hard, but he was too stubborn—and too hurt—to admit it just yet, even to himself. He kept reminding himself that any woman who thought him capable of cheating didn't deserve his love and devotion.

The trouble was, his heart refused to listen to logic.

The next few days were quiet.

Ignoring his doctor's suggestion that he take a couple more days off from work, Brash worked his schedule around Maddy's, which suddenly had gaping holes in it.

Quitting at *Boundaries* meant she was out of a job; even her surveillance on Donny Howell was over. As it turned out, when Brash passed him in the car with his friends that night, they were on the way to the emergency room. The simple dart game re-injured his back and was enough to convince the insurance company he had a legitimate claim. Her Friday afternoon runs for Miss Sybille notwithstanding, Maddy was temporarily without work.

Brash came up with a brilliant solution. He hired *In a Pinch* to do some temporary work at the police station.

He would never confess as much to Maddy, but her salary came directly from his own pocket. There was no room in the department's budget to pay someone to help with filing and organizing records, especially not with the ever-efficient Vina on top of both issues. The older black woman was the best department clerk he had ever known, but with only a minimum of begging, he convinced her to take a couple of days off to visit her newest grandbaby in Fort Worth. No one could ever fill her shoes, but Madison could at least answer the phones and do a bit of filing. And the way he saw it, it solved two issues at once: it allowed him to keep Maddy safe without pulling an officer from duty, and it gave her an income. Actually, it solved three issues, for if anyone deserved a few days off, it was Vina Jones.

With her days spent at police headquarters and her evenings surrounded by either her family, Genny, Brash, or often Cutter, Madison didn't hear from Trench Coat. There were no threatening phone calls, no suspicious vehicles circling her house or running her off the road, no dirt bikes gunning for her, nothing out of the ordinary happening around her.

The only surprise of the week was a phone call she received on Thursday.

"Madison?"

She recognized the voice immediately, even though she didn't recognize the number on her cell phone. "Derron?"

"How are you, girlfriend? I've been worried sick about you!"

Madison wondered what his mother had told him about Monday's events. She doubted Darla had mentioned her own tirade or the objects she hurled. Most likely, she had found a way to blame it all on Madison.

Madison gave an indirect answer. "Why would you be worried?"

"Mother said you came down with a severe migraine while out on the site. It must be bad, if you've been out all week! I heard you had to go to the hospital in Bryan."

"My head was definitely hurting," she agreed somewhat wryly. "But it's better now."

"Will you be coming back?"

"I don't think so. I was only scheduled through tomorrow, anyway. Won't Natalie be back on Monday?"

She heard the pout in his voice. "Yes, but she's not nearly as much fun as you. I miss you, girlfriend."

Madison laughed, surprised to know she actually missed him, as well. Derron alone had made her days at *Boundaries* bearable. "Maybe we could meet some day for lunch," she suggested.

"If Dragon Lady will unchain me from this desk." She could all but hear him rolling his eyes. "She's been breathing fire ever since she came back without you. If I didn't know better, I'd swear she missed you."

"Good thing you know better."

"You left some stuff here, dollface. Did you want to stop by and pick it up?"

The thought of returning to the office, even for a moment or two, turned her stomach. The thought of seeing Darla Mullins again made her head hurt. Putting a protective hand to the lump still tender on her skull, she did a mental inventory of the items she had left behind. Some of it she could do without, but there were a few things she hated to forfeit. "I could swing by on Monday."

"Perfect. Dragon Lady will be out that afternoon, so you might want to make it then," he suggested.

"Thanks, Derron."

"I really enjoyed working with you, dollface. Maybe you can fill in again sometime."

"I doubt that, but I enjoyed working with you, too. See you Monday. And thanks for calling."

"Sure thing, sweetie. Tootles."

"Yeah, tootles," she repeated with a smile.

Brash walked up in time to hear her salutation. "Tootles?" he questioned, eyebrows high.

By way of explanation, she merely laughed. "Derron."

"Ah, yes. So how is he? I hear his friend flew back to Paris without him."

With a groan, Madison pressed her fingers to her eyelids. "Thanks a lot," she grumbled. "With everything that has happened since, I almost forgot about that little scene we witnessed. Now that you've reminded me, I won't be able to get it out of my head!"

"Not sure how you could have forgotten it to begin with. I see it every night when I close my eyes." A shudder worked through his wide shoulders.

Madison laughed at his expression, encouraged to see him joking with her again. She worried she had done irrevocable damage to their relationship. The last thing she wanted to do was to hurt him, but her emotional state was still so fragile after her disintegrating marriage to Gray. She needed time to heal, time to learn to trust again. She only prayed that in the meantime, she didn't lose him, not when she already cared so much about him.

"So just for putting the image back in my head," she informed him smartly, keeping up the light banter, "you now owe me lunch. Genny has a new recipe on the daily special."

"Deal." His eyes twinkled. "But only because I'm starved, and because anything Genny makes is delicious."

The rest of the week went smoothly, with still no threats from Trench Coat.

Granny Bert left for her annual camping trip to Galveston with a group of friends.

Cheerleader tryouts were held Thursday afternoon. Bethani and Megan huddled on pins and needles, waiting for the results. When word came that both girls made the varsity squad, Madison was certain their victory cheer could be heard all over town. And even though she was thrilled for her daughter, new worries besieged her. Come Monday, she was out of a job again. Where would she come up with the money for cheerleader camp?

To celebrate, Shannon and Matthew Aikman hosted an impromptu barbecue on Friday night. They had mentioned getting together before now, but this gave the perfect excuse. Eager to throw Maddy and Brash together at every opportunity, the hosting couple was thrilled when the two arrived together. Maddy allowed them their moment of elation; she preferred no one knew the real reason Brash shadowed her that week. Let the rumor mill make of it what they may.

They would anyway.

28

She thought the late-night phone calls from George Gail were over. With the case surrounding Caress' death growing colder by the day, and with no one even considering her as a suspect, George Gail's obsession with being arrested seemed to lessen. Madison thought the after-hour interruptions were behind her, until her phone rang just before midnight, late Sunday night.

"Not again," she mumbled groggily.

"Madison! Something's wrong!"

It seemed something was always wrong where George Gail was concerned. By now, Madison knew to take her dramatics with a grain of salt. "What is it this time?"

"I'm not sure, but I need your help. Someone called Curtis out to the sale barn about an hour ago. Now I got this really strange text from him. It says 'Need hemp. Hurry.'"

The only things Madison knew about hemp were that it could be used to make rope and it came from the same plant as marijuana. Since Curtis Burton hardly seemed like the type to smoke pot, she made a guess. "He needs a rope?"

"I think he meant 'help.' He's not very good at typing. Fingers are too long."

"Have you called him back?"

"Goes straight to voicemail. I'm worried, Madison. Would you go with me to the sale barn?" When Madison took too long to answer, the other woman's voice took on a wheedling whine. "Please? I'm really scared, Madison. What if someone sets another fire while he's up there?"

"Maybe you should call Brash."

"Didn't you hear? There was a bad wreck out on the highway, Juliet side. Half of both towns and all the emergency crews are out there. From what I hear, it's a real mess."

"How do you always know these things?"

Halfway into the rundown of who was passing by and who called whom with the news, Madison interrupted her, "Never mind. Give me ten minutes and I'll be over."

"Thank you, Madison, you're a real lifesaver!"

"It's going to cost you."

"I only have three hundred in cash. Is that enough?" the other woman readily offered.

Madison was going to demand a promise of no more late-night calls, but cash was good. "Just be ready when I get there," she grumbled.

Brash, of course, would have a fit. He had finally agreed to drop her 'protection,' but he warned her of being extra vigilant. Madison knew rushing out into the night wouldn't meet with his approval. But, she reminded herself, he was on a call and would never know. With any luck, they would locate Curtis safe and sound and be back home within the hour.

At 12:13, Madison pulled up in front of the Burton's ranch-style home. George Gail slipped inside the moment the car rolled to a stop.

At the sight of her, Madison was taken aback. "What—What are you wearing?"

"Sweatpants and pig slippers. Don't worry, I brought boots to change into." She held up a pair of rubber boots splattered with bright flowers and peace symbols.

"Not the shoes. The coat."

She glanced down at her husband's coat she was wearing. "It's cold," she defended herself.

Trying her best to ignore the trickle of worry that pricked her skull, Madison eyed the khaki coat once more before putting the car into reverse. She couldn't freak out every time she saw a trench coat. She was being ridiculous to even consider the thoughts running through her head. George Gail was completely harmless. … Wasn't she?

Of course she was. Madison brushed away her own foolishness as she watched her passenger slip off her pink piggy slippers and stuff her feet unceremoniously inside the rubber boots.

Slightly out of breath from the exertion, George Gail leaned back with a loud, "Whew! All better now. Especially if we have to crawl around in the pens."

"Why would we crawl around in the pens?"

"I have no idea where he was calling from or what was wrong. For all I know, he's being trampled by a pen of angry bulls!"

Unsure if she were serious or merely melodramatic, Madison eyed her with skepticism. "Has that ever happened before?"

"Your Uncle Joe Bert was gorged in the thigh once by a long-horned cow. Hit a major vessel. Blood squirted all the way up to the auctioneer's box!" She used her hands to mimic the spray. "Good thing Cutter Montgomery was there selling cattle that day. He applied pressure until the ambulance could get there. You should have seen the hole. I swear, it was *this big*."

As she used her hands to demonstrate and went into some of the more gory details of the event, Madison found herself questioning her earlier assumption that George Gail was harmless. Anyone who found that much pleasure in describing a bloody wound wasn't right in the head.

"By the way, here's your money." George Gail dipped a hand into the edge of her bra and pulled out a wad of bills.

Struggling not to wrinkle her nose, Madison made no move to take the money from her hand. "You can put that in the cup holder," she suggested.

"I don't see his truck out front. Pull around to the back."

"Back there? It's pitch black. Surely he's not back there."

"Turn here beside this building. It will wind you back around."

A more nervous-type person would question the directions. A doubter would wonder why George Gail told her to drive down a dark path to the very back of the complex. A worrier would fret over the stillness of the night, the stark darkness around them.

Madison discovered she was all three of these things.

"Are you sure about this, George Gail?" she asked. Her eyes darted to the trench coat again.

"See, there's his truck!"

George Gail jumped from the car as soon as it stopped, calling her husband's name. The only answer was from the lowing cattle in a nearby pen.

"Where could he be?" she worried.

"Are there any lights you can turn on?" Madison suggested.

"Good idea! I'll go turn them on. You stay here and look for him."

Before Madison could protest, George Gail's phone buzzed with a text message. She looked down at the screen and read it aloud. "'***Put back. Hemp.***' I think he means he's out back and needs help."

"How did you…?"

George Gail shrugged. "I've been deciphering love letters and messages for forty years. His handwriting is even worse. Here, come this way."

The stockyards of the sale barn were an organized maze of pens and alleys, all tucked beneath a sprawling metal roof. For a woman of size, George Gail moved with confidence as she unlatched a gate and squeezed through its narrow frame, motioning for Madison to follow.

"Where are we going?"

"Up those stairs to the catwalk. From there, we can see out over the pens."

The beam from her car lights shone onto the rickety steps as she reluctantly followed her leader.

"Watch your step up here," George Gail advised. "This is an older section of the pens. We usually only use them when we have more than two or three thousand head of cattle, but the fire damaged the pens closer to the front. We had to go back to using these, even though they're a little woppy-jawed." She gingerly stepped over a gaping hole left by a missing plank.

The higher they went, the less light cast upon their way. As they stepped onto the catwalk that spidered off into different directions, George Gail called her husband's name. After going just a few feet, darkness surrounded them.

Perhaps it was the black all around them, perhaps it was the chill of the February breeze chasing itself through the open-sided barn. Perhaps it was the unknown, or the ambiguous text from Curtis. Perhaps it was the fact George Gail wore a trench coat and, try as she might, Madison couldn't get the stocky image of Caress' killer out of her mind. Perhaps it was a combination of it all, but something lent an air of danger to the night, a sense of foreboding.

"Do you hear anything?" Madison felt compelled to whisper, even though George Gail had been calling her husband's name at the top of her lungs.

"Just the cattle moving below."

"I can't see a thing, can you?"

"I'm not sure... Look over there. To the right, past that big beam. Could that be a person?"

The moon kept slipping behind the clouds, but if she stared hard enough, Madison thought she saw the vague outline of a large support beam against the black horizon. "I don't know," she whispered back. "I'm getting cross-eyed, staring into the darkness."

George Gail's phone buzzed again. "It's him!" she whispered excitedly, consulting the screen. "He says '***Down. Eight.***'"

She started forward, but Madison took hold of her arm. "Wait. Why did he text you instead of calling out?"

George Gail sounded frightened. "Maybe he's hurt!"

"Or maybe someone else is down there."

She could barely make out George Gail's face in front of her. She couldn't see the smear of blue eye shadow streaked across her face. She could, however, see the white of her eyes as they widened in fright.

"I'm scared, Madison," she squeaked.

Madison squeezed the other woman's hand. "Be as quiet as possible," she advised.

Somehow, Madison ended up in the lead. While George Gail brought up the rear, holding in tiny whimpers with both hands placed over her mouth, Madison led their slow procession down the long walkway. She tried to count eight pens as they passed over them but peering down into the pitch made her dizzy. Occasionally a silvery horn would reflect a bit of light, reminding her of the dangers of falling. Not only was it a long way down, some of the pens held cattle.

"Was that eight?" she whispered, turning her head toward her companion. The walkway dipped unexpectedly, and she lunged forward, falling into a handrail that felt dangerously unsteady. Feeling George Gail's hand on her back, she hissed in belief, "Did you just push me?"

"No, I stumbled! And he didn't mean eight, he meant right. We still have a way to go. Hurry up." Suddenly impatient, she shoved Madison to urge her forward.

"I can't see what I'm doing," Madison reminded her. "What about those lights?"

"I forgot. I'll have to go back to turn them on. You wait here."

"All by myself?" If Madison sounded afraid, it was because she was. There was something decidedly sinister about the night. The deeper they walked into the shadows, the worse the feeling grew. And they seemed to be no closer to the end now than they were when they began. Had she missed a cross-walk somewhere? Had she taken a wrong path and turned them in circles?

"What if he's hurt?" George Gail whined. "We need to get to him as soon as possible. You stay here, and when I turn on the lights, you locate him. You can get down to the pens faster than I can."

"Just how am I supposed to get down there?"

"Crawl down. There are ladders every so often."

"I don't know, George Gail. Maybe we should call for help."

"The wreck, remember? I'll try to get through while I go turn on the lights. You stay here and try to find Curtis. Please, just find him!"

For lack of a better plan, Madison agreed. The walkway swayed a bit as George Gail waddled back the way in which they came. In a matter of steps, the blackness swallowed her whole. Not even her trench coat glowed in the darkness.

Madison stood in the black night, trying to get her bearings. Earlier, she had seen the faintest hint of the sky to their right. She thought she had headed in that direction, toward the largest support beam, but she was no longer certain. With the moon moving behind a cloud again, there was no light to guide her steps. Perhaps if she moved on, she might get a glimpse of starlight if nothing else.

After a few steps, she heard a noise below and stopped to listen. She could hear cattle moving beneath her, a slow stir of beastly bodies in the stillness of night. Deciding it was nothing more than the cows, she took another step.

The noise came again. It sounded like 'psst.'

She waited, hearing the sound again. "Curtis?" she called in a whisper.

"Down here." The words were low, no more than the murmur of the cows.

"I can't see you. Are you all right?"

"Hurt."

Swallowing hard, Madison peered into the dark pens below. She could barely make out the backs of about two dozen head of cattle crowded inside one of the pens, but there was no indication of Curtis Burton. She crawled to her knees, trying to get a closer look.

"Crazy."

She heard his faint word as she tried to see under the catwalk. Afraid of losing her balance and falling headlong into the pen, she lay down on the wooden walk and hung her head over the edge to see beneath her. "What did you say?" she whispered.

"She's crazy," he answered, but his voice sounded weak.

"Who? Who's crazy?"

There was no answer. Madison's eyes watered with the strain of staring into black nothingness. Blinking the sting away, she slowly walked her eyes along the railings of the fence. That dark blob was a cow… so was that one… and the one in the corner was a *really* big cow, curled horns and all. And that… was that…

"Curtis?" she whispered frantically. There was a dark shape draped against the fence, squashed between the railings and a large white-faced cow.

He answered, but with a discombobulated, "George Gail."

Madison sucked in a sharp breath. Was he confused, mistaking her for his beloved wife? Was he asking about her, wondering where she was? Or, Madison wondered in dread, could he be answering her question? Was he saying George Gail was the crazy one?

No, no, no, that was impossible!

... Wasn't it?

Think, Madison! In a strange, convoluted way, it made sense. George Gail believed her husband was having an affair with Caress Ellingsworth. From the very beginning, she claimed she wanted to kill someone. She couldn't remember what happened the night Caress was murdered, only that she woke up with car keys and blood. She, herself, was worried she might have actually done it.

Or had it all been a brilliant act to pump information from Madison, to find out if she could identify her? She was wearing a trench coat, after all, just like the killer. She had directed Madison to the dark outer pens without hesitation. And she had translated her husband's mistyped text messages easily enough; too easily, perhaps? Had she known all along where he was, because she had left him there, injured and in pain?

No, that's too crazy, Madison convinced herself, even for George Gail.

Curtis said something else. She strained to hear his words. "Need to open the gate."

"How?"

"Have to crawl down here and swing it open. Stay on the fence." He struggled to get a deep breath before adding, "There's one cow in here that's plumb loco."

Madison did her best to hide the fact that she was horrified, even from herself. A man was trapped and possibly injured; this was no time to be worried about her own fears. She had to help him.

With the help of a few mumbled directions from Curtis, Madison found the 'ladder' George Gail mentioned. In truth, it was nothing more than a few strategically placed boards, nailed horizontally down the side of a support post. Madison felt like one of those people who climbed telephone poles, but without the safety belt.

The climb down was frightening enough but touching the dirt floor below was no better. She stood in almost total darkness. She prayed she was on the alley side of the fence, and not standing in a pen filled with cattle.

"Curtis?" she whispered into the darkness.

"Over here."

Even while pinned between a fence and a twelve-hundred-pound animal, the cowman had more wits about him than Madison did. He managed to press a button on his cell phone and illuminate the screen, casting a circle of light into the blackness. Madison spotted him easily enough, several feet to the right.

"Come on down the alley. The gate is about six feet this way," Curtis told her. "Work the latch, then pull it open. Get out of the way fast. Get on the fence."

"What if they stampede?" Madison worried aloud. Belatedly thinking to use her own phone, she saw that she was in a long, wide pathway that ran parallel beneath the catwalk, flanked on either side by cattle pens. Most of the pens were empty, except for the one where Curtis Burton was trapped.

"Don't get caught behind the gate," he cautioned.

As Madison neared the pen of shaggy bovine, fear collected in her belly. The odor, alone, was enough to curl her stomach. The locals all complained about the stench of the chicken houses scattered about, but when was the last time they took a good whiff of a cow pen? To her offended senses, there wasn't a huge difference between cow dung and chicken litter. And ammonia this raw and concentrated stung her nose either way, no matter which animal it came from. Add the muck and the dander and the sweat of twenty head of thousand-something-pound beasts, and the smell was every bit as rank and overwhelming as that in the chicken houses.

And cows were so much bigger than chickens! Madison was intimidated by their size, even with the security of a fence between her and them. They looked docile enough, but Curtis had mentioned a wild one. Her money was on the horned cow in the corner. While the other beasts stood quietly in the crowded pen, contentedly chewing their cuds and licking their sides with long, slobbery tongues, that one cow moved restlessly along the far fence. The other cattle left her a wide berth as she prowled the perimeter, searching for a way out.

Another cow bumped its large body into the railings near Madison. The boards bulged outward, prompting Madison to move to the center of the alley.

The latch to the gate was harder to open than she expected. Realistically, Madison knew it had to be secure enough not to give way beneath the pressure of milling cattle, but what about beneath the fumbling fingers of a frightened greenhorn? She finally lifted the gate itself, relieved when the latch gave at last.

Scrambling out of the way, she jumped onto the bottom rail of the fence. The gate was unlatched but still in its closed position. As Curtis reminded her again to stay free of the gate's swing, Madison stretched her arm out as far as she could to tug the gate outward.

"It's not budging," she complained. She was too afraid to get off the fence and open it properly, afraid she would be either trampled by the cows or squished behind the gate.

"Hit one of the cows," Curtis advised. "Slap 'em on the rump."

She climbed to the top of the fence—why did they build the sides so high?—and leaned down into the pen. Afraid she might lose her balance and fall among the cows, her first attempt was a bit lackluster.

"Harder!"

This time she slapped the cow hard enough that it jumped. The movement started a chain reaction. Cows bumped into one another, slowly at first, just enough to shift positions in the pen. The cow pressing into Curtis turned with the herd, her backside now pressed into his chest. He popped her on the flank and was rewarded with a swift kick, but she moved forward. Curtis sagged to the ground and gulped in his first deep breath since being trapped.

"Watch out for the horned piebald," he warned weakly.

Madison wasn't raised on a farm. She had no idea which one was a piebald. Too many of them had horns. And the shift in movement frightened the herd, making even the most docile creatures lumber to life. Two cows bellowed in protest, another reared up on the backside of its neighbor, riding her around the fence. Feet quickened, bodies thumped, horns slung. It took awhile, but one cow finally bumped its rear into the gate and forced it to swing open. Eyes wild, the bovine backed her way from the crowd and into freedom.

The rest of the cows quickly followed suit. There was a mad scramble for the gate, making Madison grateful for Curtis' advice. The eager herd crowded into the opening, pushing and shoving in their quest for freedom.

Madison clung to the top rail of the fence. The railings swayed as the cows fell against it, but it stood strong. As the large bodies pushed down the alley, too close for comfort, Madison swung her feet to the other side of the fence, inside the pen.

Madison took a moment to worry about George Gail. What was taking so long? The barn was still pitch black, save for the faint glow of starlight peeping in beneath the eaves.

A rancorous clatter tore her from her wanderings. She heard a low, wild bawl, the sound ominous. A lone cow remained in the pen, the crazy one with the sharp, curled horns. Did piebald mean spotted? She was thrashing into the railings opposite Madison, hurling her large body repeatedly into the wooden fence.

Paralyzed with fear, Madison watched the cow plunder her way down the fence, closer to where Madison was perched. Crazed by the commotion of the other cows, the frenzied bovine didn't realize the gate stood wide open. She was intent on making her own way out.

To Madison's utter amazement, she watched as the cow tried to jump the fence. When her hooves cleared the top railing, Madison understood why the boards reached so high. In her wildest imagination, she never would have believed a cow could reach such heights.

When the cow realized she was still trapped, she bellowed again in rage. She twisted and flung backwards against the fence.

That was when she spotted Madison.

Time played out in slow motion. Madison saw the angry cow paw the ground, flinging filth that splattered the fence behind her. She lowered her head. The whites of her eyes glowed like evil marbles as she trained her sights on Madison.

Then she plunged, and all hell broke loose.

Maddy squealed and dove over the side of the fence. Her foot hit the back of a cow still in the alley. Squealing again, she scrambled along the side of the fence, hanging by the top rail, frantically working her way toward the adjacent pen. As the angry cow threw her weight into the fence Madison clung to, the wall of boards trembled beneath her hands. The force of the second blow almost loosened Maddy's tentative hold. With the third, she heard a board crack.

If the cow jumped again…

Squealing and yelping with each blow, each angry snort, each bellow of rage, Madison sped up. When her foot slipped and contacted with another cow in the alley, she used its head to push off. The startled cow buckled and turned, causing new confusion in the alley, but Madison didn't care. The added momentum propelled her forward and just beyond the cross fence between the two pens. As she sailed over the rails and into the empty pen, she glanced to the ground below. Where had Curtis gone? The last she saw him, he was slumped along this fence, directly in the path of the crazed cow.

His voice came from the back of the empty pen. "Hurry, girl. Back here!"

Maddy jumped from the fence, her feet unsteady as she landed in the uneven clumps of dried mud. She ran toward his voice, even as the cow tracked her path. "That—That cow is insane!" she panted.

"Forget the cow." His voice was insistent. "We gotta get out of here before she comes back."

In all the excitement of the cows, Madison had forgotten her suspicions of George Gail. They came flooding back with a vengeance, just as a loud electrical hum filled the air, followed by a bright wash of light. The switch brought to life the bulbs on the far side of the barn and along part of the catwalk, but it was enough to cast partial light into the area where they stood.

Madison took stock of the situation around them. Her gaze went first to Curtis. He looked filthy and haggard, his handsome face pale and pinched with pain, but the only blood she saw was a smear across his arm. She peered into the adjacent pen, where the spotted cow was finally growing weary in her efforts to plunder the fence. The animal flung itself against the boards one more time, then stopped to rest, her sides heaving.

Unassured, Madison's voice warbled. "C—Curtis?"

"We gotta go," he said urgently. "She's armed."

"Wh—Who? Where are we going?"

"Over this fence, toward the loading pens. We can get out through the chutes."

Before she could take the first step forward, a shadow fell across their path.

29

"Oh, hell. She's back."

As Curtis muttered the words, Madison spun around in dread. She slowly lifted her gaze to the catwalk overhead.

Her heart sank down to her toes. Even though she half-expected to see her there, she was devastated to recognize George Gail's broad, squatty build silhouetted against the light. The glare of light behind her hid her face in the shadows, but the coat and hat were all too familiar.

How could she have been so wrong? Was she really so terrible a judge of character? In spite of the other woman's late-night calls and her scattered-brained personality and needy whine, Madison had actually become rather fond of George Gail. It stung, knowing she had befriended a murderess!

"What do you want, woman?" Curtis snarled. "Why don't you come down here and fight me like a real man, instead of standing up there?"

Madison's head snapped in his direction, shocked to hear him speaking to his wife in such a manner. That day at the café, he seemed so enchanted with her.

Then again, maybe she hadn't pulled a knife on him at that point.

"Why are you doing this?" Curtis asked the woman on the catwalk. "The least you could do is tell me why you want to kill me!"

The only answer was a menacing raised arm. The glint of steel winked in the light as she raised her weapon.

"She knows," Madison finally told him. "She knows about you and Caress."

"What about us?" he asked in confusion.

For the first time, George Gail spoke. Her voice was unusually low. "I know you were having an affair!"

"What in tarnation are you talking about, woman? I wasn't having an affair with that woman!"

"We saw your text messages," Madison told him.

"What messages?"

"The ones where you told her you wanted to see her boobs."

"Why would I want to see her boobs—or any other part of her scrawny little body, for that matter—when I have a woman like George Gail at home?"

"Don't you dare talk about her that way! She had gorgeous breasts! All of her was exquisite."

Why on earth was George Gail defending the woman she had murdered? Nothing was making any sense. Madison rubbed at her forehead, trying to clear her fogged brain. Could she be sleepwalking? Was all this a dream?

A very bad dream. As Curtis called his wife crazy once more, the shouting energized the cow. Somehow, the gate had swung closed again. The beast renewed its efforts to break free with renewed vigor.

"I wouldn't know, you crazy woman," Curtis insisted. "I've never laid eyes on any woman but my own wife."

"We saw the texts," Madison reminded him.

If she was talking, she couldn't be asleep, right?

"So? I can't text worth a darn. Fingers are too long and spindly." He flexed the digits in question.

Madison noticed the red swatch on his shirt was growing. She also noticed the slashed fabric, reminding her of the way Caress' clothes were similarly shredded. The same knife had done both damages, no doubt.

"You might as well know," Madison told him. "George Gail hired me to follow you and see who you were having an affair with. I followed you to the *Bumble Bee*, where you met Caress. You even took her flowers."

"That's right," the man nodded. He looked confused. And totally innocent, Madison noted, which also didn't make sense. "I wanted to make sure she got the right kind for the party."

"What party?" These words, barked from above them.

"The anniversary party, the one she was helping me plan. Our fortieth anniversary is coming up, and I wanted to throw George Gail a surprise party. Caress was helping me get it all organized. She had books with pictures and different ideas for me to choose from. I took her a sample of the pink begonias George Gail likes." Curtis' look of confusion morphed into one of disgust. "Has everyone gone plumb crazy? Why in tarnation would I cheat on a wonderful wife like George Gail?

I worship the ground that woman walks on. I'd be nothing without her."

"Then—Then she was telling the truth?" George Gail's voice sounded strangled from the catwalk, and close to hysteria. "She wasn't cheating on me?"

Madison's head snapped up. This had to be a dream! Things were getting stranger by the minute!

"*Cheating* on you?" Madison asked. "George Gail, have you gone mad? What are you talking about?"

"Yeah, what are you talking about?" Curtis demanded. "That ain't George Gail up there."

"Then who—?"

The voice from the catwalk was stronger this time, tighter. And, Madison realized, all too familiar. "Caress and I weren't just best friends. We were lovers. We've been in a relationship for years."

"D—Darla?" she gasped.

"Of course it's me, you imbecile. What, do you think a woman like Caress couldn't be involved with a woman like me?"

How could she have not recognized that snide voice? That barely controlled rage and that air of superiority? Madison felt like a fool, but at least the pieces were falling into place now.

Darla Mullins had obviously discovered the same messages as George Gail. Both women had jumped to the wrong conclusion, thanks to poor typing. Or perhaps spell-correct was the culprit. Madison knew all too well how messages could be distorted by that handy little feature. 'Can't wait to see your boobs' should have said 'books.' Even 'I like pink behinds' was probably meant to say, 'I like pink begonias.' And 'work the ride' was 'worth the risk.'

Darla, with her terrible temper and her tendency toward violence, must have confronted Caress. In a fit of rage, she stabbed her lover to death.

The surveyor's hostility toward Madison made sense now. This explained why she hired her in the first place, and why she rejected Madison's early offer to dissolve their contract. All those brushes of danger with Trench Coat… Madison realized Darla had the perfect opportunity for each of them. Darla knew Madison's schedule. She had access to Caress' car. She knew how to shut off the power at the office, and the lay of the land at the survey site.

Even Derron's words made sense now. He was so adamant about the actress not being involved with any of the local men. What was it he had said? "There weren't many people in The Sisters that met her… requirements. Caress wasn't like most people around here, if you know what I mean."

Until now, she hadn't known what he meant. She thought he meant Caress' celebrity status. But it made sense now. Even her relationship with John-Paul Noble made sense. They weren't involved romantically; they were each other's cover. In a professional world dependent upon appearances, neither performer could afford to have their personal lives exposed. Each made their living selling sex appeal to the opposite sex. Times were changing, but if their sexual preferences were known, particularly a few years ago, their careers would have been over.

Madison knew it wasn't wise to antagonize the demented woman, but she heard herself calling out the words, loud and clear. "You killed her. You killed your lover over some misspelled text message."

She saw Darla raise her hands to her head, as if to block the words from her ears. "I didn't know," she moaned. "I didn't mean to. It just happened." She kept pounding her ears, perhaps to block the deed from her mind, perhaps to block the ruckus of the mad cow below. The spotted animal reared up on her hind legs again, trying to jump the fence while making a terrible commotion. Her hooves pounded against the wood rails, her soulful cries pitched in a high keen. The tortured sound added more drama to a moment fraught with tension.

As Darla brought her hands down, Madison realized it wasn't a knife she held in her hands. It was a gun. And it was now pointed directly at Madison's chest.

There was movement on the catwalk. Another trench coat rushed up from behind. Except for the brightly flowered water boots peeking from beneath the hem of one coat, the figures looked much the same.

There wasn't even a struggle. Without pausing a beat, George Gail shoved the other woman from behind. Hard. Taken completely by surprise, Darla tumbled over the handrail and fell from the catwalk, straight atop the bellowing cow's head.

Despite the woman's considerable bulk, the enraged cow shook Darla Mullins as if she were nothing more than a rag doll. Stubby arms and legs flailed in all directions. As the cow tried to rid itself of the unexpected burden, it threw its full weight against the fence, head first. Darla was crushed between the cow and the fence, but her body was firmly wedged between the bovine's horns. The cow jumped backwards and bucked, and finally Darla's body went hurling through the air, landing with a sickening smack against the wooden fence.

All the commotion knocked the gate open once again. Seeing means of escape, the enraged cow was no longer interested in the inanimate body lying in the dirt. The beast banged through the opening, trotted several feet into the alley, and promptly stopped. Almost leisurely, the cow then ambled her way down the path toward the other cattle, showing none of her earlier signs of hostility.

"Is she—Is she... dead?" George Gail's voice wavered from the catwalk above.

Curtis answered. "If not, she's mighty close. Better call 911."

30

Darla Mullins wasn't dead, but she may have wished she were. The fall had broken her neck. The cow had broken most of her other bones. If she lived, she might be paralyzed. And if she somehow managed to pull through and recover, she would be going to prison.

Three people had heard her confession. Brash found the murder weapon at her home, tucked away in a drawer with Caress' blood dried on its blade. There was enough evidence against her to put her away for life, even without factoring in her premeditated attempts to silence Madison.

Maddy couldn't help but feel sorry for Derron. He was devastated to learn of his mother's horrific crime. He immediately closed *Boundaries*, moved out of Darla's house, and transferred his belongings into his Aunt Myrna's spare bedroom, at least until he could find something more suitable.

For her part, the opinionated self-proclaimed horticulture expert was oddly silent on her sister's secret lifestyle and involvement in Caress Ellingsworth's death. When Darla died a week later, Myrna helped Derron arrange an elaborate funeral filled with fabulous flowers, played out the part of a grieving sister whose loved one had been wrongly accused, and, as soon as the casket was closed, never spoke her name again.

Curtis Burton was crushed to know his wife suspected him of infidelity. Like Brash deCordova, the man couldn't bear the thought of his moral character being questioned by someone he cared about. It was a matter of integrity, as much as pride. Given his unconditional love for his wife, however, he soon forgave her. He seemed just as concerned that George Gail could ever doubt *herself* so much to believe she might have committed murder. He took extra efforts to convince her she was the most loving and nurturing woman he had ever known, and simply incapable of hurting another soul. He even had a logical explanation for the blood she found that night on the sheets. He had cut his hand while helping with the broken-down cattle trailer. The last Madison heard, plans were underway for a huge anniversary celebration, even bigger and better than before.

Brash, however, wasn't as forgiving as the weathered cowman. He handled the case with utmost professionalism, called Maddy several times in those first few days to make certain she was faring well, and made a point to speak to her when he ran into her around town. He was always polite and courteous, always the perfect gentleman. But in his brown eyes she saw the pain, the disappointment she knew she caused. Maddy hated herself for hurting him. After all, the man had all but admitted he was falling in love with her.

If she were honest with herself, she felt much the same way. But there were pieces of her past Brash didn't know, pieces she was not yet ready to explain. Gray had hurt her deeply, and she wasn't certain she was ready to give her heart—nor her trust—to another man, even the very worthy Brash deCordova.

Brash claimed he would wait for her.

On this, she had to trust him.

Madison was surprised when Derron showed up at her door a few days after the funeral.

"Derron, what a surprise! Please, come in. How are you?" She had been worried about her friend.

"I'm managing. Things are going well, except I have *got* to get out of that house!" As always, he dramatized his distress. "That woman is worse than the Dragon Lady, God bless her soul."

"Actually, I have a number for you," Madison announced. She rummaged around on the dining room table where her paperwork was scattered, until she found a slip of paper with a number scrawled across it. "I happen to know Wanda Shanks is considering renting out a room to help pay expenses. I put in a good word for you, just in case you decided to give her a call."

"I could just kiss you!" Derron proclaimed. With a little laugh and a flutter of his hands, he added, "But of course I won't. I wouldn't mind kissing that hunk of a boyfriend of yours, but I doubt the chief would approve. So, I'll settle for saying you are a lifesaver! Thanks, dollface."

"Brash is *not* my boyfriend," she insisted. She had barely spoken to him all week.

"Whatever. But as fascinating as your love life is, that's not why I came over."

She let the sarcasm slide. "Oh?"

"I came to apply for a job."

"A job?" Madison hooted. "With whom?"

"With you, of course."

"There is no job, Derron. *In a Pinch* isn't hiring. In fact, we're hardly even being hired." She made the distinction between the words with a wrinkle of her nose.

"That's not what I heard. I heard you have several new clients."

"How did you hear that? I just signed two of them this morning!"

"Word gets around in a small town, dollface. You know that."

Flabbergasted, Madison just stared at him.

"Seriously, do you know anything about building a picket fence?" he asked, referring to her new contract to build a fence in Miss Sybille's backyard.

"No, but I'm willing to learn."

"I not only have experience, I have all the tools."

"You?"

"My mother may not have taught me about fashion, but she made up for it by teaching me about power tools. Did you bid the fence by the job or by the hour?"

"The job."

"I'll save you a fortune by cutting the work time in half. Even paying my salary, you get to pocket the difference."

"Derron—"

"Think of the possibilities. This will expand your business into the home-repair market. I'm more than just a pretty face in a snappy wardrobe; I know my way around with a hammer and a wrench."

She had a crazy image of him in a frilly pair of overalls, armed with a decorated hammer. "I don't know, Derron…"

"You don't have to pay me a salary," he said quickly, "just by the hour, and only when you need me for a job. With two of us working, you could take on twice the clients. And once your business grows and becomes more successful and you have a full employee roster, I can become your secretary." He batted his eyelashes. "You know I have the gift, dollface. I'm a natural as a receptionist."

Madison laughed. He had a point; she had seen him in action.

"Come on, give me a try," he urged. "At least for the fence. If it works out the way I know it will, you have to promise to at least consider using me on a permanent basis." When he saw her wavering, he put his hands up to beg. "Please, please, please. I need the job, especially if I'm moving out of my aunt's house. Come on, girlfriend, you know we work great together, and you know you could use me on some of your jobs. What have you got to lose?"

"I don't know, but I can't afford to lose a thing!"

"You won't, I promise."

"Well…"

"We'll start with the fence."

Madison finally relented. She really knew nothing about building a fence. At least this would save her the expense of one of those 'how-to for dummies' books. "We'll start with the fence," she agreed.

"Oh, goody!" Derron clapped his hands and clicked his feet together, looking more like her teenage daughter than her new employee. However, he made her laugh, and she needed all the laughter she could get these days. "Wanna celebrate by going for lunch? My treat."

"I'll have to take a rain check. I'm expecting company."

"Another time then. Besides, I'll have to go shopping. I don't have a thing to wear for my new job!"

She bit her tongue before she mentioned frilly overalls.

Derron paused, a rare moment of uncertainty crossing his face. "I want to apologize to you for all my mother put you through."

"You don't have to."

"Yes, I do. I feel like you and I are friends. In a strange way, I understand how she killed Caress. My mother was a troubled soul. She suffered from bipolar issues, probably because she felt forced to live a double life. She tried to be a wife, she tried to be a mother, but it just wasn't in her. She was never really happy, not until she met Caress. Caress changed her, made her a better person. I think my mother couldn't bear the thought of going back to her old, miserable self. Without Caress, she was just a mean, bitter woman with a horrible temper. She loved Caress so completely, she couldn't bear the thought of losing her. She was out of her mind with jealousy and anger. But when she went after you… she knew exactly what she was doing. I can't forgive the Dragon Lady for trying to kill you."

"It's over now, Derron. Let's just put it all behind us."

After a comforting hug, she walked Derron to the door and bid him goodbye.

"You're not two-timing me with another carpenter, are you?" Derron asked, pretending to scowl as he watched a vehicle pull into the drive.

"What?"

"Looks like your company has arrived, dollface. And as much as I'd love to hang around and get a glimpse of that sexy Nick Vilardi up close and personal, duty calls." He put a dramatic hand to his forehead. "I'm off to buy a nice chambray to go under my Carhartt overalls. Blue and tan look good together, don't you think?" He blew a kiss her way and wiggled his fingers in parting. "Tootles."

Madison was still laughing at his antics when Nick Vilardi and Amanda Hooper got out of the *Home Again* van.

Granny, they're here!" she called for her grandmother over her shoulder. Then she turned back and greeted their guests with a nervous smile.

It did not escape her attention that Nick Vilardi was as handsome as ever and smelled as sexy as he looked. He had on a button-down white shirt, rolled up at the wrists to reveal strong, muscular arms. The contrast of color made his dark skin and blue eyes all the more vivid.

Once the formalities were out of the way and Granny Bert had served kale and watermelon shakes all around, the television duo got down to business.

"Mrs. Cessna," Nick began, "the last time we were here, you told me to go back to the city and find a way to make this remodel happen. You told me to get the numbers down and we could talk business. Well, I'm back. And I'm pleased to say that I've held up my end of the bargain." His eyes glowed with a sense of accomplishment.

"Good, good," Granny Bert beamed. "But don't be telling me. Madison is now the rightful owner of the house. All your dealings will be with her now."

"Excellent." Turning his blue gaze upon Madison, he drew out the word. His fully delighted smile should have made her nervous. It definitely got her heart pumping.

Amanda Hooper leaned forward and spoke. "Madison, I want you to know everyone at the network is *very* excited about this project."

"Good." Madison was truly pleased, but she felt compelled to make things clear, right from the start. "And I hope that excitement translates into funding, because—"

"We know." Nick broke in before she could get the words out. "You don't have any money."

Hearing the slight sting in his voice, she could only shrug. "Sad, but oh so true."

"I think we've found a solution to your pesky money problems."

"I wish!" she muttered under her breath, but she only smiled and waited for him to continue.

Amanda did the honors. "When we were here before, your friend Genesis came up with a brilliant idea. She suggested we dedicate an entire season to remodeling your house. It's a concept embraced by several other shows out there, but one we have never tried before, primarily because we had never found the right house. It has to be just the right one, a home we are passionate about, one spectacular enough to use as our centerpiece for an entire season." She flashed a smile before continuing. "I am pleased to announce that I think we have finally found the perfect house for the perfect season. Ladies, I think your house is *The One.*" Her voice softened with reverence—or perhaps merely with good salesmanship—as she smiled and announced semi-dramatically, "With your permission, we would be honored to feature the Big House as our very first theme home for the upcoming season."

While Granny oohed and aahed over the prospect, sounding appropriately shocked they would come through on the project, Nick stepped right in. "Madison, do you have any specific visions for the house?"

"Honestly? There has been so much happening around here, I haven't had time to give it much thought."

Nick looked slightly wounded by her admission. He tried not to take it personally; just because he was already obsessed with the house didn't mean everyone was. He could think of nothing else these past weeks. *Well, maybe a few other things,* he admitted to himself, sneaking a peek at the long legs beside him encased in denim. Still, if the house were his, his mind would be filled with possibilities. It already was, in fact.

"That might be a good thing," he said. "What I mean is, I have found several sponsors who are willing to fund our project, if we will work exclusively with their products. It would limit you to selection within their lines, but I think you'll be impressed with the major brands that have come forward. For instance, Valco has offered to furnish your appliances."

"I really liked my refrigerator in Dallas," she murmured, naming the brand. "I was hoping to get another one like it." Although where she would get the money for it, she had no idea.

"Did I mention Valco is furnishing all appliances, free of charge?"

Without missing a beat, Madison changed her tune. "As I said, I'm sure I'll love my new Valco refrigerator. I hear it's a wonderful brand."

Nick grinned in response. "Actually, it is. I can't imagine not finding the perfect refrigerator from within their line. And they want to supply everything, from your microwave and dishwasher to your on-demand water heater to your washer and dryer."

He took her overwhelmed expression as encouragement to continue.

"Wood Warehouse is furnishing all the wood flooring. I'm still waiting on word from Old Italy about donating the tile and granite, but if they don't come through, I think I can swing a deal with Murray. How do you feel about carpet in the bedrooms?"

"Carpet is good."

"Personally, I prefer wood, but Murray is willing to install new carpet in almost the entire second floor."

"I—I thought you weren't proposing remodeling the second floor, just adding bathrooms." Her mind swirled with the magnitude of all he said. While she tried to grasp everything at once, the word 'free' kept flashing in her mind like a neon sign.

Nick Vilardi offered a charming smile and a nonchalant shrug. "Hey, if they're willing to donate..."

Madison touched her forehead to anchor the thoughts churning inside. "Don't get me wrong, I think it's amazing—incredible, really—that so many suppliers are willing to participate. Truly, I do. But... *why* are these huge name brands so eager to help restore the Big House?" A thought occurred to her. "Wait a minute. I don't have to agree to turn the house into a museum or open a Bed and Breakfast or something like that, do I?"

"Of course not."

"Then what's the catch?" In her experience, anything that seemed too good to be true usually was. "As wonderful and generous as all this sounds, I just can't imagine all these big companies willing to donate thousands of dollars of merchandise and equipment and goods for just little ole' me and my kids. So tell me, what's the catch? I know there has to be one."

Her unease grew when she saw the look that passed between Nick and Amanda. By silent accord, the blond producer was the one to answer.

"We were fascinated by the history of the house. Of the entire town, really, and its sister community."

"That's The Sisters, all right. Fascinating," Madison muttered.

"And we understand there are quite a few well-known residents. The late Caress Ellingsworth and her longtime boyfriend, John-Paul Noble. Not to mention former Heisman trophy winner Tug Montgomery, the former Las Vegas dancer known as Glitter, the lead singer for *Cowboy Candyband,* and world-famous artist Jean Applegate. And of course, we can't forget your very own chief of police, a renowned professional football player and coach to some of the state's premier universities. That's actually quite an impressive cast of characters for such a tiny rural community. No offense," she was quick to add.

"None taken," Madison assured her with an amused smile.

"We were also very impressed with your children the last time we visited. Such well-behaved teenagers, and both so bright and cheerful and good looking. They obviously take after their mother. And grandmother, of course." Amanda flashed a bright smile at Granny Bert.

"Great-grandmother, but who's counting," the old woman beamed.

"Your entire family is very photogenic, Madison."

Something in her flowery words rang a bell of caution. "Thank you. I think." Madison looked at Nick, staring him straight in the eyes. "All the flattery is nice, but what isn't she saying? What's going on, Nick? What's the catch?"

Nick met her gaze without flinching. He appreciated her direct approach. In fact, he appreciated most everything about Madison Reynolds, but there would be time for that later. Still, he let his eyes briefly roam over her, caressing her with the warmth of his eyes.

"The truth is, Madison, we've come up with a brilliant way to make this re-model happen, without costing you a single dime."

She sucked in her breath. She was stunned but intrigued. "I'm—I'm listening."

"It's true; we do find you, your family, and your house very intriguing. Our sponsors agree. Enough to fund the entire project, start to finish. Again, with no cost to you." He flashed his tantalizing smile, as if his words weren't dazzling enough.

"There's always a cost," she said softly. "What's this one?"

"We think your life here in The Sisters would make an excellent reality television show."

NOTE FROM THE AUTHOR

Thank you for taking the time to read When the Stars Fall. If you enjoyed it, please consider telling your friends or posting a short review. Word of mouth is an author's best friend and much appreciated. Thank you, Becki.

Please feel free to contact me. I welcome your thoughts and suggestions.

E-Mail: beckiwillis.ccp@gmail.com
Webpage: www.beckiwillis.com

MORE BOOKS BY BECKI

He Kills Me, He Kills Me Not
Forgotten Boxes
Mirrors Don't Lie Series
Book 1 - The Girl from Her Mirror
Book 2 - Mirror, Mirror on Her Wall
Book 3 - Light from Her Mirror
The Sisters, Texas Mystery Series
Book 1 - Chicken Scratch
Book 3 – Stipulations and Complications Coming late 2015

CPSIA information can be obtained
at www.ICGtesting.com
Printed in the USA
BVHW041201210719
554006BV00017B/392/P

9 781947 68604